Years into Days

Years into Days

Nathan Layhe

AuthorHouse™
1663 Liberty Drive
Bloomington, IN 47403
www.authorhouse.com
Phone: 1-800-839-8640

First published by AuthorHouse 11/12/2011

ISBN: 978-1-4678-8875-2 (sc)
ISBN: 978-1-4678-8876-9 (ebk)

Printed in the United States of America

Contents

1

Slaves to Hypocrisy

'A psycho analyst who isn't in control of his own life'

There was more truth in this remark, along with negativity that came with it.

'Wow, that's a pretty blunt way of putting it'

Jane was complimented at his friend's statement about Jane's mentalist skills, and it seemed the hypocritical statement that followed never made it through to his conscious mind. Maybe he had disregarded it. The truth was he was good at reading people and aptly good at sorting out other peoples problems. But it seemed he had some lack of realistic thinking towards his own, as it was considered to him only moderately chaotic.

For a boy, Jane was an odd name, but his parents had obviously been devout believers in the meaning behind the song *Boy named Sue* by *Johnny Cash*. But he had often thought to himself: "At least it wasn't something like *Molly* . . ."

His friends had never made fun of the name, despite its oddity, he had been widely accepted. But his skill at the manipulation of socialising may have had something to do with that. His best friend knew his life was a little *risqué,* but everyone could tell he had something strange about his presence. He also seemed to have more friends in other lands than in his mother country, this fact his parents had frequently quizzed him on, but the answer always remained the same.

'I just find them nicer, and easier to get along with. Not to mention the fact they all seem to be more intelligent than everyone here in England!'

Another unfortunate truth in life. Everyone in another land seemed to work a lot harder to get somewhere than most Englishmen ever had. They seemed to be more intellectual. This was one of the main reasons he chose these friends. Intellect. Perhaps he thought he would test his human psychology skills on them, but he would later realise that these were probably the greatest friends he could ever ask for, and when it came to it, they were like him in the way that he was a unique human within his culture, a *shaped human*. But shaped by what?

In this day and age, the western man lead the rest of the world, and the Anglo-Saxon empire was one of the few governments in front, for all the wrong reasons. Media shaped lives, and anyone who didn't like what was main stream was considered minority. But Jane himself was not a follower of the people; he strongly disliked routine, order and commands. This meant he had grown a strong dislike to all religion and its beliefs. But when it came to his skills of human psychological shaping, these things were imperative. It seemed we were all slaves to hypocrisy, a little more than once in a while.

'Look I know you find enjoyment in your powers of suggestion, but I just thought I'd confirm that most people think of you the same. Anyway, the thing I most wanted to talk about is the fact that my Grandfather just died.'

'I'm sorry to hear that. Was it-' That was all Jane could get out.

'Don't worry about it, I didn't know him very well, point is, I've been left a hefty sum of money, and I was y'know, thinking . . .'

Jane was a patient person, and had little or no feel for anger, but he was leaning forward to his computer screen without realising.

'Thought maybe I could travel over there sometime, I've always wanted to experience England and-'

'Trust me, there's nothing nice about this place, after living here for the last 17 years of my life, I wish I'd been left in Ireland when I was two.'

'Well that's fair enough, but me and you could have some fun and find a good time, you could show me around, apologies for presuming, I know your rule about presumptions, but I guess you could do with the company nowadays'

'Don't worry, you're the only person I'd allow to break any of my rules, you've helped me enough'

He had a deep appreciation for his friend Lupe, he was the only person he trusted with any of his problems. Maybe it was best; after all he did live a few hundred miles away and would hardly cause any serious issues. None for him to worry about anyway. Maybe Lupe was right, a little company might kick him back into the real world. People who did know that Jane had a knack for reading people were probably sick of having him on their shoulders because no one else trusted him. He trusted Lupe, with his life, and so further trusted him this time.

'Sure, that sounds like a fine plan.'

This last statement was one of the many the two had been using to show agreement. It was a phrase from a dead language, if it was even that or just a slang term from another culture. They both laughed at this, and would be the only ones laughing if anyone were with them at the time. But of course many people gave Jane a funny look frequently, and most likely Lupe would receive something similar the moment they realised he wasn't English. That feeling that English people had, that wasn't as close as a hatred toward the other races, but never the less it was an 'I'm more important than one of your kind'. That feeling was probably the Saxon in them. Peace was considered in the military to be when you had a bigger stick than the other guy. And this had proven true over the years.

'Alright! I'll sort all the details out with my family; do you think I'd be able to crash at yours for a week or something?'

'Sure, my parents won't mind too much, they're never really indoors a lot anyway'

Jane had grown by himself a lot. He didn't know many of the childhood figures everyone else knew, he had to grow up quickly and missed out on a lot of the usual happiness most would've had. Maybe even one pet might have made a big difference, but this was out of the question, he knew what his parent's response would be to every question, so he never asked, and when his friends complained about it, he never explained their reasons. He just knew. Sometimes he wished that his skills of reading people weren't with him at some points in time. What you don't know won't break your heart. Often reading people, the people you loved, made you see them for what they really were, or what they really meant when they did or said something.

But what would humans be without irrational love? Rare, that's what they'd be.

* * *

As he continued to sit in his room, reading many books (so was his usual weekday evenings), he was constantly mulling over his friends idea. This kind of thing never really happened frequently to many people unless you were a multinational salesman, which would man going from one client to another could cost at least £300 a trip. But these days people seemed to think you had money to burn, 'make the most of now' one advert would say. These slogans he could never understand, such as the ones that directly contradicted themselves, 'bringing you the future today'. He was a picky person and knew it. But that kind of thing was in his personality, and there's no use in changing yourself for people, otherwise they don't like you for who you truly are. But the simplest of things like makeup would cause that little justice statement to appear constantly. So people throw it behind them. Everyone does it, so they say.

There could be no harm in having his friend visit. It would be a rare opportunity for him, he could learn plenty from wise old Lupe, and it would be nice for his friend to see something he considered special, even if Jane didn't think it was. He was not a selfish person. There would be no doubt that the first time they would meet would be both inspirational and a little awkward. But they had so many similarities that the ensuing days would be full of communication, what humans do best.

In any case, Lupe was a friend, and he had no desire to be in any way negative towards him. So he thought it best to welcome him with open arms, as and when he flew over.

He knew his disliked country well, and could show him what little he found worth seeing.

'That's not exactly much'

He found himself saying, but maybe he should be a little more open minded, so as not to come across as negative, that was not the effect he wanted to have. So he continued with his weekly read, with *Sum of all Fears* by *Tom Clancy*, the one that Ben Affleck so perfectly ruined with his presence on the movie. So he thought he'd read the book to redeem the seemingly sinister story line.

* * *

Never Non-Fiction. All his books had been fiction, mostly within the fantasy area, with the occasionally spy book, and perhaps a spoof here and there. He also borrowed a book from the library years ago that was a sci-fi, but if ever asked he could never remember it. Jane's stack of books was predominantly taken by fantasy novels. But not many people read true stories unless they were biographies about the latest celebrity figure, but even some knew the 'facts' in these biographies were often twisted to sell more copies.

Out of the few things Jane hated, it was always the fact that when people tried to put books into films, they always ruined the story. There were some exceptions however such as *Star Wars, The Lord of the Rings* and perhaps many others which Jane had not come across. But if someone ever recreated one of the books he read into a moving picture for Hollywood to massacre, there would almost certainly be an angry letter among the thousands that famous people burn. Should he meet one of these film directors, he'd probably chase them down the road like an angry Russian as if his vodka has just been stolen.

Jane needed to go into town to pick up some cigarette papers and rolling tobacco. He preferred the taste of fresh tobacco than the harsh taste of factory cigarettes with sawdust so generously making up a high percentage of them. Plus it was cheaper in the long run, and that was his main concern. He didn't have much of a glamorous job, but he was never short of cash to spend on the odd takeaway when the family got together and decided that no one in the room could be bothered to cook.

Many friends had discouraged him from smoking, and he did occasionally stop in order not to disappoint a certain someone in his life at the time, but he soon realised this was a pointless ritual to have, as it was never really appreciated. But the thing about it was the fact that he chose not to quit to gain himself a few years in his life, but to continue, and just stick the way he was. He enjoyed it, and it got him some of his friends in life, and one of his favourite characters in a book was frequently described rolling a smoke, and this was near enough reason for his habit. This came to be quite a difficult habit once publics bans had come in place, and his parents had never let him smoke inside. He often made use of the nicer scenery outside of his town when the urge came on, and it helped him with many personal issues.

But even being as skilled as he was with human sociology, it often didn't help much when it came to his problems. But he had had Lupe for that over the last 2 years. And his friend made a good job of helping him through.

* * *

'I think it's sorted' Lupe sounded just as excited as he was the day he told him of his interesting idea.

'Everything that needed to be done on this side is done, to a surety' Jane hadn't spoken like this for a while, and it seemed he was still in one of his fantasy book moods.

'Which one was it this time? King? Nathan Fillion? Or am I way off the mark on this one' these were authors that Lupe tried to grasp from the air in his head.

'Yeah it was a King one'

'You know I'm way behind you on those ones, I only just started a few weeks ago, and I have a slightly more partial love to Tobaco' this was a book written only in Bulgarian, and in 1960 they had made a black and white film (for the American population obviously) which didn't quite capture the same feeling the book did.

'You know my language barrier doesn't quite breach into Bulgarian, that would be quite adventurous, and not nearly as exotic as I'd like'

He secretly wished he did have the time to learn another language, but it would become another hard task he could do without. He did learn random little things, that can make a stranger of that language appreciate you more, but he didn't try much else that sounded more advanced than a basic greeting. Even *that* he didn't know in Bulgarian.

The evening went fast, which never normally happened, but he was trying to concentrate on conjuring some kind of image of what the next few weeks would entail. But even if he had a wild imagination, he could never guess what was to come. What he would lose, and what would eventually be a new direction for him, if that was an advert punch line, it would be "his future, today!"

Sometimes it was the simplest of things with irony that could scare people and affect them the most. It was only now that Jane realised he had been completely silent to Lupe for the past 15mins (time tended to have that effect), and he felt the need to redeem himself for his unexplained lack of speech.

'Sorry, I lost myself'

'Literally? Wow, never knew anyone could do that . . ."

'You know what I mean'

This last sentence came out with no aggressiveness in it, but sounded like it should have. Even if he did try a little aggressive behaviour, it would only make him seem more hopeless. He wasn't one for making much of a stand, which had its advantages sometimes. However many people found more cons than pros.

'Try not to go *todash* on me like that, it's enough to make a friend uncomfortable about his social standing' Lupe laughed after making this statement. He meant well and then added,

'Got another problem for us to have a palaver about?'

'Nah, it's all good, I got myself covered this time around'

This was the kind of thing someone would say then wink shortly after, and didn't take a genius to realise. But the truth was he didn't have it covered, and didn't know what he was trying to cover. "Great not another problem" he thought to himself. He didn't want to sit and think about this and further disappoint his friend by becoming anti-social while he made sense of the worries his mind had created, for no apparent reason, so it seemed.

'Lets get through these next few days and worry about things when your countries foreign population goes up by point one of a percent eh?'

'It's not my country, but that definitely sounds like a sound plan'

At this point Jane exited the video conference, and laid back on the pillows on his bed that were against the wall.

He continued his nightly ritual of reading and getting lost in his books, but he never slept until early the next morning. This was nothing a perfect cup of tea couldn't cure. What wishful thinking that was.

2

A Little Like *Lost,* No?

It just wasn't quite right. He had attempted the usual backwards sweep of the hair that made up his fringe, but this time around, it seemed like the day would start off bad and end up worse. Everyone had been puzzled about an Irishman with the hair of an Australian; that blonde looking highlight with brown roots. Kind of like one of those pretty boy surfers on the adverts and movies, that consisted of more clichés than a 60's cop series. But this made him look more approachable, until the voice that followed the seemingly fair face, crushed their hopes of a typical English friend. Their disappointment was not much his concern. But he had a good feeling, something he rarely had the luxury of feeling, that his new friend would not much mind how he sounded; he had heard and seen him before on video conferencing, but apparently the camera adds 20lbs.

Was it always so necessary for him to feel so negative? Surely it was everyone's right to lose their optimism once in a while. But Lupe was not one to worry about things going bad, he had a way with himself that was enough to make everyone feel comfortable with him. Or so Jane thought. Maybe not everyone appreciated the laid back: if optimism doesn't work, try more optimism and virtual violence, attitude. Quite a novel way of thinking, but it worked well for him. Although Jane hadn't ever quite got the hang of most computer games other than solitaire, which even he found extremely boring, but in desperate situations where it was necessary to waste time, it suited him just fine.

He'd have to grab a taxi to Coventry airport, one of the smallest and, in Jane's mind, a very pointless airport. But it was perfect for someone who was coming in to England for the first time. It was small and very few people came in through it. Heathrow wouldn't exactly be a perfect atmosphere for his friend, but Jane had no doubt that Lupe would somehow befriend a passing by innocent. Or worse, a crazed airline passenger that had had a very aggravating flight (maybe the ones that got refused that "last one" spirit on the flight to calm the old nerves). He knew thinking such things would do him no good, so he continued with the strict routine of his "awakening" as his father sometimes jokingly put it. Except this time that routine was a few hours earlier than usual and his body would soon make him pay for the sleep he missed out on at a later date.

He dressed sluggishly, knowing full well as soon as he walked past a mirror he would perfect everything with a few minor tweaks. What can go wrong with simple jeans and a shirt? Everything and yet nothing, maybe. Although he had little hopes for the success of his hair turning out remotely presentable. But he wouldn't dwell on that fact, not because he didn't want to, but because there was other things on his mind. This feeling had been one that he hadn't thought of in an age so it seemed. Jane was worried.

* * *

He wasn't much of a fan of taxis, because of that lingering musty smell of cheap car cleaner that all drivers had stuck in some compartment in the car, just in case a passenger they picked up was one of the people who had just come from a party. The thought of what things had happened in a taxi plagued his mind. And he guessed that money wasn't the only thing these taxi drivers accepted as payment. But this taxi wasn't so bad, the smell was there, but it looked as though this driver had taken much pride in keeping his vehicle in good nick.

The driver himself was Scottish, and quite a chatty fellow. Even though Jane was Irish, he still found it incredibly difficult to understand some of the things he said in his broad accent, but he got the general gist. He was just another man that wasn't from England, with good intentions. This only fuelled his opinion of the poor stereotypical English attitude. But the Scot, Brinkley was his name; spoke too frequently for Jane to focus on any particular thought. Perhaps that was for the best. He imagined he would eventually find out, would he ever stop talking?

'Tis a fine day fu' travelin' aye?'

"How on earth do I reply to that?" Jane thought.

'Yeah I guess the weather isn't too bad, not warm, and not cold, there's clouds but no rain. Pretty much ninety percent England's weather right?'

Although there was some humour in this, Jane was actually meaning it negatively. But the Brinkley took it as the former and simply laughed, in that big harsh voice that so obviously showed every bit of Scottish blood in the man.

'Up in Inverness, that where I come from, the weather be far worse, and more frequent. But that's nothin' we canny handle!'

Jane held back a laugh, he found the last few words Brinkley had used far too typical of a man from up north, and found it moderately amusing. He'd never met a Scot before, and he'd have to spend the next three hours getting used to them. He even thought with a bit of practice, he might be able to mimic the accent too. But he'd better not try, the driver knew he was Irish, and would probably not take much of liking to someone who could potentially be making fun of his birth.

'Ye must be tired, looks like ya could do with a wee sleep, feel free to nod off, I'll not disturb ya if ye need shuteye'

Jane had decided this man had absolutely no English blood in his body. He was far too nice, but Jane did recognise that this man was quite well built, so he was most definitely not harmless.

'Thankee, I just might do that' Jane said with a little compassion in his voice.

'Thank-what?' Brinkley questioned.

'It doesn't matter'

Before Jane actually fell asleep, he was staring out the window, where all the natural fields and trees were typically merged with pylons and out-of-the-way industrial factories. These things weren't here naturally, but the things that were there before had had no trouble accompanying them over the vast miles of semi natural farmland. He was looking at all the factory names as they passed like a blur. But one caught his eye. It was a particularly new looking factory which hadn't yet been consumed by moss and damp. He had never heard of the name of it before either. On the right of the motorway he saw a sign that directed a route towards it that had been securely lock with a "No Admittance" sign posted on it. Jane read:

Interior Union Corp.
Wide services from Home to worlds end!
Tel: 03422—11-11-11

He felt a little uncomfortable with the saying, but also the fact that even the area code at the beginning of the number added up to eleven as well. The day was perfectly normal, and there was plenty of natural light even at this time in the morning. But the factory looked dark, even in all its new and modern walls which looked to be made of some metal. Zinc perhaps? Maybe it was time to sleep and forget about this. But maybe always meant no. Not that he wasn't going to sleep, but he wasn't going to forget this strange company that didn't belong. Then he noticed a van driving down the path towards the building. It was just a plain silver van, but it was new and had some kind of picture of a man on the side in complete black, no details. All it said on the side was "Omni".

"Most definitely time to sleep", he thought. It didn't take long to slip. He felt more comfortable sleeping in this taxi than any other vehicle. But he'd soon regret it.

* * *

As usual, Lupe had a mighty smile on his face. He was a man of much optimism and happiness. Even though his friend circle was small, his spare time was mostly spent inside doing work for all his upcoming finals. He was always working, but never struggled to find time to talk to Jane every night. He had black hair which looked slightly unkempt, and looked like a bit of a hedge on his head. But he enjoyed having outlandish hair. His partner at the time had been his first and would no doubt be the last, as he was very much so in love with her. But she would be the last, not out of choice, but from unfortunate circumstances.

The plane had just landed, and although a little bumpy on the way down (all those clouds in England, from their typical weather, Jane would have thought) he had no fear of anything going wrong. Naivety was seldom seen in Lupe's personality, but he'd never feared for the worst without a little smirk. He made his way out onto the tarmac, down a set of stairs that were driven to the plane. All these passengers had just woken up, including the man that had sat next to him, who had pretended to fall asleep in the first place in order to attempt to stop this Bulgarian from talking. But Lupe had watched films he'd never seen before on the TV's placed on the back of the chairs. He had watched a few things he'd already seen, like the films with the spy hamsters in. That had kept him occupied for a long while. If anyone were to have a lot of wrinkles on their face at the age of fifty, Lupe would probably have the most due to using his facial muscles to pull off hundreds of cheery expressions each day.

He made his way through to the tiny baggage claims room, to collect his *Samsonite* luggage, and thought to buy a quick sandwich on the way out. Never had he heard of a BLT sandwich, but it looked like quite a tasty snack. "May as well try the food while I'm here" he thought. He did feel a little uneasy, placing all his trust in signs telling him how to get out of this building, but his English was word perfect, so there was no way he could have got it wrong.

Again he was greeted with the natural light of the sun attempting to shine through more clouds than he'd seen since the last rainstorm in Bulgaria, but these ones weren't rain, just those irritating ones that sometimes covered the warmth of the sun. Except here there was more than just the occasional irritating one. He took a quick scan of the surrounding area to check for his friend, but was surprised to see very few people, and Jane was none of them. But then a man holding a sign with "Lupe Delgado" written on it caught his eye. This was strange; he thought Jane himself would be here to greet him. So he innocently walked over and the man met his gaze, appearing to recognise him.

'Are ye Lupe? The one here to meet Mr. Jane?'

'Yes, I thought he would be here to-'before he could finish the man interrupted him with a bit of an odd accent.

'I am to take ya to meet him on the way back to his home. Can I take ye luggage sir?'

'I guess so . . .'

This all made Lupe feel uneasy, but he tried to block it out. This was a perfectly good explanation. Maybe Jane had arranged something to eat before they returned to his place. Maybe he shouldn't have eaten that BLT. He'd lost his appetite, and lost his surety of this whole situation. But he remained optimistic, and continued to follow the man who had taken the luggage from his very palms in the blink of an eye. He jumped into the rear passenger side; he hated being sat right next to a driver, especially one as odd as this man. He certainly wasn't English. Perhaps that's why Jane chose him. This made Lupe giggle inside his head, but he quickly put it aside and felt tiredness making its move on him. "No I can't sleep just yet" he thought. "I want to see a bit of this countryside before I miss it all".

It was halfway through the journey when the tiredness was making the part of his head behind his eyes hurt. So he decided that maybe it was time to sleep for a little while. As he started to drift he saw a very odd looking factory. But he took no notice. The driver had started to talk to him.

'Where are ye from?'

'A little place called Bulgaria my friend'

'Ah, I see, well your Lupe right? My name's Brinkley'

'Thanks . . . Brinkley'

With that short burst of conversation, Lupe slipped out. But in his subconscious mind he didn't notice that the taxi wasn't going on continuously. It slowed, and then turned down somewhere. The sound of a gate opening almost woke him from his sleep. But he remained oblivious to the actions that would change his life forever.

* * *

His sight made a scene that looked all too familiar to the films where they had scenes of heaven, mainly complete whiteness. But this wasn't quite as calming. It felt more like disarray and brokenness. Jane soon realised that he wasn't in a big white room at all, but in fact his eyesight was getting accustomed to the light on the ceiling above him. He squinted and turned over, to see someone here who he didn't expect to see the moment he woke up. There, lying on a makeshift bench that had been placed in this lockup was Lupe, fast asleep. What made Jane confused was the fact he looked rather peaceful. He was too dysfunctional to say anything at this moment, and all he could do was take in the surroundings. This was most definitely not Coventry airport. Nor was it the taxi he had slept in.

What he did see was a small slit, but three inches wide and nine inches across in the door that kept them presumably locked in. He tried to get up and walk over, but it seemed not only his eyes had taken a vacation. He lost his balance and keeled over near the bench. He was lucky not to have broken his jaw on the corner of it. With this thud of a body hitting the floor, Lupe almost instantly shot up.

'Werhah!!' this made no sense, and Jane thought perhaps the speech of his friend had not quite returned to him after all this surprise.

'Hey there sai, y'alright?' Jane tried to reassure him, but it seemed what he said came out with a particularly groggy voice.

'Yeah I think I am. I'm guessing this isn't your house. And if my assumptions are correct, I sure as hell knew I shouldn't have trusted that taxi driver! He had the most evil accent I've ever heard!'

'You talking about our man Brinkley?' Jane inquired

'Yeah! Don't you think he was odd, and a little scary?'

'He's not odd, he's just Scottish, and he seemed quite nice to me, but I don't believe that after what has happened to the both of us. Let me take a look at what's out there'

Jane nodded at the opening in the door, and attempted once more to walk to it. But this time he tried this action considerably more slowly. As he got to the door he saw no one outside of the room. But he did see a sign on the wall in the hall. And it did not comfort him one bit. In fact, the irony was, it was the first thing he expected to see, but he didn't understand why.

Interior Union
Rift subject holding area

He certainly hoped that they weren't the subjects, but this looked unmistakably like a holding area. But what was this Rift? And why were they chosen out of all the people in the world? Surely it's not that hard to find some homeless guy who needs the collateral pay to keep up one of the many habits he so eagerly contrives. But as Jane leant against the door to try and get a view of the rest of the corridor in his blind spot, the door clicked and swayed open. Again, Jane hadn't expected this and fell forward as the door swung open. But this time he didn't hit the floor. He was held up nothing short of five inches from the concrete ground.

Lupe has got used to using his feet again quicker than Jane, and had walked up behind him silently as Jane was reading the sign. He caught him just as the door made a decision to give up its hold on them. It was a good job he did, if Jane had continued to fall, his nose would be planted about 2 centimetres to the left of his face by the unwelcoming floor.

'Watch out there buddy, I'm better at helping with words not actions, consider yourself lucky' Lupe said this jokingly, but had surprised himself when he reacted so quickly.

'I'll not consider myself lucky until we finally get out of this place'

The look on Jane's face was a little unnerving, but given the situation, Lupe counted it as a suitable look for the given situation. But why would you kidnap two people and then fail to lock them up properly? Perhaps that was a question for the scary Scot that had brought them here. But Lupe doubted this was entirely the taxi driver's doing. Maybe it was some kind of greater plan, but Lupe often thought of things in a more fantasising way, so he guessed it couldn't be that complicated. Then again, the situation was a little strange, so nothing could be ruled out just yet.

'Maybe we should take our chances and try and get out of here' Lupe suggested.

'They left the door open for a reason, they want us to get out and come to them, but I agree, I see no other realistic choice' Jane understood they couldn't just sit there and eventually waste away, but he feared what their escape would bring upon them.

'Not to sound too hasty, but let's get a damned move on' Lupe smiled and nodded for Jane to lead the way; this was his country, so he would be leader for now.

They headed off into the only direction they could go, and follow the signs to this mysterious Rift. This left Jane a little bewildered as to how they actually got inside this place, as there was no clearly shown exit route. He supposed this was the idea, so the plans they were unfortunately included in went as the creator of them wanted. They were heading along the blue route, as the arrow showed, Jane had an idea there weren't just blue arrows, as there were different coloured lines on the floor which followed, but no signs to direct them to where they lead. This made Lupe feel particularly uncomfortable as he had no control of anything, this was the first time Jane saw these emotions from his friend, but imagined that he was showing some that were much the same. But he wasn't. Lupe noticed a strange calmness come over his friend as they made their way through this maze. But he was glad someone had some control, it would help keep them on top of things.

'My ears popped' Jane said in awe.

'That means . . .'

'Yeah, we're just going further down'

The conversation did not continue, it seemed they both had agreed there was no other choice, but to follow the path that lay before them. They had no choice, and saw no point in making an effort to undermine whoever had so aptly taken them. There was clearly no reason to believe the person who had taken them would kill them; why would someone make you walk this far just to meet a short and unnecessary death. They were part of a much larger plan that probably had something to do with this Rift. That was the main thing that scared Lupe, not knowing what purpose they were brought here, but knowing that a word defined it.

They came a across an odd looking door at the end of their path. By now all the multicoloured lines on the floor had split off into solid brick walls. Maybe they were put there as some sick joke to make them think that there would be an alternative way out. Or maybe the walls were illusions. Jane suspected that this door was also unlocked, but he saw no handle. Only a small note saying:

Verbal Access Required

Jane didn't stop to think.

'Eleven'

'Oh yeah as if a random-' Lupe was cut off by another clicking sound as the strange looking door unlocked what kept it solidly in place.

'How did you . . .'

'Just a guess' Jane knew Lupe wouldn't believe this, but now wasn't the time for questions. Lupe understood this as well as Jane did.

Jane opened the door, and had never felt so much tension. The door may have been plain in look, but Jane could feel something emanating from behind it, but he wasn't too sure whether Lupe could feel it too. Something there, that should not be. The door made no attempt at squeaking like a typical door of importance would, but Jane made attempts to ensure that if it did, he could stop it as and when it began. As Jane slowly opened it, Lupe leaning ever closer behind his shoulder, they slowly peered around the growing opening from the side of the plain door. But as the door opened, nothing but pink light flooded their eyes, leaving them partially blind. But beyond this pink light were silhouettes of three tall, and heavily built figures.

Despite tiptoeing over Jane's shoulder, Lupe seemed to have clear vision of sight over it, just to make out three. One of them pointing what seemed to be a gun at the other. He thought he recognised the figure who took the bullet to the chest. He heard no noise; this pink light was also giving a low hum that seemed to drown out almost everything. Jane and Lupe soon realised that the man lying in the pool of his Scottish blood, was Brinkley, the taxi driver who was full of surprises. In a way Jane felt sorry for him, but Lupe, having not shared a word with him felt very different about the man. All logic and sanity was temporarily lost from Lupe's head.

"Welcome to the Rift room, young one, glad to see you made it here with such impeccable timing.". The voice was being sent through to Jane's mind, and he looked over to see Lupe was just as astonished. "Follow us if you will, for you are one of the few that may, you and your puzzling friend here." Jane attempted to send back "Who are you?" And at first he thought he had failed, but in actual fact these spectres had ignored his seemingly logical question. "You need not know a thing, follow if you will, but understand that you can either attempt to stop our plans of killing this monster, which I assure you will fail, but if you do I guarantee your questions will be answered.". Both of the boys thought there was a clear answer to this. Run. But what if this thing was something more important than they thought? What if it was some part of a larger plan? They would never know unless they took the chance. But they would never come back, but neither of them thought about this fact they had been graciously told, as they ran for the men before them, without even engaging in a debate. But Jane felt they had, in their mind.

The men walked slowly towards the light, and soon became engulfed in it. Both the boys became a little apprehensive about following them, but never the less, they continued on the charge. They were soon being pulled forward, into this pink hum of light, the Rift, so the signs had said. They were being pulled to a place, they would forever be lost in. Discordia incarnate.

* * *

"My head hurts like hell". Jane thought

'Yeah mine too; maybe this wasn't such a great idea in hindsight'

Lupe had spoken without thinking, as he lay on the smooth floor.

'How did you hear what I was thinking?'

'I thought you said it out loud, I just heard it'

Jane gave a horrified look, and soon Lupe was looking back with a similar look. Had he really just heard his thoughts? Perhaps this place was a lot stranger than the floor gave away.

'He said we'd not be able to get back' Jane had said this with a tone more along the lines of realisation. Realisation of a bad choice, but this wasn't one they should waste time on thinking about. But Lupe had left behind something a little more important to him. If he couldn't go back, he could see his beloved again. Jane could feel his thoughts, not just using techniques he had long learnt, but could literally hear them in his head. “We’ll find a way to get back, I can’t promise, but we can try”. He sent this over and saw that it had registered with Lupe. But promises didn’t seem to make up for it.

When Jane looked over to Lupe again after getting to his feet, all he saw was a grin on his friends face. Was this all in his head or had the craziest thing just happened to them and now his friend was smiling as if it was for the better?

‘What is there to smile about?’

‘Reminds me of that awful TV show the western world watches so much, the one with the people stranded on the island’

‘You mean *Lost*?’

‘Exactly, it’s a little like *Lost,* no?’

That remark had Lupe written all over it. Mr. Optimism.

3

That's Love. No Rhyme, No Reason

Despite the optimism Lupe showed, they still showed much in the way of confusion. *Fear*, Jane thought. This place they had been taken to, had been lured into, was neither pretty nor forgiving. The terrain was nothing short of rocky, and looked like some kind of desert. Although the patch they were in was some kind of flat, smooth, pink tinged metal. But it didn't feel cold, as Jane expected, and it didn't feel warm either. All it seemed to do was amplify the low hum that they had felt when they ran towards the light. But they knew it wasn't just light.

Lupe wondered why they had been encouraged to follow these strange men to this place. What made them ones of the very few that could travel through it? Lupe supposed that they were important in some way, the ones that could make a difference in this world. Yet, these men wanted to achieve something, and they knew Jane and Lupe would be the ones to try and stop them. So why encourage them to follow? These were questions that could only be answered by chasing down these men of the pink light. The Members of *Interior Union.* And that brought up another question. Just who was Interior Union? Lupe knew they had certainly not originated in their world, but this one they were apparently trapped in. But if this company had got through into their world, then they must have found a way back. Perhaps only certain people could go back.

All this was far too much for Jane to process, he could feel Lupe's mind at work and felt all his thoughts, and he decided that this was all best left for a more pressing time. It clouded his mind and he could feel his own emotions swelling inside his brain for Lupe's loss. It was time to make some priorities and decided just what they were going to do. It was then when Jane saw a flash and a faint plume of smoke over the horizon. Lupe had seen this kind of thing before.

'That's got incineration plant written all over it. At last this place and our world have something in common.'

'Yeah, mindless pollution' Jane replied in a bitter tone

'Looks like a little more pollution wouldn't make much difference to the land in this place. But one thing gets me-'

'Where are those two men who managed to go through seconds before us?'

'This psychic thing is gonna grow on me, at least I hope it will, but right now it's moderately scary'

Jane hadn't understood why this had happened to him, hearing thought as clear as day. It disturbed him, but at the same time, he imagined it being quite useful for their times ahead. But if this had happened to him, then what had happened to Lupe? Jane could feel Lupe's feelings of remorse and sadness, and understood how he missed his partner. It was understandable, but it would get them nowhere in their seemingly new quest. But right now they didn't know what that quest was. It was as if they were pulled into something prematurely, doing something that they shouldn't have done for another few years, when they understood more. Maybe that was the men's plan. Apparently they were told by the men themselves that they were to stop them from doing something. But this seemed all too convenient for both their liking.

'I think it's time we went to find some answers, and that little industrial plant over there is where the questions begin. After that, we get on the trail of Interior Union.' Jane took on a leadership role straight away, without any appointment.

'You're the boss. I should imagine you might like England more than you like this place.'

'There's still a chance for this place yet.'

With that halt of conversation, they began the trek toward the civilisation they saw miles before them. There were miles and miles of strange murky desert, with next to no visible life among the seemingly random rocks across the plains. But there was little else they could do, unless they sat and twiddled their thumbs at the idea that had become their life. But Jane continued to read Lupe's thoughts, and found little comfort in them. He felt so sorry for Lupe, he had lost what meant most to him, and now on their journey, they saw no means of getting back what they lost.

* * *

Strangers in the strangest land, a song which flooded into Jane's mind, and reminded him of all those so called "mellow" songs that *Tom McRae* had released. In his opinion, they were some of the best songs he'd heard, songs which had a true sense of meaning and the kind of albums you could listen to all the way through. But those days of quality music were dead and gone. He wasn't even too sure if this place they had been taken to had even got such a thing as music. But he thought he shouldn't assume that just because the land looked different, meant that it was entirely different. But what they were walking towards showed some similarities.

As Lupe looked across the plains they walked upon, he had been secretly hoping that this would not become the last land they would ever know of. He couldn't stop thinking about what he had left behind, and had a constant weight on his mind. Regardless of what questions they wanted answering, what task they had in this place, he just wanted to go back home, to his beloved and hold her once more and tell her just how much he appreciated her. This little accidental trip had taught him plenty in the space of a few hours. He knew not to take so much for granted before. In his head, he was hoping there would be an answer, but sense told him there would be nothing of the sort.

When you see something on the horizon, it's easy to focus on at first, as it seems so close. But as you gradually begin to walk and realise that what you thought was in reaching distance, is actually further away than you once thought, it becomes harder to keep your optimism and hopes on the goal ahead. It seems like nothing ever gets bigger, just clearer in your head. The problems don't solve themselves; they simply make themselves better known to you. It made them more of a problem. But both boys seemed to have a limitless supply of optimism, despite how much hey wavered on their way. Jane knew as well as Lupe did, this was not the only hardship they'd go through, and was probably the easiest they'd come across. But everyone starts somewhere on the ladder. But this wasn't a ladder any ordinary man wanted to climb. Only the seldom seen man was enough of a fool to try.

'You ever thought why rich people are always the ones that go for long runs?'

Lupe looked puzzled at this outburst, and didn't know what to say, but managed:

'To keep fit?'

'You see, the rich man has to break a lot of morals everyday to earn the large sum he does every year, lie to his employers, his family and most of his friends, just to get where he wants. With this type of lifestyle, you can imagine that the rich man has a lot of problems on his mind.'

'Ok I think I'm following here.' And Lupe was.

'So the rich man sought a way to help clear the problems from his mind, and no one widely accepts self punishment. So they soon found that putting their body limit to the test by running for miles in the country, often helped them think about these problems, and sometimes even solve them. So they'd go back to their homes and have an honest life. But only for so long before they go back to their dishonest lifestyle. So that's why you see them so frequently on those scenic routes, running their hearts out.'

'I think perhaps you might know this from experience. But I get the point, and how does this help us?' But Lupe had some insane idea of what Jane was thinking.

'Do you think you have a problem right now?' Jane asked.

'I think so yes, so your solution is . . . to run'

'Absolutely'

And with that lesson, they put into practice to see if the rich man had indeed found a solution to the problems in life. Then they ran, towards that ever closer goal, with nothing but the clothes on their back, the trust in their hearts, and the shoes on their feet to keep them going. They, like the rich man of the story, ran their hearts out. To find answers, and cling on to that ever more appealing hope that seemed so out of reach.

* * *

At first Lupe thought he couldn't continue at this speed for such sustained periods of time. But it seemed this place gave him an all new burst of vigour. Despite the trials he was having within his mind, he found the energy to continue on through the stitch that was developing near the lower part of his abdominals. After spending so much time doing school work and socialising with his friends and beloved, he rarely got any occasion where it as necessary for him to be so active. So to have this feeling of pure stamina was quite exhilarating. He did not expect it to last, and he simply thought it could be down to the adrenalin still making its way through his system after their entrance to this world, but even that must have been gone after this amount of time. They kept up this pace for quite some time, and found their goal (as unwelcoming as it looked) getting ever closer, and more desirable as it protruded into most of their vision.

'This place . . .' Lupe managed the first part with a gasp between for more breath.

' . . . does something to the people in it, don't you feel it? Like your little mind reading thing.'

Jane looked a little disappointed at himself, perhaps because he didn't feel comfortable with this little gift of mind reading this place had given him.

'I think it does certain things to certain people. For example, it enhanced my skills, but in your case, it gave you something you were particularly bad at before'

Lupe didn't look hurt at his friends comment about his fitness, but did feel a little dissatisfied with Jane's remark.

'I guess I wasn't the fittest of guys beforehand. Seems like it didn't do much else to us though'

'Perhaps we'll find out a little more about this once we find someone, preferably one that speaks a similar language'

'You don't think they'll speak like us?' Lupe seemed a little unsure.

'I think maybe we should keep an open mind, but then again, that is a lot easier for me to say lately' and with that remark, Jane turned his attention back to their goal, with a smile on his face. How long that would last was the first question in Lupe's mind, the second was, what if this place was automated? He dared not think this, but he had a strange feeling of dismay in his mind, a little doubt creeping into his dwindling optimistic frame of mind.

Aside from its surroundings, the building looked fairly normal, as if it would quite easily fit into Jane's world quite well. Unlike the Interior Union building which had stuck out rather morosely in the field it was stuck in. almost as if it shouldn't be there, and was so incredibly hard to miss. This one seemed almost identical to a typical industrial build, aside from the fact that it had not been consumed by rust or mould as of yet. It could've been a new building but the boys doubted it. This place felt as old as it was strange, but they knew a lot less than they thought.

From the distance they had come from, the factory looked like it was a fairly small place, but as they got closer and closer it began to hit Jane that it was in actual fact a leviathan of a building. The walls must have been a few hundred feet high, made of reformed brick, kept in rather good condition, and the smoke turrets on top seemed as though they were about the size of two average buses.

"No way could someone have made this with basic building tools" Lupe thought. "And there's definitely no way this could be automated". He turned to Jane.

'Imagine the amount of people that must be employed to operate this thing'

Jane replied with 'Dozens I could imagine, if not hundreds, but where could the workers have possibly come from, there's no civilisation within miles of eyesight.'

This brought a thought to Jane's mind. Eyesight. Maybe these people weren't in blatant eyesight. If this land was as bas as it looked, maybe the only place that could be permanently inhabited was *underground.*

By this time the boys pace had slowed to a brisk walk, and both of them showed increasing tiredness, felt as though the world was pulling them down that slightest bit, to make them work harder with each action. But there could be no pause for rest at this point, both of them were hungry and tired, and they didn't know how welcoming this environment was at night.

At first it didn't look as if the building actually had an entrance, until Lupe look a little higher than ground level. It appeared as if the people of this place were a little paranoid about general ground. If they were in fact living below ground. But now Jane thought they either chose to live beneath the earth, or far above the clouds in cradle like ships, suspended permanently in the air. "No, that's going a little bit too far I think" Jane thought. Maybe his imagination was getting the better of him, trying to use the new abilities he had received. He had now realised that this was an idea from one of the games he had played on his friend's console, the mechanical warrior robot type thing.

He wasn't someone who remembered things like that much; he preferred to conserve his memory for more important things.

'After such a run, a ladder never looked so unappealing to me.' Lupe said this jokingly, but meant it at the same time. It was nothing a smile couldn't wear off.

'No rest for the wicked' Jane said as if it were a question.

'I thought we were being the good guys here'?' Lupe seemed a little astonished at first.

'Well you never know until the end, for all we know we could be fighting for the wrong thing.'

'Y'know a little optimism never hurt anyone. I'd rather not know that I ran for a dozen miles, just to take over the world or something, Id rather pay minions to do that for me. Now let's get up this ladder, before I start to complain.'

At first Lupe looked nothing short of unwilling to start the climb, as if he doubted himself, but soon trundled up before Jane thought to take the lead. By now their legs should have been aching from all the lactic acid building up in their muscles, but it felt like they had only taken a short run.

When Lupe looked up, he thought the ladder was never ending, but saw a small panel which seemed to be big enough for a few men, that looked like it was held up by string sized wires. That would do nothing for their confidence, but this place wasn't exactly a walk in the park, and Jane had been right. The run was the first and probably the easiest challenge this world would throw at them. Lupe was hoping the next one wouldn't be quite as harsh as he could imagine.

One thing they noticed about this place was the climate. Everything seemed all too perfect; there was no wind at all, even at the height they had reached at this point. There were clouds but no visible sign of any sort of sun or star that emanated light. There was a light source of sorts, but behind it seemed to feel like darkness when you tried to look deep into the sky. That was another thing that puzzled Jane. The clouds were incredibly high up, far higher than those from home. Perhaps this place was altogether bigger than where they had come from. Maybe this was a bigger *planet* with a different atmosphere. But why and how it was here was another question, because both boys felt as though this place was not natural, but man made.

Sometimes when you walk on ground, it feels like there should be some kind of sturdiness in it, and no sense of give. But as they ran across the plains, they noticed some kind of bounce, but not an elastic type. It was more of a subtle measure put in place to remove any type of hindrance ground would normally give. The ground looked natural but felt all wrong. Lupe was somewhat glad to be on ladder of all places, and felt that some kind of blatant man made object would make him feel a little safer in this place, a little more in control. He needed to understand things to feel safe. This place gave him no security.

It seemed this high up that the part of the brain that was used for speech was being put aside, as the boys had kept silent since making their way up. Silence was never an option for Jane so he opened first.

'Everything going on ok up there?' It was a desperate attempt, but Jane felt it was necessary.

'Tip top, literally. A few more minutes and we'll be on top of this thing.'

Jane sympathised with Lupe's courageous effort at keeping good posture, but noticed that the humour in his voice was slowly waning. He remembered looking out of the taxi window, at the countryside that was mixed with wild flowers and trees, along with pylons and power cables, not to mention the occasional car wreckage. But as he looked over this desolate place, he noticed nothing but the strange ground they had travelled. Neither did he notice any other form of civilisation in this place. This made him think of the possibilities. Had they been too late after these strange men somehow? Maybe they had destroyed this place in a matter of minutes, but failed to take down this last building. That would explain the wasteland state of this world.

"Far too many questions for one mind to answer" Jane thought. He had questioned everything that had happened so far, and doubt was rising in his feelings like a rush of blood to the head. But he refused to let the image of this place crush his hopes of some answers. He knew he would have to constantly reassure Lupe of his intentions to help him get back. But that could be more difficult as the days passed. His own mind was becoming difficult, and he did not know the reason why. But still they climbed.

4

Glory Skies

They had approached from a different side. If the boys made it to the top and did for some reason decide to walk over to the other edge of the building, they would notice three lines of disturbed ground, about three meters wide, each one going in a different direction, but completely straight, seeming to continue to the horizon. Whether this would give them a sense of purpose was another matter. But fate knew that they would not do what seemed so obvious. Someone watching from another place could clearly see a path for someone to go. But when they were in such a position as Jane and Lupe, sense was replaced with questions and the need to survive.

Neither of the boys had so much as mentioned anything about food. It seemed as though the feeling was forgotten here, and that it wasn't necessary. But as they reached the top of the ladder, onto the platform which rattled Jane's nerves at every slight waver in the air, Lupe brought up this odd fact.

'I haven't eaten in hours.'

'Neither have I, but I'm not hungry, and I know your not either. In fact you're wondering why we're not hungry. Weird huh?'

Lupe wasn't too pleased at Jane letting himself into his thoughts, and as Jane asked the last question, he noticed and immediately felt himself being thrown out. This was a strange feeling, and a first.

'This place is the definition of weird' Lupe said 'and I'm not too keen on wasting away like a man who doesn't know how to eat, wouldn't exactly be a courageous way to die now would it.'

'Best that we achieved something before that happens then. Let's get cracking through this place, let's hope for some normal people.'

As Jane turned to open the door, he remembered what happened last time he let himself in a door, and thought he would prefer to keep his nose in one piece. He gave a "lead the way" gesture to Lupe.

'You got the honours this time my friend.'

'Why thankee'

As Lupe opened the door, the way they usually did with the strange click from nowhere, they were surprised by something they did not expect to see in this world.

* * *

It was like a reminder of the long years that had passed since those TV shows where the hero of the story was inevitably and animal, of some highly adorable factor. Although the surprise was not from the memories (cheesy though they may have been), but it was the fact that the sheer chance of something like this arising in this world was incredibly slim. But this world had a brilliant way of asking many questions and answering none, one of which was, how on earth did something like this get here? Perhaps it was the same way the boys had, except it could not be on purpose. No one would have brought something like this through without any real reason. It would be most likely that this had broken in and came through by accident, or by chance, depending on how this thing would aid them in answering their questions.

If it were in fact some cruel version of fate working its' course on their lives, they had hoped it was a gift, and not a burden. Although in its present state they were not entirely sure which, as they had only milliseconds before it launched itself at them.

They were often considered to be the closest looking animals to demons; however they weren't in short supply in their own world, in more domestic forms. With their strange blue ringed eyes that so many people found mesmerising, and their double coat of white and black, these looked like animals far from ordinary.

However this was no ordinary one, and was clear that it had part of its anatomy missing. But this 3 legged wonder had no falter in its leap. Despite the condition of this place, its front canines seemed in perfect form, as if new and never used. This lead the boys to believe in the time they had to think, that the animal had not used those teeth before, and in a long time, so just how was it in such good condition? It had no signs of malnutrition at all.

Jane had a particular liking to Siberian huskies, but his feelings had been all but gone as this disabled dog seemed to lurch towards them. How on earth had this husky got here? And where was its front left leg? After all this thought the dog was all but in Jane's face, and had already made contact with his upper chest. But it made no effort to take a bite out of his face, rather it continued to launch at him and push him harshly to the ground. It seemed Jane would be spending more time being thrown to the ground than he thought. Maybe one time it would be from higher up, and do a little more damage than a disabled animal.

'Get this-' was all Jane managed before a burst of barking broke out in his face

The mouth of the canine was so close to his face, the barks pierced the eardrums in his ears with such a pain that his face contracted as he winced and screamed deep inside his head. Rattling his brain within his skull, sending shivers down every nerve in his body. But the thing that shocked his brain the most was that he could hear thoughts inside the animals head. Human thoughts. Despite the density of the sound going through his mind, he only held a shocked expression as some kind of twisted realisation came to his mind.

"This cannot be . . ." Jane thought, and as if he had sent that sentence through into the dogs mind, it stopped as if thrown off by something it did not understand. "Are you *supposed* to be a dog?" and as if the blue eyed beast understood what happened, it sent back "I . . . I don't believe so"

'What the-, get away from him!' Lupe shouted, but neither his friend nor the creature seemed to be paying attention to anything other than each other.

"Hello there young man, my apologies, you're the first person I've seen since I was sent here, and I felt the need to protect myself, my name, is Roland"

5

Glory Skies Part 2

Its not everyday you get kidnapped, sent through a portal you don't know how it came into existence that you cant come back from, and seemingly eternally lost from your beloved forever. But what he was seeing was something he did not expect.

By this point Lupe had thought of the fact that Jane could be communicating to the creature through thought. But the puzzling look on both the faces of his friend and this dog looked human. And unless he was not mistaken, it looked as though they were *talking*. It didn't take a psychic to see this.

'What's going on? Lupe seemed to beg more than ask. 'Who are you?' he was talking to Roland now, as if he expected some answer from the well bodied dog.

'His name is Roland, and I don't think he was a dog at birth.' Jane said this calmly but with the same look of shock on his face.

'I don't follow. Not born a dog?'

'He was once a man, in this place-' Roland interrupted Jane's speech by sending "That's quite right young fellow!

The men of Interior Union caused this, but that I must cover on another occasion."

'I think the men that captured you and me are the ones responsible for Roland's change.'

In normal circumstances, this would be all too much for one man to comprehend all at once. But given the situation, there was no time to stop and think. Lupe would just have to take what was being said to him, as crazy as it all sounded. However this place had taught him one thing. Nothing was crazy. If anything in this world was crazy, then back in his home world, it should be considered as utterly insane by all standards. "These days aren't easy anymore" he thought. "And they'll only get harder, until eventually, they get too hard."

'How can you be so sure?' he questioned. ' For all you know he could be a sort of trap they set for us.'

By the look on Jane's face, Roland could see the recognition of an absurdity and immediately felt the need to send "I assure you I mean no harm upon you two, I just want to get back to my former self." This came across in a particularly whiney way, and Jane thought of the dog making that whining sound an animal would make when feeling moderately upset about something. However this was not the time for them to get upset. They needed to move on.

First, however, Jane needed to ask Roland something.

"Are there any people here?"

"Many, but not in plain sight, nor are they below us, I presume you thought of that." Roland seemed to answer in a matter of fact tone, which messed with Jane's mind, after all he was a dog.

"That leaves only one thing, if there are people here at all."

“The Glory Skies young man.”

Jane had been stuck in his place of concentration, it wasn’t every day you talk to someone, or some*thing* with your mind. He had not noticed Lupe just standing there with an ever growing look of bewilderment on his face. Lupe must have felt left out; he hadn’t seen any sign of something special happening to him yet. Right now he was the odd one out. But was he? He had lost something he loved and was told frequently he could never get it back. It seemed Roland had too; after all, he had been taken from his human form. Perhaps right now, Jane was the odd one out, but harnessed a skill that both of them needed.

‘Sorry.’ At this point Jane had noticed that Lupe standing there awkwardly.

‘No need to apologise, do what you need to do then-’

‘We need to move on, I know. Roland says the people in this world-’

‘Ah so there are people around here!’ That was the best news Lupe had heard all day.

‘Yeah, but they are up there.’ Jane pointed his right thumb up to the sky. Along with that gesture, came a look of surprise from Lupe’s face.

“That’s quite right young man” Roland butted in, or so it seemed to Jane. When you hear someone’s thoughts inside your head, things seem a little different.

‘Ok so, your saying, the people of this world, whatever world it is, are living in the sky. Somehow’

‘Sorry if that sounds a little vague to you, but it seems either Roland here doesn’t know much or he doesn’t want to say anything more.’ Jane’s tone had changed a little. He felt like questioning Roland’s integrity, Jane wasn’t quite sure how much truth Roland was showing in his thoughts.

"We don't have time to discuss such things as these luxuries, I promise, when the time comes I'll tell you what's necessary." Roland sounded a little desperate, but Jane felt he could trust him for now.

Even though the dog Lupe saw before him had lost one of its legs, it still stood proud, and majestic, as though it were constantly in need to impress. That made Lupe think that the person this dog was before, could've been someone important. Maybe someone they *needed.* "Hell it could just be some poor guy who thinks too much of himself" Lupe thought. Then he realised that Jane could've been reading his mind. He looked over and saw he was too busy concentrating on the canine before them.

'How do we get up there?' Lupe asked.

'Roland said there's some sort of a lift device that takes you up, and it's in this building. But apparently the building doesn't stay in the same place.'

'It *moves?*' Lupe seemed a little shocked. 'How does something this big *move* across these damned wastelands?'

'And I'm afraid our thoughts came true. This whole place is automated. Something about it collected the resources necessary to keep those things in the skies above ground.'

'Yeah I can imagine that something that holds millions of people a few miles above ground must have one hell of a drain on batteries.' Jane thought it was good to see Lupe's humour was still their. That would keep him sane for long enough.

Lupe didn't entirely trust Roland, and for good reason. The last person that had caused their paths to crash together was an evil man who had soon met his end when his boss' didn't need him anymore. But something made Lupe feel a little more welcoming to this person. "No not a person, a *dog*" he thought, but he knew it was a person deep down.

He just needed time to adjust and take in everything that had happened to them.

Jane felt a little more welcoming to the new member in their party. Roland could help them, he probably knew more about this place than they did, and this knowledge could greatly help them in times to come.

"I think it's time we got going through this place, it's a bit of a maze and we have a while to walk before we're out of this leviathan."

'Agreed' Jane said out loud

'Excuse me?' Lupe had not heard Roland's thoughts and wondered exactly what Jane was agreeing with.

'We need to get going through this place, before it moves out of the way of place above.'

'Ah, yeah, of course.' There was a little doubt in Lupe's voice, and Jane guessed he felt a little left out of the conversation. Jane knew Lupe's time would come, when he would need to take the lead, and Jane would be in a similar position of feeling a little useless. It seemed like this place had a bit of equality in it. Or so Jane hoped.

* * *

The inside of this moving industrial plant was nothing to be raved about. There was a constant hum of whatever this thing had in replacement of engines. It has the smell of fuel, but it wasn't one either of the boys had smelled before. Despite the fact it was automated, it had clearly been designed to hold people and transport them temporarily, because Lupe noticed overhead lights buzzing in their sockets, sounding (and looking) as if they would just fizzle out. The place looked rusted and was probably older than either of the boys could guess. Regardless of its condition, it clearly served its purpose well, as it hadn't broken down yet, and it helped power whatever the people of this land needed.

Jane wondered just what this thing could find on the plains that would power anything. No knowledge in the world could help him discover this. At least no knowledge in *his* world could. As they walked through the ramble of wires, halls, and seemingly dead lights, the boys had nothing but the hum of the slow, constant engines, powering away at the ground beneath their feet. Or more to the point, a few hundred metres below their feet.

Behind the light in this plant, it looked continuously dark beyond, just like it had seemed outside this world. It was one of the uncertainties, one of the questions, that had truly unnerved Jane, because it was so inexplicable. Then Roland decided to reveal a piece of information while they were clambering through the plant. Daunting information.

* * *

"I presume your wondering what, where and most importantly *when* this place is" Roland began.

'What do you mean when? As in, the timescale of this place?' Jane replied without so much as a thought about Lupe hearing only a random out burst of dialogue that Jane was seemingly saying to himself.

"To put things bluntly, this is a world you know, but has since been scorched by earthling man, and has moved on many times since."

'You wanna fill me in on what he's talking about?' Lupe seemed a little more interested in what Roland had to say, as it had aroused a little perk in Jane's attention. But he was only ignored. Jane started again.

'What do you mean moved on? There's no way this place was once earth. Just look at it!" the anger in Jane's voice was rising, and it pierced through Lupe's skull like a knife.

"Us humans did a little more damage than just a simple A-bomb, young man. We found weapons far beneath the sea bed while drilling for oil. Ones we didn't know the power of until we used them. As soon as that happened it was too late."

At this point the tone had gone down to a grave one in seconds. It was odd how someone's thoughts could portray a different feeling, after all they weren't said as such, but Jane could feel conversational thoughts in a different way. Far more intricately. What Jane was hearing was the equivalent of on of those notices you get from a cold hearted, stone faced man, who is due to tell you of the death of a loved one. This made Jane think. Maybe his parents would get a similar message back home. Back in his timescale. But was that time gone now he had travelled through to this barren place?

'Does this world and ours coexist, or is it just one?' Jane felt the need for the answer, more than he showed.

'It has to!' Lupe butted in. Jane knew why his friend sounded so desperate for this to be the truth. If it wasn't, his hopes of a reunion would be crushed, and so would his feelings.

"Your friend looks like he could do with this answer" Roland began, "and yes, it does coexist with yours. Without one, there is no other. Just blackness, like the one you clearly see behind the light in this one."

'Good news Lupe, they both have to coexist' Jane felt a tremendous weight off his chest, and sensed a great sigh of relief from Lupe, but there was still more weight to be rid of yet. Jane felt like the middle man for Lupe and Roland, but didn't mind. Sometimes someone had to make some sacrifices, and there were some things which just had to be done. There was no use in complaining about anything. It would get them nowhere.

'There's still more we need to know' Lupe said, but he somehow knew they wouldn't get much more information from their new comrade. 'But let me guess, all at the right time?'

Roland made a nodding gesture, but as a dog, it looked for trivial than anything else. It was odd conversing with a dog. It was even more strange realising that it understood everything they did and said. But what they didn't know, was that the answers they wanted, couldn't simply be explained. They didn't know just how long Roland had been here, or the extent of knowledge he had. But this was something he wanted to keep to himself. They hadn't considered whether or not he trusted *them*. At this point Roland wanted to keep some important things to himself, just in case the information he held was the only thing keeping him from being killed. But the boys showed no intention of threat. "Other than that one." He thought, thinking of Jane with his mental abilities. Just what could he do with his mind? Maybe even the boys didn't know that. Neither had Roland seen what the other boy possessed, although both of them seemed to have very different regional accents. The taller and older one seemed to speak the language as though it wasn't his own.

It was interesting for the boys to see a dog missing a leg make its way through a mountain of mangled metal and other waste products. It had obviously been used to being a tripod instead of a quadruped. Maybe it had had been missing a leg for quite some time, showing his age. Nevertheless, Roland made no struggling about hopping over rather sharp and dangerous looking objects. "Perhaps the guy's been making his way round this place frequently" Jane thought.

As simple as Roland made it look, Jane and Lupe still had difficulty making it through the extremely narrow corridors. After all, Roland was about a third of their size and weight. This led Lupe to think. Roland weighed considerably less, so what if the floors in this moving building had deteriorated. It might not take the combined weight of them all. "Now's not the time for negativity!" Lupe would think to himself quite often. He didn't much care if Jane was weeding around his head. Nothing would change their present course. Thinking to himself was the only shelter he could take from exploding all of his emotions out of proportion.

"I can see you're both looking a little exasperated, there's not long to go now. If I can make it with three quarters of myself, I'm sure you two young boys can keep up." Roland sounded as though he was attempting to reassure Jane, but by the simple look of tiredness, he saw it had not helped. But this did give an insight to Jane that Roland was a sight older than them. With age came maturity . . . and knowledge.

If this had been said to Lupe, he would have almost instantly taken it as pessimism, and reacted quite differently. But Jane had simply showed how unimpressed he was, by showing no emotion at all. It seemed to Lupe, that Jane was quite good at this. Although he seemed a perfectly nice friend at all other times, Lupe was now beginning to think his friend was a little less caring than he thought. He *needed*

Jane to care though, if they were to have any chance of getting back to their own world, and carrying on the life he loved to live. He thought by now that he should accept the way things had turned out, but acceptance wasn't a luxury that Love liked to give.

The main thing that made Jane nervous about this building was the fact that it was so old and yet so *advanced.* He was pretty sure that cables and lights hadn't been invented thousands of years ago, let alone massed together in such a large form. He guessed this was easily bigger than the pyramid in Giza, and altogether higher than any of the buildings he had ever his laid eyes upon. "And on top of all that it moves!" he told himself. What kind of people could have the advanced mind, and the time required to make this kind of thing? He felt he had to stop asking questions, even though it was the natural human thing to do. It only worsened their state of mind, and made some things evermore difficult.

'If I'm right about the size of this thing, it'd take us quite a while to reach the centre, if this lift is dead in the centre.' Lupe had decided to share his negativity with the other two, in hopes it would encourage Roland to tell them more about this *thing.*

'Well?' Jane aimed this at Roland with the type of look you would give a child if they had something to say for themselves.

"Your friend would be right, however the lift isn't quite in the centre. Luckily for us it's on this side of the plant"

By the look on Jane's face, he had clearly realised what Lupe had meant to do. If they could strip any knowledge from Roland, now would be the time to do it.

'I'll take that as a "It's closer to us than the centre" then' Lupe didn't like to presume, but knew if anything negative would come of it, Jane would have told him.

'Looks like your learning to read peoples minds too'

As they walked on, they came across what looked to be a flat plate wall. It didn't have the features of a door or anything else. Just a plain wall, blocking their path. Not the first thing to do that to them. But despite the boys weariness to walk on, Roland seemed to simply ignore it. He kept walking, and walking. He showed no remorse, never faltered and then as he reached the wall, Lupe let out;

'Watch out old man!'

But he walked through the wall.

'A hologram' Jane presumed. However, he presumed wrong.

They took a few reluctant steps forward and then made what seemed to them to be a giant step into something they knew nothing about. Jane half expected to just simply hit the wall, and Lupe expected to feel something when they went through.

But they both felt nothing, as if it were never there.

* * *

"Do you boys remember how you got here?"

'Yeah, we ran through some weird pink light'

Again, Lupe just looked over his shoulder at them and decided to walk ahead instead of trying to make sense of a one sided conversation. He hoped they'd find some way to change Roland back or at least some device so they could understand him.

"Well in case the people who lured you here didn't tell you, you're very unique people."

'Meaning?'

"Well, only certain people can come into this world, and in turn only those people can get through these mental blocks."

'So the wall we just walked through, is a *mental* block?'

"Indeed, one way of keeping the lowly ones out." Roland made a very odd chuckling sound as a dog and it came out like a dog dreaming.

Lowly. Jane hated the sound of that word. As if some people were superior to others, in some false or corrupt way. This made him wonder if this was some world made for people who claimed to be of higher intelligence or better wealth. If this was so, where *were* all the so called "lowly" people of this world? "Stop asking yourself questions" he thought, then as if from nowhere, ahead Lupe said.

'What questions?'

Jane had obviously thought too strongly and accidentally sent it to Lupe.

'Sorry, I guess I was thinking out loud.' This expression seemed to make more sense now.

* * *

No different to every other door they had encountered in this place. Grey, rust covered, no door handle (it seemed the people of this time used their hands little), it looked ancient and as if it would never work. Doors seemed to be the only thing in their path, and as simple as they may be, the way in which to unlock each one would either be very similar (if not the same) or completely different. "I can see this getting frustrating" Lupe thought.

'May not look like much, but Roland claims this is the lift.' Jane took one glance at Lupe and continued, "don't look too overjoyed to see it.' Sarcasm was all that was the hope he had left right now.

That look of "Say anything like that again and I'll plant my foot between your knees" made its way to Lupe's face as he slowly turned his head, and those tired, weary eyes. It wasn't that he wasn't glad to have finally got somewhere. The problem was that it didn't get them any closer to some sort of hope. More to the point, it didn't give *Lupe* any hope for his goals. A selfish but understandable attitude which most would have taken. Nevertheless, that kind of attitude wasn't particularly constructive in these circumstances, and unless Lupe gave it a backseat, then it could destroy what little unity they had forged in such little time.

Truth be told, to Roland it may have looked a seemly sight, but to the boys (Lupe especially for some reason) it was something quite different altogether. It reminded Jane of something from sputnik. It was a simple yet majestic square platform, with a raised part in the middle, from which it was presumably activated. Like the rest of the plant, it looked aged, almost magical. Instead of the metal they had expected, it seemed to be of some carved stone, with patterns and images placed upon its every face. Below it was as somewhat heavenly glow that sent shivers down the boy's spines. It was pink. As both their eyes went up to the proclamation of its name on a plaque-like surface, they read:

Displacer, Vertical Class A
From Interior Union Corp.

'Those guys seem to make just about everything here' Lupe exclaimed in hopes of some explanation.

'Yeah, they make problems too. I'll bet they created the problem that made this place what it is now' and as Jane finished talking, Roland made a statement which Jane did not pass onto Lupe.

"You're quite right, now they're attempting to cover over their mistakes. God knows what they'll think of next."

Jane thought to himself, "they're going to *kill* something, that's what's going to happen next".

Reluctance was prominent in both the boys' body language, yet Roland showed no such dismay or mistrust of the mysterious lift like machine. He simply walked upon it, and it seemed to compensate for the weight that was now upon it temporarily. Once again, standing upon an ancient piece of technology, like a dog in its prime, but without its dignity. Which made Lupe wonder, if he were turned back, would he be missing and arm?

"It won't explode in your face you know, come on let's get up there." The well mannered tone was slowly fading in Roland's mental voice; it seemed to Jane as if he was becoming accustomed to their way of talking. But that kind of thing doesn't happen fast, so perhaps Roland wasn't as pompous as he thought.

'He said let's jump on, apparently it's not known for exploding.'

'There's a first for everything, and this place is full of 'em" Lupe's humour had obviously made its return.

An estranged glow lit up the carvings on the Displacer, but only faintly. The central part of it twisted and became raised, as if it were of importance.

"Press it if you will." It was impatience from Roland.

'Want to do the honours, old friend?' Jane gestured to Lupe.

'Gladly, and hey, I'm not Wise Old Lupe. I'm just Wise Lupe for now' and he smiled as he pushed down wearily on the raised stone portion. The glow was light at first and then the brightness erupted. The stone began to smoothly waver.

And up they went . . .

* * *

Whenever you went over a small hill in a car and then back down again, there was always that lurch, the uncomfortable feeling you got in you stomach. The feeling so many people classed as excitement on a rollercoaster. The Displacer gave a similar feeling, but the boys were not so trustworthy of its safety. It appeared to go incredibly fast, yet they weren't thrust down to their knees due to the ordinary effect of forces upon the body. Instead the three of them watched as the rush of air went by, the sight of the plant which drew some sort of resource from the ground grew smaller. That strange ground that was neither rock nor sand, and had the colour of something unnatural was now metres, no, miles below them. Yet further up they went, higher and higher, past the point Jane thought it would be safe to breathe.

As he looked up (Lupe's face soon followed the gaze), something drew closer, but it was far larger, far vaster than that plant they had made their way through. They had not even explored the industrial building; they had only walked through unimportant sections of it. Now, as they were drawn up closer, this shelter in the sky (A Cradle was what

Jane had thought before), began to show its full size. Like a floating city, supporting millions . . .

(But not the lowly ones)

. . . and providing all that was required from no doubt dozens of similar power plants below.

They drifted towards a square section of the Cradle on its underneath. It was like entering the mouth of a hostile creature which you knew nothing about. Like a Kracken. Then as the Displacer seemed to dock into a chamber which made the noise that some pressurising machines would make, they were welcomed with none other than:

"Welcome to Glory Skies, Cradle 11"

6

Lucky number: 11

'Well now Mr. Finch, this is rather interesting news.'

'You don't seem so surprised Sayre, doesn't this bring up complications?'

'Oh no, no my good man it doesn't. In fact, it may make some things easier in the long run, all it takes is a little control. Incentive, if you will.'

Sayre smiled grimly at this prospect, the ideas he had in his mind, all planned out to perfection in almost every case. Almost. Despite being a powerful being in the side of the world, even half-god-like figures got things wrong sometimes. It was the power that went to their heads, and the mere prospect that something could overturn their ideas did nothing but enrage them.

He was a tall man, feared by his underlings, like Tailen Finch. None had seen his face, none that still lived. He was almost always concealed with a dark shroud like mask. With long draping black cloth tightly hung against his body, showing a rather well formed human body. Only a fool would attempt to quarrel with such a man physically, but an even bigger fool would dare challenge him mentally.

Tailen had seen a man fall to his knee's after having his brain seemingly melted inside his head after having claimed Sayre to be a Maverick, and a genocide inciting warlord. This was all true, but Sayre preferred it when people didn't make such a fuss about it. It wasn't good for public association.

'Alright sir, it sounds like you have everything in control. Would you like me to keep a permanent spy on their movement?' Tailen never appeared to come across as frightened of his master, he was not proud, but new his master looked upon him highly.

'No, I'd prefer a more experienced and reliable eye kept on them.'

'A psyche watcher then?' Tailen appeared confused but tried to grasp what Sayre was putting forward.

'You misunderstand, I mean you.'

Tailen rarely disagreed with Sayre. No one disagreed with him apart from the more governmental figures that were responsible for the Cradle projects, but they were entangled in their own wars with each other over resources. Tailen had questioned him once before and had been punished for it. He watched his own brother lose his body. But at the time his brother did not know he was related to Sayre's number one man. He had drifted through from the other world like so many others, but had lost a portion of his arm in a war of some sorts, over resources no doubt. "Narrow minded we were, thinking oil was everything" Tailen thought to himself.

He was quickly brought back to the matter at hand as Sayre's partially covered face cocked to the right a little, as if in contemplation.

'Er . . . Yes master, if you think that's the wisest choice of action.'

'Good, now go and shadow them. Oh and if any security officers question you, tell them your following protocol-'

'Eleven sir?' Tailen butted in, and then lowered his head in apology.

'Yes, that's right.' Sayre took the apology made by body language and dismissed it immediately.

'I wondered, why eleven?'

'You could say it's my lucky number, but it means far more than that. However we'll go into that at a more suitable and during a pressing time like this' There was a strange expressing in the dark masters face, or what he could see in it. As if he were contemplating.

'Very good master, I'll be on my way.'

Tailen made his way out the room, aware that Sayre's eyes were closely trailing him. Not just his eyes, but his *mind* as well. When someone knew you could manipulate minds, it made them keener to be honest with you. In such positions as Sayre's, honesty was a handy luxury to have from lower ones. He stopped his mind gaze at the end of the hallway outside his large and somewhat plain, black room. He had more important plans to think about.

"Not long now" he thought

He began to unravel his face mask, which revealed more than the boy's would ever be able to cope with.

More than Jane could ever strive understand.

7

The Shadow You Don't Notice

It was somewhat easy to lose their sense of ground. Being on some city that was suspended by nothing, perhaps dozens of miles above ground made Lupe sick to a lot more than his stomach. The boys experienced immense body ache, down to their bodies attempting to accustom themselves to this new habitat.

It had an extremely different look for something that was supposed to be technologically advanced. Granted there were no tarmac roads, just large metallic looking rooms met by corridors that would no doubt end in more rooms. But there was an outside to it, an external part the Displacer had docked with. They were sat on the very edge of a kind of arm of the Cradle. But it wasn't a basic arm, it was far larger than could be described, and there were a gratuitous amount of them coming off this gargantuan city.

One thing they did not expect was the fact there was life growing on the outside of the iron beast. Flower beds, trees and other such things were draping over the edge, and covering vast midsections of these arms. Aside from these docking arms, which to Jane seemed to contain stations for various Displacers to dock onto, the main body of this suspended city had great depth. It went higher the further in the middle you got, like a pyramid, except far less brick-like; It was more industrial, more manufactured.

What they did not expect was for the so called paths on the arm they had come on to be empty. There was no one to be seen. Most unexpected on something as big and intrusive as this. The boys expected to see some kind of security officer, perhaps along the lines of some military to ensure the safety. Security obviously wasn't a concern.

Roland appeared a little uncomfortable up here. Jane noticed a small shift in his body weight where his front leg should've been. He had been here before, but perhaps only once. There had to be a reason for this. "He'll cover that at a more pressing time" Jane thought sarcastically in his mind. Best that they aimed to keep low profile around here, just because security wasn't a key concern didn't mean the place welcomed any odd person. If they followed Roland's line of thinking about low people, they might not take so kindly to them.

This made Jane think. Maybe Roland didn't have that point of view. It could have been a point of view *against* him. Perhaps Roland was a low person to these people. It did explain a few things. But Jane didn't want to jump to conclusions right now. It wouldn't be fair, especially if he was wrong for whatever reason.

Both of them wished they knew Roland a little better. *A lot better* in fact. There was so much he could tell them, and some things they wished they knew about him. Like just who he was and what he was like before.

There are two sides to every story, however right now they wanted his.

"A little subtlety and tact would be greatly appreciated around here. It's not a place you want to get too involved with when it comes to opinionated people."

Jane repeated this to Lupe, and got a predictable response.

'Well that I could've guessed on first sight. You don't go letting any old person into your own house now do ya?'

'I suppose that depends on some things' Jane matter of factly said.

'Oh yeah? Like what?'

'Like which world your in.' He winked.

This response left utter silence between them. It was like mentioning something to someone that touched a nerve and brought a vow of silence over them. The kind you dare not bring up in case of causing some sort of offense. But it was a response that was fact.

'I hope that's not gonna be an excuse for too many things now you've discovered it' Lupe remarked.

'I'll try not to, but if it helps some things I might just hang on to it' This was one thing they could smile about, if only for seconds before Roland once again decided to press forward, to a destination neither of them knew. Hopefully somewhere where they could find a few answers. Plus, with any luck, it might bring a solution to the issue of Roland talking through Jane.

The distance from where they were to the seemingly short glorified entrance to the city seemed vast, but nowhere near as bad as the trek they had taken to get here. It did not arouse any reluctance. They had had their fair share of trials on the way here; at least they could walk with the pleasure of striding past the plants to their destination. Regardless of the trials that lay ahead.

* * *

The vegetation concealed many things on the visitor's arrival. Tall, healthy trees hid the dark body which consumed the shadows of a watcher, who so aptly kept a trained eye, ear *and* mind on the strangers from the other world. Tailen had learnt many concealing tricks over the years and some mental abilities which kept people from paying attention to certain objects. But that was not necessary on this occasion, however it may be in future, when the boy's subconscious minds made note of a constant reoccurring face among many.

Sayre had not completely mention the part in his plans where these people who were invaders to their world came in. however in this case he would not question the ideas of his master, as these people proved more resourceful than any low men he had encountered on his rare trips to the surface below. The dog however was an unexpected addition. The boys had obviously found the fool and decided to use his knowledge to get here. Sayre would no doubt deal with the depressed old dog. But it hurt Tailen to see his brother being used by such people who did not respect things here as they were.

'I'll not let you lose your dignity like this' he muttered to himself. Wishing deeply that Roland could see him and understand the regret he felt so deeply. Roland had followed him wrongly to this place through the doorway. Then he had got himself involved with an opposing party and caused such an upset with Sayre. He brought this upon himself, but how was he to know?

He hoped Roland showed no remaining hostility to him, but it was obvious human nature that he would. That was understandable at least.

There was only one way Roland could have got through. He couldn't possibly be a low man. He must possess some power. A mental one, if he had managed to communicate with his friends. That meant they could talk to him somehow. The devices made to amplify personal thought that the Union had created to keep tabs on the psyches could help.

Tailen wanted to do more than just allow communication. He wanted to change his brother back. Maybe Sayre would forgive him and offer him services to his sect. But Tailen remembered how truthful and pure Roland was. He'd never support something that was so disagreeable. If only he could see the greater long term effects. "Everyone is entitled to their opinion" he thought. "But Sayre doesn't believe so". His thoughts betrayed him. It would do him no good to keep on this track of thought. So he continued through the plants who kept him concealed, staying ever close to the ones he saw before him. Sometimes it's hard to love someone, until the day that they are gone. He could hold no grudge against his own brother.

He could only pity him, silently in his head.

* * *

"I think there is a great need for us to rest somewhere, and soon. We'll address the people of this place accordingly when we're a little more . . . refreshed and alive hmm?" Roland said this with a little more friendliness as he reached the end of the statement. It was true however that they were in great need of a rest. They had worn themselves out and it seemed liked they had travelled for an age.

'Where an earth can newcomers sleep, without even alarming anyone? We can't just break into someone's house, or whatever it is these people live in.' Jane exclaimed, as it seemed he misunderstood the place which Roland knew so much more aptly than the boys did.

'Beats me, why are you asking me?" Lupe questioningly butted in until he came to the realisation of what was happening. 'Oh, Roland thinks we should sleep somewhere, my mistake.' He seemed a little ashamed, until Jane reassured him.

'No worries, I know it's a pain in the ass, but we'll find a solution soon. If anywhere, this place will hold a few solutions for us.' The second that last statement came out Lupe was quick to react with:

'Yeah plenty of solutions followed by a few more questions no doubt.' Lupe appeared negative but he then felt regret of this emotion and showed little more than grim sadness in the following look. A little regret was enough to humble any man. 'Where's he got in mind to stay?'

"Well, I know as well as any other Glory Skies citizen does that they have an overnight stay wing on the North-East arm. So I think it would be advisable to start to that place." Roland certainly appeared to know how to stay calm in an awkward situation. It was quit calming to the boys, and he easily answered or dismissed any question they raised.

'So where are we now?' Jane felt a little out of touch when he was in someplace familiar. The feeling was all too lost. Both mentally and physically.

"By the time we get to the end of this Arm we'll know. Most of the Arms are developed symmetrically so they look the same. In fact, with any luck we might be on the right one."

At this point Lupe simply stood staring awaiting a response or a little information as to where the hell they could place themselves.

'Care to share the masses of wisdom old Roland has here?' Lupe said with good hearted sarcasm.

'You're the only "Wise Old . . ." here, and yeah, we're aiming for the North-East Arm for a place to sleep. We'll know our whereabouts when we get to the end.' Jane felt more confident as information was passed to him. He wasn't a born leader, but he did enjoy providing hope for people. However he hated the occasions when it was necessary to let people down.

'So we're on the lookout for a map saying "You are HERE" with a big red arrow right?' Lupe said, still smiling a little.

'This ain't England, at least not as we know it.' Jane said, showing a little smirk at his friend's whit. He looked ahead, a little dismayed about how far they'd have to go just to get to the end of this Arm. "God please let this be the right Arm, I can't do with walking much more today" he thought. But was it still "today"? Or was it another day? Time was hard to grasp around here, and it seemed to change whenever you tried to concentrate. Behind that seemingly light sky was black. It seemed like day and night shared the skies.

As usual Roland took the lead in directing them to the entrance, with a bit more bounce in his three legged steps. It was nice to see the little guy had a little more hope in his mind. So they followed, both the boys and the shadow closely behind.

8

The First Signs

'World Time, it s about quarter to nine in the evenin' sir.'

'Thanks, good evening to you then' Brax said.

'You too.' The clerk didn't seem to appreciate his whit as much as Brax thought he should. With that he took his leave from the North-East arm public store.

He was one of the few people that hated the fact you could never tell the time by the light, and had to use some mechanical means, which for all you could know, might in fact be wrong. It was always light and *dark* here. A little sunshine for some hours followed by a regular night would've been nice. They were luxuries of an old time though. Most people, if not all, had gotten used to this strange sky condition over the last dozen years.

Brax went to fiddle in his right jean pocket for the security card for his home. He was one of the few that still wore jeans; he had brought them over to this world with him, whereas everyone else wore the more practical clothing. He was an older man with stubborn taste. Was there a punishment for that? Other than a few looks of disgust? No. It was at this point that as he realised his jean pocket went no deeper and there was no card to be found. So instead of panicking he simply put it down to the fact it must be in another pocket about his body. But after but exploration of all the crevices of his clothing, he soon realised he didn't have it.

In the boys' world this would have been cause for mass panic. This, however, was Glory Skies. He would just stay in the overnight rooms tonight and request a reprint of his card the next morning, there wasn't much of a fee for it. Luckily the overnight accommodation was only a short walk away, and the evening (so time said it was) never brought much of a threat, unless the rivalling corps decided to wage war suddenly. So he trundled down the quiet, lifeless streets of this city.

Then something caught his eye. A shadowed man. He had obviously not seen Brax as he simply sneaked in a brisk fashion to the other side of the path, which concealed himself from vision.

"How odd" Was all he could think. The dark figure however showed no immediate aggression to him, and had disappeared almost as fast as he had appeared. So he walked on, with the permanent wonder stored to the back of his subconscious. A thirty minute walk would be simple enough.

Brax may have been pressing on fifty, but he looked a little younger, so assault on the older and "less able" was most unlikely. Cases had been heard of years ago, but he wasn't worried about this. He could handle a young man who thought of himself as some kind of superspy. Not a very good one if a forty nine year old man spotted him instantly.

* * *

'Well look at that, isn't this our lucky . . . well . . . it feels like night.' Lupe said, as he spotted a rather well placed sign stated the first piece of good luck they'd had since they came here.

North East Arm
Arm 2/8 of Interior Union
Cradle 11

'Ah I knew we'd be on it, it was about time we got a break anyway. So Roland, which direction is it to our much deserved bed?' Jane had said with a little more uplifted feeling inside. He felt like he could talk to Roland openly with Lupe, but every time he got a response in his head instead of out loud.

"I'd say a little less than and hour, maybe forty five minutes."

Lupe raised his eyebrows in a 'well, what did he say?' fashion. He was ready for some rest, but in this place he felt he might sleep a little less easily, no matter how tired his legs were. He didn't exactly feel safe.

'Forty five.' Jane mentioned shortly. Then he continued on to follow Roland on his path. This time they weren't being followed, no, the shadow was ahead of them, knowing exactly where they were headed. He had decided to make his way back for further orders from Sayre. Perhaps they could be monitored in their temporary home.

Jane was the only one who seemed to have complete faith and a safe feeling about the place. For people so sure of their own authority over other people, it was bound to be free of the usual violence. Provided there was no sign of low people on the cradle. If it was anything like how politics were in his world, he could imagine a few of them hiding amongst the city, planning their attack internally. He had no clue how scheming these people were, or just how sure the Glory Skies citizens were of their safety.

Roland had spoken of other corps that were in a war against the Interior Union, but failed to mention any details. Maybe he'd enlighten them soon, maybe even tonight.

* * *

As Tailen had rushed through the streets in his faint shroud, he had not noticed anyone about. On one occasion though, he had made a mistake. He was so confident of no one being around to see a figure rush towards the more central parts, he had dashed past what he saw as a man, carrying a bag of items which had no doubt been purchased from the nearest store.

Any old citizen didn't prove to be anywhere near as fatal as an enemy military member. The man would probably forget about it, after all he was gone in milliseconds, and didn't raise much suspicion. That was a chance Tailen would have to take, in hopes that Sayre would not be aware of his silly slip-up. If any trouble were to be aroused, the man could be dealt with easily.

He progressed hastily towards Sayre's over glorified living accommodations. He was of course a powerful man, but he did not strike any as a lover of material posessions. His house showed otherwise. It was a seemingly majestic piece of reinforced ecological titanium steel alloy (most of the city was created with such a metal due to structural integrity). Despite the plain colour, it had balconies to overlook the advanced city, which was at this time quiet.

Tailen frequently chose the more challenging approach to enter the place: Scaling the wall up to the balcony that lead back into his living quarters. He had no desire to take the entrance to his bedroom and enrage him, or that would result in Tailen becoming a bloody mess on the falsified carpet on the floor.

As he approached the door (which itself had a handle on the side unlike most doors in the city) and noticed Sayre waiting inside on a chair, sipping some steaming brew that had recently been made.

He opened the door awkwardly; he rarely had to see a handle and had only got to grips with it recently. As he walked into the room silently, Sayre facing him he was greeted with a short glance, a steady and small sip of what smelled like coffee, and then 'Do make your self comfortable.' This was said with upmost respect.

At first Tailen stared bemused, then made his way to a strict looking chair. He wished to keep his posture in a perfected state. Tailen soon realised Sayre knew he had much to report as he just sat there awaiting the information.

'I can either glean as much information as I can from your thoughts or you can update me through speech. I presume you would prefer the latter?' Sayre promoted no impatience.

Tailen did not want Sayre to know about his small mistake so went on to tell him of the events. He further went on about his brother being with them. That part raised a small change in his master's face, but after a controlled sip of his drink, he returned to normal.

'It would appear they are most resourceful in their travels to a new and strange land.' Sayre grinned a little, but it was hard to tell much else from the concealed face.

'Would you like me to monitor them in the sleeping quarter?' This seemed a prudent plan of action to Tailen.

'Leave them be for now, we'll continue our watch tomorrow.' Sayre finally decided.

This surprised Tailen but he did not wish to disagree. He obviously had a plan of action that would follow the course of the next few days. Perhaps their eyes were misplaced on these new people. It would be more advisable to monitor the other corps in the long run.

Cradle's F-Freedom and F-Decadence, both in control of the Serenity Union showed signs of aggression towards Interior's plans of action as to the collection of power on the ground. They were after all winning in the race of collecting more than any other rival Unions could. But they constantly blamed the outcome of this world on Interior. It was half true in fact, but Interior seemed confident that all in all it had led them to a better height of advancement.

'Alright, I wish you goodnight sir.' Tailen added then took his leave, this time out the main entrance to Sayre's estate.

As he made it out the room Sayre had captured onto a part of his mind Tailen had obviously wanted to be kept hidden. Someone had seen him.

Sayre locked onto this and searched deeper into the man, who had been out that night. A close watch will be kept on him. He had clearly shown some sort of curiosity. This could prove no good, but Tailen would not be punished for this. Something like that could happen to anyone. However not anyone had Sayre to cover their tracks. Sayre did this quite well compared to anyone of his stature. This is what he would do, when the time came.

If this mysterious man was in any possibility, a spy, or a low man, it could be a sight more dangerous than Tailen had thought.

*   *   *

An odd feeling had become of Jane. He had never travelled at night before, when the light in the sky was at a constant brightness. It was both unsettling, and made him wonder how easily you could find sleep in a world of permanent dark-light. In honesty he didn't want to sleep. Another thing that struck him was that the need to eat had left him entirely since they got here, and his body wasn't punishing him for it. He noticed none of the party seemed to bother about it, especially so since they have arrived on this Cradle. His emotions were raised to a brim, he felt so frustrated with himself, and so doubtful of everything he felt. It all felt real, but in his world, what this would be considered as was plain wrong. No control made him feel helpless, and permanently unsettled. A constant presence was on his mind but he simply could not pin it.

"I felt it too."

Everything suddenly rushed back into proportion as his well of emotions was struck back by surprise. Roland had overheard his mind. This was a startling prospect.

"The presence, we're being watched, but we're strong enough to break the shroud in our minds." In a way, Roland seemed to lose his comfort and stride. He tensed up, but felt better that Jane felt he did.

"Let's keep this between us." Jane suggested. "I don't want anything else playing on Lupe's mind. He's gonna have a tough time here."

"I can't tell him anyway." Roland said, but not in a spiteful voice, at least not the way his mind portrayed it. It seemed Roland had a voice of none. One that both lacked sensitivity, but the very smoothness of it calmed anyone. The kind of voice that screamed the sound of rescue, and offered aid. That was only a thought Jane could hope was true.

"Do we know who it was?" The sound of Jane's portrayed sound showed his lack of contempt. He was scared, and they all knew it. They all felt the same.

"I have a good idea, but let's leave it until we're in safer places." Roland commanded. It was in fact a masked statement, sounding like a suggestion, but the truth was, it was an order. He lacked patience at this time; they all lacked something over here.

They walked on, revealing building after building on these fake, metalic streets. Everything looked the same; everything was equal, showing that maybe people here were either naive or simply idealists. Each door was identical, having some kind of voice mechanism incorporated. Every wall had the same greyish metal finish. Was there anything unique about this place? Nothing seemed real and natural other than the plant life they had seen. But maybe even they weren't entirely natural. It wouldn't surprise them if they were genetically modified. The Cradle lacked any kind of personal touch, the kind of thing that would relax an ordinary citizen, allowing them to show pride in their floating city. This world it seemed, had many ideals, but little in the way of homeliness. That was it. It didn't feel like home.

Right now Jane could feel himself yearning to see those fields he had constantly criticised in his mind. Those fields, that had been so carelessly incorporated with manufactured pylons, steel giants of the twenty first century. Maybe, after all, he had the wrong idea of things. England might not have been so bad after all. It had what everyone needed, personality, uniqueness, a little twist in living. Perfection proved to be insufficient in this case. He reminded himself, "give a man rain and he'll complain its wet, give him sun, he'll complain it's too hot. Give him neither of the two, simple overcast weather, he'll ask for one of the former." It was time to buck up his ideas. They had no way of getting back, so they needed to do something here to save whatever they had left to live on. No matter what it would take? That would be something he might regret in future.

Lupe had not noticed the silence while they were walking, it was in fact a waste of energy, but he had his own thoughts of home. Sure things weren't exactly luxurious at home, but he had one thing that made his world tick. The very thing he yearned for everyday, any time the feeling took. He longed for one more day with his beloved. One last chance to prove his worth, that he had never taken what feelings he had for granted. This was after all, the most important feeling to him in the world. *Both* worlds. He dare not speak her name in front of anyone, as it would no doubt bring up a torrent of tears and emotion at the very prospect of being lost forever without her. He felt that he was no longer worth anything, his purpose in life was for her, and now he was to go on through a path that would end only in disappointment. Not to mention his own blind ignorance would lead him to a treacherous path none of them could afford to go down.

As they approached a larger more protruding building, Roland felt a need in his head. A wealth of information, no, a story, must be told. It was time for him to stop putting things off, and time to reveal all to the two boys who so aptly adopted him as more than just a guide. He felt a connection to them, friendship. He hadn't had a friend or a soul to confide in for two years. The time he'd been stuck here, had been a lonely man in another organisms body, unable to do anything but whine to himself every supposed night.

'This the place?' Lupe pointed a thumb at the odd looking place. It had blanked out windows and a seemingly clean looking exterior for a building designed for allowed rest for those not in homes.

'How would you know?' At first Jane was confused as to how Lupe knew, until his friend smiled eerily and moved out of the way of the sign clearly stating its purpose. 'Ah, I see.'

As they entered it through the door with no handle, Jane expected a voice recognition password as usual. But this door simply opened. Except they were shocked to have the face of a stranger greeting them in a startled nature and nervousness. The way a guilty child would look after its parents had just observed it doing the opposite of its parent's orders. The man fumbled out the words.

'Oh, well er . . . Hi there, seems we've both got some home issues.' Brax forced a smile. The sweat now appearing on his upper lip. He felt exposed. Perhaps these people were here to catch him. Then as he came to realise they were no more than two boys in late teens along with a triped dog, he relaxed a little.

'I guess you could say so, friend. We'll just take this side and leave you to your business, we don't wanna intrude.' Lupe said, and he felt he handled the situation well enough, and popped himself down on a bed in the far corner of this seemingly large central room, filled with enough beds for a family and relatives. They expected to see some kind of homeless shelter. However they were greatly mistaken, it was in fact so well tended, and not a speck of dust was out of place.

Jane followed Lupe awkwardly, and Roland did the same willingly enough. Lupe lay down, not wanting to say a word. He only wanted to sleep instead of risking making the others aware of his problems. Jane however took a look across the room, and saw their new found loner, lying like Lupe on a bed in the other corner.

"I feel I need to explain a great many things to you." Roland suddenly stated out of the blue. He sounded earnest enough.

"About your early life, before this?" Jane gestured towards Roland, emphasising Roland's appearance.

"Indeed, if this night will allow. A little trust could be good for the both of us." Roland sounded more and more distressed as he went on. Then Jane spoke.

'Tell me your story, I'll not interrupt, only listen.'

Roland went on, and began where he thought best.

"It was four years ago . . ."

9

Dog Tails

Roland had just *finished his usual night out on a Friday evening to the movies he loved, with his brother Tailen. Everyone had always said how odd their names were, but in truth the boys themselves loved their names. Uniqueness was certainly a positive aspect. Roland had just finished working an extremely low paid job at the local pub collecting glasses at a small village public house in Maine. One he was not necessarily embarrassed about, but nonetheless, at twenty two it wasn't the kind of job security you dreamed of for supporting yourself and a partner. Getting a family was always a priority, but finding someone to start that with, never came easy.*

They had just finished watching the film creation of The Shining, *a very disturbing horror written by some man they had never heard of. Roland only remembered that the authors' second name was* King. *It had struck Roland deep, when the disturbing scenes of twins covered in blood had flashed in his eyes. So much so that he looked down in some sort of inexplicable shame and shock. Apparently the author was well known for his disturbing books along the lines of horror. Even though Roland could not stand the sight of desecrated children, something about the writers' style intrigued him. Perhaps he should read up on him.*

As he walked down the long and worn tarmac of an ancient road that hadn't been re-laid despite large cracks, Tailen walked beside him with a grim look upon his face. He walked with a slouch, hands in his pockets, forever looking down, as if the floor held some comfort in whatever was paining him.

"What's the matter bro?" Roland said, with a croak in his throat, as he had not used his voice in quite some time now.

"Nothing for you to set your worries on, just leave it." Tailen replied, quite clearly knowing that this phrase would not only cause the opposite of its requests, but it would also cause a long term issue that would forever sit on Roland's mind. 'Never mind' was always a pair of words that left the listener in a state of wonder. One that always meant something was wrong, that it hit deep, and more to the point, meant everything in the world to that person at that time. Yet still humans continued to use it.

"Well if you're sure, I guess we can leave it for a bit, you'll feel better in the morning I'm sure. How is work treating you? I never thought to ask earlier." Roland attempted to revive the conversation, expecting a short answer that would thwart his efforts, but was surprised at the results.

"Yeah maybe I'm just tired. You know how the hotel business is. Head security has its up days, and the utter shit days, everyone knows that. But still we soldier on right?" Tailen showed a brief effort at a small smile, but with no real emotion. And it showed.

"Well at least its work huh! A sight better than-" Roland never did finish the sentence that was demeaning himself deliberately to make his brother feel better. Something else, more meaningful had appeared in front of him.

Tailen needed no hint, he briefly nodded at Roland and this time gave a more meaningful smile. He crossed the road and took a cut off onto a narrower road. It would lead him home, just with an extra five minutes journey. Tailen had his times when he showed good favour to Roland, but on a more often occasion he acted like a typical older brother and made use of every second to mock and ridicule him.

He had swallowed his voice, or so it seemed. Sweat broke above his lips and brow, and his legs seemed to both lock up and quiver as he attempted a smooth and effortless walk. But little did she know, it took far more effort to make those simple steps towards her than it would have to give his life. In this case, beauty was indeed a killer; one worth all the while, and the immense effort. It looked as if she had not yet seen him. Women did that so well. That act of surprise when they saw someone, as if chance itself had put an object in their path that they claimed to have no clue about. That didn't matter; Roland never thought too much into it, he wasn't concerned with the attitude to which she had formed. He was genuinely glad and surprised to see her at this point. But words still did not come to his mouth.

As if a saviour from heaven, she noticed his failure to let out sound, and simply moved her head forward in anticipation. At that point she understood his situation, and made that understanding smile a parent would normally make at a child when it had embarrassed itself.

"Hey, Roland?" she said, in her ever perfect tone of voice. One that caught Roland off guard in every situation. He forced the sound and thought at first he had croaked out the first word. In pure heated intuition he carried on, rather hurriedly in his words.

"Hi Lucy, how's this past week been, pretty tiring eh?" He blurted. He thought what an idiot he had made of himself,

saying so much at once within what? Seconds? He felt like crawling back inside a cave and never showing his face again, in order to not further show his feelings.

She showed a little more of an understanding and tried to reassure him. As a woman so well thought of by Roland, she reassured him more than anyone ever could.

"Aha, yeah I guess it was tiring, but y'know we all get by somehow, every week, just keeping things up. Where is it you were working again?"

It took what had to be the longest thirty seconds in Roland's life before he had comprehended the fact she had just openly asked him a question. He shook his head in a twitch like fashion as if he had just woken up and quickly burst out with:

"Yeah we keep on going! Well me? I'm working at the uh . . ."

"Hawg Heaven, that's it!" she said, before he could finish his stuttering words. This made him think to himself. Had she really paid attention to find out where he worked? How wonderful . . . but in a way it wasn't, his job was nothing short of bog standard. He certainly never raved about it.

"That's right" he said as he laughed nervously "A bit of a crap-hole but it does me just fine." He lied about that last part, and he hoped she wouldn't notice. In Roland's opinion, there was nothing impressive about his current employment, he need something to really catch her attention, something he could prove to her, to show he could do *something with his life. He spent most of his time working on how to make himself worthy to her. Nothing meant more to him than to have her respect, and maybe a little more. Again, he noticed he was silently dialoguing with himself and not concentrating that someone he felt so deeply for was standing beyond him, silently waiting for a little response from the figure that stood so awkwardly in front of her.*

He stood like a proud and well treated man, back straight, with an altogether good posture. His hair seemed worn away, straight brown, and yet straggly and greying and his tender age. His face looked weary. Permanently. But she didn't know this; she had never spent much social time with him, just the odd occasion of an eye catcher, and a friendly smile, that in fact, meant so much more to the both of them. His blue eyes seemed deep, but troubled. His body reflected exactly how his life had been going. He was an altogether tired and weary soul, looking for an escape from this life he lead, appearing to be a different person than what he actually was. He disliked himself, but showed no fear; utter determination to achieve his goal drove him forward and kept him going in his unending toil of a lifestyle.

"So er . . ." the words seems as though they would never come, but to his surprise they boomed out in a more solemn fashion. "What did you get up to this evening? . . . If of course you don't mind me asking!" He felt the need to add this last part in order to not seem nosey. The last thing he wanted to put across was a stalker-like feeling.

"Nothing much really . . ." Roland knew this was the usual lie people told you when it was something they didn't want to share. " . . . I just went out with the girls and things, just the usual kind of thing." She showed a brief smile to attach on to the white lie she had just told, in attempts to make the blow to his standing a little less harsh.

She didn't want to lie to him, she genuinely did like him, but her personal life was nothing to be proud of at this moment in time. Therefore she felt no need to include people into her chaotic and eventful life. It was understandable, but only so much so to the people that didn't know it all. They were left wondering, hoping to know what they were never told. Roland didn't seem to mind the fact she had been vague with her answer, and thought about it a lot less than she expected, instead he simply moved on to a more difficult part of the conversation. The end.

"Well I hope yours was a little more interesting than mine, I gotta say, The Shining is what I expected . . . film producers just seem to murder books!" Roland made this simple attempt at humour rather flawlessly, and managed to laugh like and ordinary human being, without so much as a squeak or grunt. All in all, in his head, it was a success. He laughed at himself, inside his head. Making conversation with this person felt a lot harder than the landing on D-day. He hadn't been there, but nothing could match up to his nerves that day. Leaving the safety of his trenches, just to gain a few meters ground. A classic war situation.

"I did thanks. Likewise, see you later." She made no falter in her way of ending conversation. But little did she know that one of the words she used struck Roland as rather odd, but nevertheless it made him laugh in his head.

As quick as they had spotted each other, they both parted with no real grace. Roland felt incredibly awkward walking away, and tried to walk as naturally as possible. Instead he managed no more than a brisk and edgy walk. He must have been close to running speed. He'd beat himself up about that the next morning. Not everything can go as smoothly as it can, but this was just plain disorganised. At least he thought so.

He hoped she wouldn't pick up on too much, all those mistakes he genuinely believed he'd made, but in actual fact, were not noticeable at all. The chill of the night hadn't reached his bones as yet, he had been too preoccupied trying to keep his cool, and not let himself turn into a rattling wreck of nerves. It was useless to plan things like that, because no matter what you try to do, they always end up sideways. He almost missed the road he was supposed to be taking to get back home because he was still concentrating on walking ordinarily. Roland jerked to the right, to get down the small side road that cut through to his smaller block. What he saw shocked him at first, then just plain confused him. " . . . No Roland, he's not getting mugged at all . . ." he murmured to himself. He quick fled to the side where the darkness would hopefully conceal him, as he looked upon these people.

* * *

Tailen had taken no great displeasure in leaving Roland to his antics with Lucy, the girl he had adored since he could remember. He knew by just being there would make Roland swallow his tongue, and shit out his nerves ten times over. That was him all over; little courage ever existed in his body. The small road he took didn't strike him as hostile or dangerous, he had taken it a thousand times, as and when the need was there. It probably served a handy purpose for any of the locals who took a liking to the white stuff, or any or substances they could get high on to leave their troubles behind them.

He had been walking for a good five minutes, and in his head thought that by now Roland was either lying in a gutter in shock, or had actually served his purpose and talked to the damn girl like a respectable man. God help him if he were to continue look into things a little too much. It wouldn't surprise Tailen if she had somehow got irritated with him, the guy was sensitive, and with that came emotions that took a pin drop to set off.

"Good look to him . . ." he said to himself. He'd need it if he had any possible chance of achieving anything in his life, let alone telling the girl he liked just what's what.

As he continued, he saw no one in the shadows that so aptly made horrifying shapes to anyone with a nerve threshold of a small child. But this was Tailen; he was a respectable boy from Maine who had never done wrong, as yet. In any case, he didn't expect to find someone and have them jump out a dumpster at him. At least not unless he was some stupid wealthy person that was well known, walking through the dark streets in a suburban town. He kept his head down and hands tucked tightly in his pockets. He, at least, felt the cold a lot easier than Roland did. The air was still, but the chill of a cloudless night needed no breeze to reach the innermost parts of your body.

The road was different, but not to the blind eye of an ordinary human being. It forever remained a simple backstreet. But there was in fact an extra building on it that didn't seem to catch anyone's attention. It had a kind of aura that made people not want to notice it, as if it tried to keep itself hidden in plain sight. This time, however, someone wanted Tailen to notice it. That someone slowly and coolly stepped out of the mental shroud he had been hidden in. He turned towards the unsuspecting young man that was walking towards him. Tailen had his head down and didn't immediately notice the figure, until it was but a few meters away. At that point he had opened his mouth, but nothing came out. At least he shared that much with Roland.

* * *

As Roland looked on, he only just established to himself that one of these people was his brother. *The other man standing, no, towering above him, was much too concealed to make anything out. Dressed in draping black, no facial features showing other than the eyes, behind a sanguine mask that seemed to weightlessly cling to his face. It was hard to make anything out other than a murmur. But Roland continued to yearn to understand just what they were saying to each other. He hoped his brother had not got in the wrong crowd that involved drugs. The look of the man he was with quickly dismissed that thought. This was all too serious.*

As he leaned forward to try and hear as much as his ears could make out, he noticed he was leaning towards a rather precarious looking trash pile. If he leant over any further, he'd end up knocking something over, something loud *over. Either he moved towards them and hope they didn't notice or he could stay where he was and catch the occasionally word.*

He went against his better judgement and moved his body slowly, controlling his breathing in case that would give him away. His breath was, after all, resulting in condensation in front of him. He edged along the wall, trying to avoid every object that had be carelessly thrown or dumped into this ally, for whatever reason the litterer decided was necessary. For a moment, he heard a low scuffing sound and quickly realised his navy coat was rubbing against the wall with every careful movement he made. He had to move a millimetre away, or risk having himself found out for eavesdropping. If there was a simple explanation for Talien's odd behaviour, then Roland would be quickly scorned for making a mess of things. Instead of trying to press on, Roland decided the dumpster ahead would provide necessary cover. His own courage at this point amazed him. Who would've guessed he'd be this drawn to his brother's situation?

He only heard partial sentences, as the two men spoke to each other. Roland then realised it was more along the lines of this masked figure talking, and Tailen simply nodding or agreeing in some worried and grim fashion. That was enough to tell Roland something wasn't quite right, and this wasn't just a friendly chat with someone you hadn't seen in a while. Roland could hear faint parts of dialogue which he couldn't make much sense of.

" . . . I understand you're in a difficult situation which you haven't told anyone about . . . If you just come to the other side we can solve everything . . ." Then a pause as Tailen said something, and mentioned what Roland thought was his own name. " . . . We can do nothing about that . . . it's impossible to come back . . . leave things how they are and follow me." The figure turned in Roland's direction briefly, and then turned to somewhere just out of Roland's sight.

As if he had no other choice, Tailen seemed to walk behind the tall dark man, towards a large security fence with a gate just large enough to fit a van through. Roland desperately wanted to know just what they were speaking about and what was so grave that gave Tailen no choice but to follow. Suddenly Roland's senses became heightened, and his adrenal glands began pumping. This time he wouldn't take flight as an option. Instead of rushing forward like a disconcerted madman, he crept forward, remaining ever silent in his steps to pursue his brother and this man who had seemingly taken control of Tailen in an instant.

At this point Roland then came to realise he never noticed a building. The one they were walking towards. It had been there all this time, but his brain had told him not to pay any attention to it. But how couldn't *he? It was so . . . strange, out of place. Not to mention clean. The same couldn't be said of the small ally it came off. He thought to himself it should have been impossible not to notice.*

As he approached the gate that his brother and his captor had walked through, a sign became barely legible in this darkness.

Interior Union
11th Science Facility of Travel
Where Every Year Seems Like a Day!

The last part made no sense, unless they were trying to make it seem like the employees enjoyed them selves at this place so much that time went fast. But company slogans were never to be trusted. The way a company described itself was about as true as a cheap Chinese watch.

Movement made hi forget about the strangeness of the sign, and Roland concentrated on the figures moving into the building ahead. As if from nowhere Roland heard another rustling from behind. Something was in here with him. As his nerves began to shoot messages of fear to his head, an abandoned dog seemed to trundle out from the overgrown grass that lay behind the fence connecting to the ally. No doubt it had just eaten something quite dead from there. It made its way toward Roland, seeming quite contented, simply looking to inspect just what this person was doing.

"Go away, don't touch me, god knows what your living on!" Roland gasped, in an attempt to whisper loudly at the animal. Maybe he'd get it to go away. But it didn't work entirely; instead the dog just looked at him in bewilderment. Roland decided to ignore it, hoping the creature wouldn't follow him.

There was no light other than one that clearly stated that there was a door below it, and it seemed to shine brightly, despite the little area that it actually managed to shed light upon. Roland walked carefully up to it, hoping his poor attempts at sneaking up to the building hadn't cause alarm within the building. If he was caught he didn't know what the hell he'd do. He didn't even know why he was following Tailen. Nothing could possibly bring him this far.

The door which stood before him seemed almost lost in its place. It held no real logical position on the building. It was neither in the centre nor equally to one side. It was as if someone had just stuck it on the end in a blind rush to get a door on. It held no real colour, just a grey mass of some metal, bulked together in a square shape. Hell, the designers didn't even think to put a handle on it.

It was at that point when the door simply, slid open. With no real expectation, Roland was greeted with a blow to the head from someone behind the door, and was swiftly carried off whilst he remained unconscious for quite some time.

Then the dog edged its way in the door, secretively, and followed the strange person that had made some attempts at communicating with it.

* * *

In his head, he felt nothing but ache and confusion. Nothing would come to mind, and he couldn't draw any ideas in his mind as to where he could place himself. He felt the tingling in his head, that giveaway ache of a drug manufactured purely for knockout purposes. The place where the needle had entered his neck, to transfer the liquid substance that would prevent him from struggling or causing any undue damage to any equipment on the way to holding. The place before he was brought before Sayre to decide the fate he had seemingly widely accepted after trespassing on land that was apparently kept locked, both by gates and *mental blocks.*

Roland felt as though he was just a consciousness, floating on his back, noticing the spotlight above him moving across the ceiling ever few feet he moved. He came to realise that this was in fact a corridor he was going down, with gratuitous amounts of overhead florescent lights.

It wasn't the drug that made his body feel that pulsating effect; it seemed the adrenaline in his body was still being pumped around since he was grabbed at the door. His body obviously thought instead of flight it would take the fight option. But right now it looked like his body had the wrong idea. If he could break through the tough leather restraints against his wrists, neck and ankles, then maybe, just maybe, he could have made a little use of the increased heart rate his body had adopted. Clearly, that wasn't going to happen, so he hoped his body could save the minor enhancement a while longer for when a time arose that meant he needed a little more running speed.

That was when he smelled it. It wasn't strong as such; it was more of a tinge in the air that caught his nostrils by surprise for a split second. That ally-trash like doggy smell could reach the inner core of anyone's senses. But it seemed Roland was the only one that realised that his little acquaintance was following him. For what reason, he didn't know, probably just curiosity.

He tried to turn his head slightly round without alerting suspicion to the figure pushing the stretcher, but his head was firmly tied down along with the rest of his body, to prevent damage to anyone, maybe even himself. He thought it was hard for any normal human being not to notice the strange tapping of dog claws against a seemingly cold and hard floor. This surprised him, but then again, a lot of today wasn't exactly normal, and had happened nevertheless.

He heard the sound of smooth hydraulics, doing their job to open a large heavy door they had come to, and without any further distraction, the trolley pusher simply walked straight through, into a room filled with warming light.

* * *

Tailen's mouth simply stopped in astonishment as the realisation of what had just entered the room struck him. At first he saw one of Sayre's men pushing a man strapped down, no doubt an intruder. Then he came to understand, that intruder was none other than Roland. Just as the door went to close automatically on itself, Tailen caught a sudden glimpse of fur dash in behind them. But the surprise of what he saw before him made Tailen forget all about it in an instant.

"What are you doing here?! Why did you follow me?" he said. However his questions were answered with complete silence, as Roland was tied and gagged about the throat.

The room itself seemed to share its silence with the victim of the situation, everyone was shocked to see someone come in uninvited, even Sayre.

"Loosen him, and unbind his voice" Sayre said, with complete composure.

Like a robotic switch, one of the few men in the room rushed over to do as they were told. The man pushing the stretcher simply stood like a rock, as if he required further orders just to operate himself.

As one of Sayre's minions untied the prisoner, Roland made careful moves as he slid off the hard board. The canine however that remained hidden beneath the stretcher stayed as it was probably in its best interests.

"Sayre . . . this is my brother. I ask of you to simply let him go, he knows nothing and he means no wrong" Tailen seemed to beg.

"This is a very awkward and unexpected situation, I'll admit, however, we must leave now, and your brother holds no place in our plans." Sayre said, with remained calm. He had struggled enough to get this far, and gather the people that his own master had requested. "I cannot say for sure whether he can follow us through, but I doubt it. Everyone, its time to go through." Then he turned his attention to Roland, giving a stern and long hard look into his eyes, as if reading deep into his head.

Roland just stood, still puzzled as to the situation he was in, wondering what this bright pink light was before him, and who this man was who was the ring leader of this place. His body remained frozen as Sayre decided to make his way towards him, with his cold hearted, half covered face ever remaining on Roland's eyes. But as if from nowhere, he turned his attention onto the vehicle that had brought Roland into the room. Roland then began to realise what Sayre had noticed. But it wasn't the slight waver of the sheet that covered the body board that gave it away. Sayre could feel the presence.

As if it could feel it had been detected, the dog leapt out of the board, and was instantly greeted with a 9mm shot, that, given the situation, was not well aimed, and simply maimed the creatures front leg. The howl of pain it gave lasted only seconds before it was met with a scream of pain as a second bullet from Sayre's gun met Roland's flesh in his torso.

Tailen screamed his thoughts about what had just happened, but all that came out was a loud scramble of words, met by a short phase of blubbering, until Sayre grabbed Tailen's arm and fled through the pink light within the room, closely followed by all the other minions.

"We do not have time for this, leave it all behind" Sayre shouted.

Within seconds the room was empty as most of the fully living people departed. Roland however, lay holding his lower abdomen, but remaining his focus on the animal that now limped towards him despite his pain. Like a motherly companion, the dog put its snout gently around his collar and steadily dragged him towards the light, with great difficulty, due to its missing leg. Roland moved a bloody hand to greet the dog, and was met by an equally bloody patch of fur as they slowly were pulled in.

Blood mixed with blood . . .

10

Spy Among Spies

Jane listened as Roland spoke within his head for what seemed like an eternity. But the night that did not exist outside had almost allowed time for him to finish before it set its spell on his tired, heavy eyes. Roland showed no signs of weariness throughout, and sat with elegance still. Lupe seemed to have been fast asleep for an age now, and looked as though he could stay there on that bad for another lifetime. However, they could not stay here long, for they had answers to glean.

Jane had intently met Roland's gaze, and listened earnestly as the dog told its tale of his loss of embodiment, and his pride. But he had lost something altogether more valuable: The trust of his fellow sibling, who had seemingly betrayed him for nothing. Another thing was left unanswered. How Roland had been causing Sayre further problems in this world, to other parties rivalling Sayre's. Jane also wondered just how Roland got into the plant that they had travelled up in. presumably he had fled the cradle and found that place one of security, and hiding.

"When I was in the city in this form, people noticed me quite blatantly, and wondered just what had happened. I soon asked questions which people reluctantly gave to a mind talking dog, and found some contacts that could help me fight back. The Independents soon showed themselves." Roland went on.

'What did you guys end up doing to get force you into hiding in that massive machine?' Jane said, not realising that he had spoken out loud until Lupe's slumber was partially interrupted. He turned over and continued to drift.

"Sayre was more powerful in places we did not imagine. My state showed the Independents that something had going very wrong, but they were brought down by people working inside them. It seemed there were spies who worked against their own Union. Most of us were silenced" Roland's head nodded down with a grim look of defeat "Some fled to other Cradles where they were out of his reach, and I decided to survive where there were no people."

'That's when we came all these years later' Jane said, making sure his voice was kept down. 'How long has it been?'

"Many years, I know your wondering, I am about thirty eight years of age now."

'Sounds like you were down there for a while. What would people think if you're walking around this Cradle now?' Jane seemed a little cautious all of a sudden. If Roland's presence would draw a mass amount of attention they would surely be in trouble sooner than they thought.

"After what happened last time, no one will raise any question; they would no doubt wish to stay neutral at this time of aggravation between the Unions." A tone of helplessness made its appearance, but was soon covered by a sense of will.

Jane looked a little disappointed, but it was at least a good thing to know that the people here would no doubt see that something would happen. It was just a case of backing the right side this time. The last time, however, might make the people choose the one Roland had no place in. with a grave look on his face, Jane continued.

'At least the people know of you. Maybe this time, we'll get something done about, and these people might find their faith in democracy again.'

One issue Jane had was that in his experience, democracy widely failed. Capitalism, Communism, even idealism failed. All of this was due to the simple fact that humans were easily corrupted, no doubt about it. The people that lived here were different though. They were the only ones that *could* get to this place. In any case, they were different in some way. And so were Jane and Lupe. Roland, on the other hand, was invaluably different. He had an image that no one could turn a blind eye to. What person wouldn't question either their sanity or the Union running this place, when confronted by a dog that spoke through its mind?

'Guess we'll have to use what we've got right here then guys' Lupe broke in, followed by a wide mouthed yawn. He had clearly got his fair share of sleep. 'I'll bet you two didn't get any sleep did you. If you get slow and caught up in something due to tiredness, I won't say I told you later.'

'We'll have to trust that you watch our back for the meantime then' Jane said 'But I don't intend on getting caught up in anything today, I think it's time for us to talk to some locals.'

'If it's a few contacts and people you can trust, I can set you boys up-' The man that had been across the room must have had an acute sense of hearing, and he had heard the entire dialogue Jane had seemingly had with the dog they were with. 'I'm guessing that's no ordinary dog' Brax said.

All three showed a shocked expression, or at least Roland attempted one. They had been careless to fail to see the danger of the people around them. Jane felt a sudden embarrassment as the realisation that he had been talking to a dog must have seemed strange to any ordinary person, but Brax knew.

'I've heard, that a while back, a man in an animals body caused a lot of heartache for the Interior Union, and I'd be betting my lifestyle that you're him little man.' Brax gestured towards their canine companion.

"You'd be right there." He sensed in reply.

'Excuse me for not being Mr 'Oh So Trustful', but who might you be?' Lupe butted in.

'I don't expect you to trust me right away, but I'm a spy working for the Independents, and it's just my luck that I found you guys. I think I could certainly use your help.' Brax said.

He felt the opportunity. The rivalling Unions had been earnestly trying to bring down Sayre and his regime, but he had been backed by some unstoppable force that allowed him to continue with whatever plans he had. Now that the dog-man had shown up, people would be sure to raise a few silent questions in their mind. But you could never count on the will of the people. They only let you down when hope seemed lost, but not necessarily gone. The people of this world may be different, but were just as fickle as the world they had come from.

'This isn't a good place to make palaver, I think perhaps we should move to a more secure location.' Brax suggested.

'Let me guess, a secret hideout? Please let that cliché be real' Lupe gave a sarcastic grin.

"I wouldn't be too surprised if that were the case, these people do things by any means necessary, as long as the price is large." Roland sent to Lupe, and Lupe's gaze on Brax was broken as he turned towards the dog. This was enough of a sign to show Brax that the dog was talking to him.

'I reckon we can do something about your friend's dialogue, seems like it might be making a nuisance of itself to the three of you.' Brax said

'That *would* be greatly appreciated' Jane started 'So where's this secure location you have in mind-'

'My house. Curtsey of Interior Union.' Brax smiled as though he had achieved some battle against his rival Union already, but the feeling wouldn't last while he was still on this Cradle that was formidably known to everyone from the other Unions as a shithole. Corruption, murder and all things that everyone worked away from was the state of Cradle 11. It was as if Sayre wanted it like that, just to prove a point. Or maybe he didn't care about the Cradle; it was just a tool in one of his larger plans.

'Come, now I have my very own informants-' Brax directed a hand at the three of them 'We have no time to waste, things must be done, gather what you have and come with me.'

He soon realised the three of them had nothing, and knew he would need to offer them something once they reached their destination.

'One question I have, why aren't I hungry?' Lupe said with sincerity. Jane couldn't help but hold in a small laugh, but he secretly wondered the same in his mind.

'I'll cover that once we're at my place, you people aren't very good at keeping the dialogue down, I think I'd better give you a bit of guidance on that too.'

They gathered together, all of them looking weary, even Lupe despite the sleep he had had. The room was looking as empty as it had before as they began to depart out of the door into the everlasting dark-light that greeted all outside. This was perhaps the only place they had not been watched, but it would no doubt be the last place of privacy in a long time.

* * *

When fantasising about the extraordinary things that spies did in their day to day lives in films and books, imagining just how complicated and action packed very living day was for *James Bond* and other such antagonists, people often crept past the fact that maybe spies *do* in fact have their own lives. One filled with ordinary experiences, like having a family, mowing the lawn, cleaning the house and even taking the occasional stroll to clear their mind, not to "silence" the local loud mouth who knew too much. But in this world, not many of those things were possible. Only that of having a family was remotely possible to people here, but Tailen, no. He had distanced himself from everyone, no one knew him, and he lacked anything in the way of a social life and friends. His life consisted of *being* a spy. But it was not out of choice.

He lost his brother, due to a deal made with his master. He had left everything behind. And now, working for the Union that everyone hated with such passion, yet they let it live on for so long, he was devoting his life to a cause he had not fully understood.

'A balance is in order' Sayre would say to him. Tailen knew nothing of this balance, only that Sayre wished to disrupt it somehow. In *both* worlds. One of the people travelling with his brother also interested him greatly when it came to balance. Something important struck Sayre about him, but he had made a point of keeping that secret, even to Tailen and his most trusted employees. It puzzled Tailen that it could be something with utmost value and importance. Something he would never understand until death. Or *Jane's* death so Sayre had told him. The odd thing was that Sayre didn't wish for him to die, under any circumstances.

It was then that Tailen was interrupted in his thoughts by a man stood in front of him (Tailen could not tell just how long he had requested his attention) and seemed to bring out a big smile.

'HELLO! Can I interest you-'

'Do not interrupt a busy man or I will have your testicles hanging from the nearest pole.'

(No thank you, in other words)

After this is did not take long for this absent minded man to realise he had tried to sell to a very serious man. One not to be trifled with. All Tailen could hear as he hurried off with no time to loose, looking for the next likely buyer was, 'Very well! Very well sir!'

Tailen was onto something when he was thinking, but that crazy man had killed his flow. At this time he felt like killing *his* flow. But this place didn't tolerate much in the way of disorder. Even on the Cradle of his own Union, he could be struck off. So he continued on his silent walk down the North-West side of the Cradle, staying near the centre as opposed to walking near the Arms. That was hen he felt it brush along his leg.

Tailen was not Wearing his usual shroud of clothing. He looked fairly ordinary, apart from his well fitted upper clothing which seemed halfway between a folder over vest and a shirt. No one could have been able to tell he was a spy off duty, no one knew him. But one.

He felt what no human could have come across in this world, brush lightly against his right foot. As far as anyone knew, no one in this world had *fur* aside from the deranged abominations over in Cradle 1, the ever infamous science platform. He tried to hide his ideas, but knew for sure in his mind.

"*Roland?*"

But as he turned his head and tried to make out the canine figure, all he could see was a crowd walking, as if it were purposefully trying to block his sight of the ground and all else. What he did see, however, were some oddly clothed boys, either following someone, or simply trying to find a pattern in the crowds movement. It took no genius to know they blatantly did not belong here. That was when Tailen's mind truly began racing, trying to think of a suitable course of action of how to deal with them.

"I cannot kill them" He thought, "Especially not the other boy, Jane." He thought maybe he could get away with silently dealing with the other boy, the crowd would not notice until someone were to trample on his lifeless skull, and Roland, he thought, he could not throw harm upon, despite his "Please Remove Him From The Eyes of the Crowd" status. Harm was out of the question. The only other thing would be to immediately report to Sayre about their movements. Either follow the fantasy spy way of life and interrupt his walk, or continue to get on with a poor excuse of spare time. He was no *James Bond,* but neither did he have a life to which he could fall back on, and claim to his non-existent friends that he could not in fact go and do a side job for them, because he had family plans. Instead he chose to blindly follow his logic, instead of his peace of mind.

H e began a brisk walk back toward where Sayre would no doubt be waiting for a report on the actions of the travellers. Acting like a primary school teacher-teller, going to tell on his friends, his *brother,* to the teacher, waiting for his much deserved reward, which he knew he would never receive, not even through death.

"*Not quite James Bond, a sell-out version.*" He thought. How long could he live with *that* status.

* * *

Crowded though it seemed, no one particularly took notice of the boys, who were blatantly following the man they had put a moderate amount of trust in, after having spoken to him only briefly. The handy thing with this place was that the crowds made it impossible for anyone to notice the boys following anyone, or even notice the *boys* themselves. After previous accounts of people trying to fight against the Interior Union, people very rarely showed an interest in anything that could be considered as an attempt of an attack. It was better for their *own* interests.

That was very much the attitude in this place. Life was mediocre, but considered good by most standards, and anything that could possible interrupt their peace of life here would be given no more than a quick glance followed by instant dismissal. *Fear* did that to people here. The world was not what it once was, not for a long time. They had strived for so long to survive and come out on top. And they had. Now was not the time to go about trying to change what was already satisfactory. Some, however, knew things could be made more that satisfactory. Without the Union controlling their conscience so strenuously they could have perhaps made things better in the first place, and living in the skies, afraid of muties, lesser humes and other such living dangers that could not reach the skies, would not have been an issue.

No one pitied the men and women lost to the strain of a parasite on Cradle One. Nor did they feel the slightest bit of regret when they referred to humans living on the ground as *lesser*. They were very much an indecisive population for a Cradle. All the rest owned by rivalling Unions lived in at least *some* dignity and choice, free to say as they wanted. But here, they realised they could get away with much more. Nothing was quite obvious on this Cradle to the naked eye and the naive mind. Quite a number of people however, who were not spies, knew just how corrupt and violent this place was. But luxury proved to be a perfect bribe. And when temptation failed, threats did not.

Lupe strongly disliked the vibe he was getting from the place. The feeling of being noticed and looked upon, but no one showed a direct interest. It was like being watched from every angle, but not knowing when or where exactly. Every face he turned to he would be greeted by the other side of it. Jane and Roland, however, *basked* in it. The feeling of not being seen and the blatant fact of no one caring why or how they were here was a perfect way to go unscathed. The last thing they needed was for someone to kick up a fuss and make their job of following Brax with subtlety was extremely undesirable by all means.

Roland had made frequent attempts to not brush his fur against any unsuspecting people, for he feared anyone could be allergic, and that would have been a difficult situation indeed to get out of. Every other person he avoided would only cause him to almost bump head first into another, then when he tried to correct himself in the compact crowd he would overcompensate and almost bash into an innocent shin. This made his job very difficult, but he remained at the side of at least one companion at once. He favoured Brax due to his larger build, people were more likely to move out of his way, and he had a kind of aura that made people simply part slightly for him. Roland and Jane however were very slight and had little of a force behind them physically, and this was made obvious by the amount of dodging they themselves did through the streets.

It all reminded Jane of the streets on Manhattan when he had visiting New York so long ago, staying in a Panamerican hotel remembered distinctly how hard it was to walk across a ten foot wide path. It was almost as if people purposefully walked in the opposite direction to make your tourist life harder. Although Jane always hated the idea of being a typical tourist, it seemed too typical. He noted the way the New Yorkers never waited for the green man like in England, they simply came to the edge of the path, saw an inch gap between a truck and a mountain sized saloon and simply stepped out despite there being a police car parked so closely outside the Empire State Building. It was never just one person either, it was an entire multitude of bodies moving across a black floored slaughtering ring. It would only have taken a careless taxi driver, or an unprepared driver to miss or slip on the break pedal to take out a number of souls. But still, they walked.

That holiday was a good one. One of the better ones in fact. Although nearer the end he had unknowingly been cut in the back by someone, but a no one. It was like the person had cut him for nothing, and scarred his back for no apparent reason. But the most disturbing part was, Jane didn't feel a thing, only saw the blood pouring down his back in the shower. Jane hated hospital though. Not once in his life had he been to one for any of his own injuries. He had been knocked out by a friend accidentally, and rushed to hospital. It ended by them saying he was completely fine, however six months later he had a mysterious bony lump on his shoulder and had been made to see a doctor. As it turned out, the bony lump was the result of the joint of his shoulder being split in half and bleeding internally.

The doctor had said it must have been due to a heavy hit to the ground in previous months. Jane had that same feeling when he found out. He never even *felt* it. He quickly dismissed this frequently on all occasions of it happening, he felt the pain of everything, falls, bashes, even *love*. These larger more visible scars however, he had not felt. As the years went on he had multiple signs of scars on his body, but could not recollect how any of them had gotten there. The only ones he *did* feel were the ones made by a car hitting him, breaking the windshield of the car with his back. But the pain lasted no more than a few hours.

He had been told he had been dropped on his head as child. He could always feel the slight ridge in his skull where it had clearly been misshapen, but his mane of hair clearly covered it.

All this was brought to the forefront of his mind, by what? A simple crowd situation? He knew there was a much deeper meaning why his brain had purposefully made his attention focused, but he did not want to risk worrying anyone else in the party. His brain had enough psychic tricks of its own, which it had so aptly reminded him of every time he had communicated with Roland.

Roland . . .

Jane looked around, noticing he had not felt the frequent bash of a dog's body on his legs as the poor canine had attempted to make little of a scene while they followed Brax. But he could not make out the figure anywhere. He passed the message on to his companions.

"*Roland. Where's Roland? I haven't noticed him anywhere. Look for him!*"

As their heads turned facing the floor, looking so intently for just a small shine of fur, their eyes went unanswered as to the whereabouts of their friend. As the feet and lower bodies of the people walked by, never once stopping to wonder what the newcomers were doing, standing there, staring at the ground. They had more important, *luxurious* lives to live, which would remain so whilst they kept their curiosity in check.

Each of the boys and Brax had their own mini heart attacks, and the feeling was felt throughout the group of them. Constantly pacing back and forth, scanning all they could. But no sign, no slight idea was found. They had been tricked by the security of the crowds.

* * *

The lady had scooped him up ever so quickly, slapped on a restraining belt across the dogs mouth and popped him into her vegetable sack. No one had noticed her little deed, and no one would, not in these crowds. She had caught the sight of the thing and knew his importance *immediately.* She hadn't looked like she knew what to do straight away, but Tailen nevertheless saw the awe in her eyes; an unnatural look on her face, one of temptation. He knew this day, he would not allow the brother he had betrayed to be *property* of anyone. He had made the decision; he would follow, and deal with her in a quiet place.

She then hurried off, and he went into his spy mode, like a natural reaction.

* * *

"*Where is he?!*" Jane shouted within their heads.

Then he felt a hand drag him from behind, into a nearby empty door way. Then his heart sank, thinking it was all a setup for them to be dragged and taken away, but was greeted by a familiar face.

'Don't worry so much, I had to do things that way, to make sure that no one tried anything.' He spoke with utter calm, as if nothing had happened. Although Jane thought men like him would not show emotion at a lost friend, betting he had lost many. Then the realisation came to him.

'You *faked* a kidnapping?'

'It was for the best, now we have achieved some sort of worry within the crowds mind, someone will have noticed, not to mention if we kidnap him, no one else will be able to.' Brax seemed confident at the plan he had draw out with such short notice.

'Why weren't we told?' Jane said, wishing he had been let in, to save him the temporary worry he had felt.

'It was best you reacted as close to real life as possible, if not, the effect we wanted might not have come across properly.' Spoken like a true politician on the subject of "Collateral Damage". Seemingly heartless to the public, but a necessity any president would have to make at some point in his life.

The instant mistrust hit Jane deep. He had been tricked so quickly by someone he and Lupe had put a great deal of trust in, and it almost backfired on them.

'I think Lupe is still searching for him, we better go make him aware that it was all a rouse.' Jane spoke with disappointment, and it was evident in his face.

'Try not to take it so personally, it was necessary, trust me.' Brax tried to reassure.

'It's kinda hard to trust someone after something like that, you have to admit.' Jane said, the anger still remaining in the back of his mind as he tried to control it. His way of solving the problem was to simply go and look for Lupe. He'd break the news to him as coldheartedly as Brax did, only this time with a more emotional state of mind.

It was not hard to find Lupe. All he had to look for was a rather protruding mass of curly black hair, constantly bobbing about in a circle. Then Jane shouted over to him.

'Lupe! Come over here, we need to talk.'

Lupe remained just as clueless as he was while searching for his friend who wasn't there when he heard Jane calling from behind the multitudes. He strolled over as any innocent would, but saw the face on his friend as he walked towards him.

'Something I missed?' Said Lupe

'It was just a farce. Roland . . . missing, none of its serious' Jan replied as gravely as he looked.

'Sorry if I'm missing the greater picture here, but I don't quite see where you're getting' He tried to grasp at the point but his mind couldn't understand why Roland was missing and what they were to do about it.

'Brax set up a false kidnap, so no one else could do it for real. So that nothing bad could happen to him. However he failed to see the greater idea of telling us, and saving s the confusion.' the latter half was said with a school boy's attitude. As if he were a child being deprived of what was necessary.

'Oh, well . . . good idea, I guess.' Lupe still showed confusion, but gradually grasped the idea of a political "We know what's best for you" state of mind. 'Gotta admit, he got me worried for a second there.' The confident smile he faked told Jane more than necessary about his ideas of the situation

'You weren't the only one . . .' Jane then turned around without even so much of a second glance back. Lupe could see that deception had obviously gotten to him. He could read minds, but he had failed to find this vital event hidden within Brax's mind. He hadn't even so much as thought to do it. Now, however, he wouldn't think twice about it.

Jane's face showed every part of his disappointment in what had happened, and the realisation he had been tricked into doing something that had made his heart stop. He *felt* for Roland, both him and Lupe, and they both had some connection of friendship despite the oddities of the way they communicated with one another. But Brax had shown no feeling or care towards the boys' feelings, and had nevertheless made them feel they had placed their trust wrongly.

"We trusted him the moment he told us his standing in this place, and now we can trust him no more than any other person here." The thought in Jane's head was more than understandable, but they *had* to put their trust in Brax, more so than they felt comfortable with, because it seemed like he was the one that could help. After all he claimed he had the situation in his control for the time being. But the problem Jane had with it was that in a place where neither he nor Lupe was familiar, plenty of things could go wrong.

* * *

"What a trivial job *this* is!" Sandra thought.

Not since times of tension between heavily armed Unions had she had a job like this to do. The idea of it both excited her and scared her, but her mental needs had overpowered her sense of fear of what could go wrong, because she desperately wanted the action, the thrill of making a catch in a completely crowded area, and yet, no one noticed.

At the time her nerves were failing her. Her legs were shaking, her hands were sweating, and most importantly, her resolve was failing. In this day and age, whatever this date *was*, this kind of thing was considered dangerous, especially on a Cradle where they were not welcome on. But when the time came, she simply strode up with great courage in her long smooth strides. At first she had considered the weight. What if she couldn't pick up the beast? And what on earth did she plan on doing if it barked or signalled? Hell, it could have even bitten her hand off! But no, she had smoothly grabbed it by the scruff of the neck and simply lifted it into her extremely large sack, which was in itself, a very odd carrier bag to be using I this kind of place.

It seemed like the animal was on some bad turn, the air on the Cradle that was supposed to provide the living this with nutrients and energy while they breathed had obviously failed to affect the dog in some way, but it still carried some muscle on it. This place was not entirely designed for anything but humans. However some . . . mistakes . . . were made with the air dispersing design, and the people on the Science Cradle 1 had gone mad, their skin had taken a bad change, and their minds had gone almost completely as they tore each other to pieces. The people on this Cradle were considered similar to the abominations on Cradle 1, with their corruption and secret deeds that were done when the people slept during the permanent sunlight. Other Unions looked down upon this place, and yet no one dared to confront it, in case the leader, Sayre, had spies in amongst all the other Unions. It would turn into a backstabbing mess.

But the idea of cutting the head off of the snake had come to mind. Sayre, however, was more difficult to find than an ant on a mountain. Although in this world, there wasn't a great deal of mountains *left* after the destruction wrought upon the surface.

The sack on her back was slowly wearing the endurance of her shoulder away, yet the dog inside had made no attempt to move. Sandra had checked numerous times that she was not drawing attention to herself, and found herself walking along one of the metallic streets filled with no one other than herself. And yet, she still had the horrible, skin crawling sense, that she was being watched. Or followed, and *examined.* This feeling struck her harshly, and she changed her stride to an extremely brisk walk. She hesitated at every turnoff and alley, in case there was someone there, standing, waiting for her face to make recognition of the long barrel of a rifle aiming at the soft part of her skull.

A corner came up, only this one was shadowed, and the sunlight made no attempt to light it up on its never moving axis. She had a feeling about this one, a *bad* feeling. Her pace slowed, she was almost at a crawl, and as she went to check the corner she heard something: a flapping noise, similar to that of paper in the wind. But she doubted it was as simple as paper. It would more likely be a sound of a madman's clothing, stuck in an odd position against a hard calibre, wavering every time he moved and the many drafts if this place blew.

She turned and saw a vague outline of a man. There was no coat. Just the psychotic grin on his harsh skinned face, yellow teeth gleaming despite their condition, and his eyes, *burning* with an orange tinge. He moved his hand toward where the weapon would be tucked into his belt, and as her impending doom hit her, like the bullet that would go to her face, at first smashing the bone and then plunging into her frontal lobe, shattering bone into her screaming eyes, her nightmare of a daydream broke.

But it was not broken peacefully. She stared at the empty dead end of the alley, waiting for what her mind had made up, expecting the scenario to go as her brain had told her. Only at the sight of this blank space on the Cradle, she felt slightly more settled. Her nerves, however, had not failed her entirely. Stood behind her with a silence matched only by that of a rock, was Tailen, and his brother safety blazing in his mind as this woman simply stood there, awe struck at some empty space.

Sandra turned, to face the way she intended to flee, only to see the real trouble which her mind had failed to imagine. There stood a man, in clothing as sanguine as the night. There was no hard calibre. Only the shock of what had struck her body, causing a great sensation in her abdominals.

Tailen had plunged a master looking cutlass blade into her, the blade plunging through her stomach, piercing her liver and scraping the lower part of her right lung, and protruded out the other end of her body. She could not feel the blade at first, but then the explosion of the pain in her body was great, but not great enough to force her body to push out a scream. She could say nothing, and she could do nothing, other than stare at the cold face of a haggard trooper. He looked like a young man, professional at whatever it was the Union had employed him for, but he still looked *tired.*

Her neck felt limp, and all the remained was to stare down at the object that had penetrated her body, and then allowed the attacker to *lift* her body in the air, as he slowly tilted the blade to the sides, in order to cause her torturous pain in her final seconds. As the blood slid down the blade to the hilt, each dropped to the ground measuring the seconds left of her consciousness. Once there was a small pool at the place on the ground where her feet once were, her face was stone cold, stopped, dead.

Tailen merely tilted his alloy forged cutlass at an angle, and allowed the body to simply fall off from its own weight, and it dropped to the ground with a gentle thud on the hard cold floor. The bag itself lay next to her body, in a mass that could be barely identified as a dog. Thought still it simply sat there, still, looking almost as dead as its previous captor. It was at this stage where Tailen had to decide just what to do with the situation. To take and hide his brother, or to simply leave the sack here with the body and allow him to make his own way back to the hole her perhaps once lived, so as no to be caught my the Interior Union and tested with unnatural tools.

This was a decision Tailen himself could not make.

11

Unwanted Reunions

There was never any clear way to describe the situation that a family member was put in when they hadn't seen someone for years; even more so when the cause of that situation was something of another's doing, something forced and yet chosen, necessary, and yet not desirable. It was difficult for Tailen to focus on anything at all. The situation he had now put himself in was dire. He had murdered in mid day, not that anyone could tell by the sun, but no doubt someone would come across his deed. But this was something he had not been told to do, and unexpected deaths on the cradle were not the kind of news people in high places like Sayre liked to hear about. The worst part was, he couldn't stay and look after Roland, he had betrayed him, and his honour was stick weak from shame, but also the fact he worked for what could be considered as an evil force made things ever so more difficult. Roland was practically fighting against what Tailen was working for, and there was no room to accommodate both.

He had to make a decision. Go behind Sayre's back, which was next to impossible, and help Roland on his journey with his friends, whatever their aim may be, in spite of a dire future. The other, was a simple one. He could return to Sayre and his usual job duties as if nothing had ever happened, until of course, someone became aware of what had happened, then he'd be in a great deal of trouble.

He was fighting both heart and mind to make a heartless logical and heartless decision, or one which would change, and in the end, perhaps end his life entirely. Each giving moment only made him feel more and more uneasy about his standing. Essentially, anyone could walk round the corner at any moment and see the ragdoll-like body of a woman on the floor, with a gaunt and shadowed figure standing over her body with a large rucksack as part of his claim.

He did what the coward inside him did. He took the sack, ensured the captive inside it was still unconscious, and ran.

* * *

As Brax and the boys continued to walk, with a mistrustful silence between the three of them, they began to notice that the crowds of this place quickly died down depending on the area. It was almost as if people had created a society here where specific road became high streets, like tourist attractions, and they made the choice of which roads were considered back alleys. But regardless of their views in the minds of the people who lived here, each street, road, or path was identical, being no different in quality or size then the previous or next. And yet, the people here made it . . . as if it were like the earth Jane and Lupe new. A typical society, clinging to its views and values, shaping their different world around what they had before.

As they walked down the invisible end of the high street path, the crowds died down, less and less did they have to fight through hordes of seemingly busy people, focused on their own selfish needs on this Cradle where no one seemed to have a care in the world. *Their new world.* Without any cause for such behaviour, people seemed to actively avoid the route they began to take, down any normal road, that went straight like any other, had corners like any other, but had the aura of cold death at a seemingly random point.

'Even though this place looks the same everywhere, it gives me one shit storm feeling of creepiness. Something just isn't right.' Lupe broke the silence with his usual musings.

'People seem to avoid us, or wherever we're going, why?' Jane posed the question at Brax, who seemed like he was unaware of ay attempts to create conversation. Finally he answered after a minute of silent consideration.

'They know something isn't right about these parts of the Cradle. It's not Sayre, they just seem to know our hideout is round here, but don't exactly make a point of getting involved. They've seen what happened in the past, if you get my drift.'

'I'll bet they saw more parts of that person than they wanted to, bodily I mean.' Lupe made an appalled face of childish disgust. Then was astonished at the reply he got from Brax.

'I'm afraid it wasn't just Sayre's men who caused the mutilation of innocent people who knew things' He looked down in apparent shame, but Jane thought he saw some fake quality in his looks. 'The Independents did have to get involved once or twice to keep people from revealing too much. Mind you, it wasn't just this cradle that faced some pretty harsh destruction . . .'

Jane seemed to read his mind without even attempting to force on his skilful use of the mind. 'What happened on one of the Cradles?'

Lupe seemed all too astonished at the question Jane broke out with, but simply stared at Brax in anticipation of the answer that might come forth.

'Cradle 1, it was a . . . heavily experimental science vessel, a little smaller than your average Cradle, but it was possibly the most important.' Brax changed direction down a very similar looking path, and gestured for the boys to follow him while he continued. 'Most of the technology we have on these Cradles is from the development on Cradle 1, for example it designed this air system, which feeds the population with intense economy use.' At this point, Jane and Lupe were particularly focused on their breathing patterns. 'However, at one point they came across a very basic compound to attempt to . . . suppress certain diseases this world could cause, like cancerous organs and the like. But, something went all too wrong.'

Brax's voice faltered slightly, as if he couldn't bare the thought of whatever had happened. It was like this world had had more dark days within the first few years of its very existence, far before Jane's world had encountered the so called "first murder". 'They tested in on about five thousand volunteers from every Union. Then the chief scientist, who developed it seemed to lock himself away in the deep central part of the Cradle, raving and screaming about "inexplicable results" being the doom of the science vessel. That's when the madness broke out in all of the volunteers.'

Lupe broke in. 'Please don't tell me they all turned into mindless flesh eating zombies, that would be the biggest cliché ever, not that I wouldn't respect the countless people who might have died in such a case . . .' Lupe felt the need to add the final part, in case his thought might have hurt Brax's feelings. Maybe Brax knew some of those people.

'Not zombies, but they are no longer men either. Just mindless killers, who don't think, all they do is want to kill the living. Some of the Union leaders say that some of them escaped and ravage across the very ground of this world, hunting down the lesser men.' This was another time Jane had heard people talk of the people not fortunate enough to get on the Cradles when the world was massacred.

'Hang on one moment; you said "are" not "were". Are you saying that there's a Cradle, number 1, that's floating a few miles above the ground, with a few thousand mindless killers on it, that just so happens to be the crème de crème of all science facilities? Which just so happens to have all the amazing technology *we* might need to get wherever we're going, or at last *help* us get there.' Lupe's mind began to scheme.

'Well, anything that would be incredibly valuable to living on this planet comfortably is on there . . . although I could imagine, something along the lines of helping your friend become a human again is something more on your mind' Brax was wrong to assume Lupe wanted this kind of thing, but he was not wrong that *someone* was thinking about it. Lupe only wanted to get back home, back into normal life and see his woman once more and proclaim his love to her indefinitely. Jane however, felt more inclined to help Roland with his condition. It was the least they could do to aid the friend that had so aptly helped them in this unfamiliar place.

'Well, that wasn't entirely what I was thinking, but its an idea, I just want to get out of here.' Lupe seemed to put his point across to Brax very efficiently. "I want out *now*" it screamed at him.

'Well if that's what's in your mind, then maybe, that science Cradle held many unknown and unpublished discoveries and breakthroughs. But we sent men there to clear the place, but all of them fell, and were tortured and ravaged like this world's surface. No one will be going there anytime soon. If any of the Unions could be bothered to spare the resources and do something about it, they could blow the place off the face of *this* second world, but there are so many valuable things on there which all of them would sacrifice plenty to get their hands on. Trouble is, no one wants to risk it after our try.'

Now it wasn't just Lupe's mind that was scheming. It seemed apparent to Jane that this Cradle was their invaluable source of answers and help. If they could get there and get their hands on some form of technology, they could defend themselves and perhaps get closer to whatever it was that they had been urged to fight for by the very person who wanted to fight against them. As his mind went on processing every aspect of their chances, he and Lupe followed Brax who had just led them round a corner when he stopped, amidst all his nightmares and imagination of the machinations he had been talking about.

And now he was faced with this daunting prospect.

* * *

"Drowning . . . in blood." Was what Jane could only hope to think at this sight. And it could have almost been true. The body looked liked it had been emptied of almost the entire percentage of blood, and was left with nothing but a bled out husk. It was a woman, as well. Her face pushed hard against the floor, with her hair messed up and strewn across her head. She looked in no good condition, and hadn't even died in a dignified fashion. Although the gaping whole that had perforated through her spine, lungs, heart and eventually the chest, had been made by a brutal blade, which in old medieval times, would have been considered a majestic death. She however, Jane thought, would not have agreed.

There was no grace in her crumpled body, almost floating now on the thick, almost crusted liquid that the body now lay on. On and on, the blood seemed to trickle further afar, as if trying to escape from the place where her body was, trying to find some soft, rich soil to seep into. But in this world, there was only man made industrial soil, and even that must have been out of the blood's reach. Despite his grave concern for the woman, Jane had not yet noticed Brax's expression in reaction to finding her. Lupe did. He made quick work of finding out just *why* this was such a grave sight, for Brax, and seemingly the boys themselves.

'You know her?' He asked, trying to maintain some form of respect for the dead, but still only thinking of his concern for their own situation. Why did this woman matter to them? It wasn't as if they had any business with the bad atmosphere. But it could have been them, lying in their own entrails, robbed of their possessions, and perhaps a different type of dignity.

'This is . . . not even describable. This woman, yes . . . I know her . . . this is not good, for us . . . you or your friend.' It looked as if his blood was being drained now, from his face, hands, and all other visible skin. It had changed from the raw red of a man with moderate cholesterol, to one with a more haggard and gaunt expression, wearing the colour of a mucky white upon his skin. Yet still, Lupe's own thoughts pressed on.

'What exactly does this have to do with Roland? If that was the friend you were talking about. I mean, who was she?'

'The one who staged the kidnapping in that busy area.' He replied with a blunt and yet emotionless response, his mind still focused on the outpour.

The blood, oh the *blood.*

His stomach tightened, thought he outlasted Jane and Lupe's determined state of strength, but he was the first and only one to lurch and release the sickening bile pitted at the bottom of his stomach which has so rarely been used in this place. It seemed as if despite the fact no one *needed* to eat here, their stomachs still functions a little, enough to make the grotesque smelling mixture of acid and stomach lining.

Jane had felt like heaving himself, and releasing the tension in his gut, but his mind had kept him firm. He felt now was a time to lead onto his own questioning, however harsh it seemed in the situation. He and Lupe were in a dire situation, now faced with mass death, but still they needed answers, if only to keep them sane and press on to the greater scheme of things.

'This means Roland is gone. And we don't know where. This may be a question we could answer for ourselves easily, but could you be sure that Sayre or men from the Interior Union did this?'

'I have no doubt about that, but this was not ordered, no one could have known about it. I personally spoke to Sandra about this job, and it was only a short while ago. Someone *must* have stumbled across her, and either panicked, or made good use of the opportunity. Whatever the choice, they made a point of making her suffer.' His voiced croaked as he uttered his last word, and he was holding back a crashing wave of emotion.

Jane looked deep into him, and found not love, but a long standing respect between Brax and this friend. He had obviously asked her personally, as she was the one he'd entrust these kinds of sensitive jobs. One question arose, as it did in almost every situation that the boys had come across. And Jane made short work of it, and he felt the frustration, even as he listened to himself say it.

'What now?' It felt like a hopeless question, open to any form of defeat. But there was nothing else they could aim for at this point. Unless someone had a plan of action.

'We need to continue down to our base of operations here. It's not big, but it's where we need to head if we have a situation. Though I'm not sure what we can do with ourselves now . . . we need guidance.' The logic in Brax's mind had faltered slightly, but he knew what had to be done, and what orders he should follow. He would need his good sense of mind to make it through the rest of the day, regardless of how intense it got.

'And um . . . what do we do with her?' Lupe gestured to the lifeless doll of a corpse.

'The Interior Union will find it, and if they did not order the hit on her, then it will cause uproar within the party. Right now, we could do with that kind of distraction on their part. It just might help us slip by without them believing we are here.' The shame struck him as he uttered those words, but it was what had to be done. It was their only hope of getting by unscathed by the wrath of the Interior Union once they discovered the fate of this woman.

'It seems a little . . . cruel, but I understand. *We* understand, right Lupe?' Jane nodded toward Lupe. 'Let's get to this hideout of yours; I think we need the time inside, and the time to rest.'

There was no reply from Brax; it was evident that this discovery had struck him hard in a place that was left unsuspecting. There was nothing he could do; it was just a case of facing the dangers that you put yourself in on this Cradle. It was a dangerous job being a spy, but someone had to do it, or life for millions of other people aboard different Cradles could be as corrupt as the ones the people led here. They reversed around the corner they had taken, and instead took the wider and clear route. It seemed they had taken the frame of mind of a suspicious psychotic, believing danger lurked around every corner. But in this world, that kind of psychotic person was probably considered as a very wise individual. Very wise indeed.

* * *

They had only walked a matter of minutes before they had come to a place where the crowd seemed to pick up again. This was another of the hotspots in the Cradle, and it seemed like the Independents had decided to set up camp here, where things were busy. But busy meant unnoticeable on this floating city. As if they did not exist, the people still took no notice of the two boys, who were blatantly following the larger man in front, with the grim look of a man who had seen no better days in perhaps years. Although right now, the trio did not seem to care about being noticed or not, they simply wanted to get inside.

It had been the first time Lupe had seen a dead person, the second for Jane. The defence mechanisms in Lupe's brain had kicked in, urging him not to take any memorable note of the dead body, with the gaping whole and clotted blood. He had his mind focused on random things he saw, grasping at them like a life ring, as if they could save his memory from collapsing on its self as it tried to deal with cold blooded ruination. He had imagined dead people being simply normal looking, nothing out of the ordinary, just with no breathing going on. But it had been entirely different to how he could imagine it. It had been careless, bloody, and *mangled.* The body's shape had seemed unnatural and forced. It wasn't something he could deal with on a long term basis. He needed to forget.

Jane however, had felt much less emotion. He had felt minor remorse purely for the fact that if they hadn't come here, they wouldn't have created this mess. They had no other choice though, they were urged on by their own brain's curiosity. His memory of death however, was one more graphic and atrocious. The sound of a persons bones being shattered as their body hits the ground and immediately becomes limp, was something that haunted him some nights.

He had been walking back from a routine run along the river, when a man, a psychotic, had been stood atop one of the roofs on the department store on the high street. With no cause whatsoever, or so Jane thought, he had not after all known the man or even heard any news of the event afterwards, the man didn't jump, but rather let himself keel over onto the thin air. He looked as if he did not expect the death which met him so flatly, and as cold as concrete could be. Jane saw no blood other than the few specks on his head and face, he had been far away, but not far away enough to not notice the unnatural bodily fluids that were leaking out of his smashed brain and organs. It had slowly oozed, but Jane left the scene quicker, feeling the weight on his mind and heart as he hurried home to try and scrub the event out of his mind. No scrubbing could get it out.

The worst however, was Brax. He had still not said a word since they had departed the fallen body of his friend. It was evident that he would not say anything until they reached the next waypoint in their journey. He soon did stop though, as if noticing something out of the ordinary. It wasn't something he had newly discovered though, it was the well hidden, seemingly normal entrance to where they had been heading.

Independent Services Offered

It took no wits for either of the boys to understand the simplicity of the disguise. But no one would question a simple shop, after all, very few of these places had windows, and were lit with a sun replicating light inside. It was in fact, just like every other building. Inside however, they imagined it would come across quite different. They followed Brax as he headed in like a regular customer.

Upon first sight, it looked as if he were a genuine customer. As the clerk saw the boys follow in behind Brax, it seemed like he intended to treat Brax like a proper customer, and not even Jane or Lupe heard any sign of code talk as they spoke to each other, as if figuring out what kind of service they required.

'Afternoon, or whatever it is up here, makes n' difference.' The shop clerk said.

'Hi, I think I'm looking for a commodity cleaner, I have a few things in my place which need tending to.' Brax seemed to get right down to business, ignoring the remark about the time of day. 'Is there anyone you have in mind for sensitive ornaments such as the ones in my possession?' This was where Jane and Lupe caught on, but couldn't make any guesses as to what on earth they were intending to do.

'Sure.' The clerk said, and like any typical backdoor dealer, he continued with, 'Just follow me out back here, I'll introduce ya.'

As if serious about the business he was asking for, Brax gestured for the moderately mannered clerk to go through the door that lay at the back end of the place. That door, Jane knew, wasn't supposed to be there if all the buildings were the same as the one they had slept in. But it almost looked as genuine as the services offered in this shop. For a short period of time, the boys actually thought Brax had stopped off to run some quizzical errand, something entirely out of the ordinary. Something not quite in the plan they expected to formulate.

'I believe the man you're after is Sir Pedley, he'll be right up your street, 'specially with the type of work you're r'questin'.' The clerk unlocked the door, with an old fashioned looking key, something which no other doors in this place had. The key however, was most definitely old fashioned if this was the hideout they were interested in. If they were lucky, maybe Brax could explain the use of it later.

'Thanks for pointing me in the right direction; I do believe I know my way to him from here.' And unlike any usual customer's request, the clerk paid no mind to the statement, and simply walked back out through the door, and they heard it lock behind them. The tunnel that lay ahead of them was not carved to perfection, nor was it particularly high tech. It looked like some sort of escapee tunnel that people in films like the great escape made, only tall enough for a normal sized man to walk through without having to focus too much on watching his head space.

Without any speech, Brax simply led them on through the tunnel, which was too dark to see any end. Like a man on a mission, but with no fear of the dark path, he walked along the awkward tunnel, without even so much as a small falter in his step, despite the fact that the ground was in no good condition for someone who could barely see where they were going. It was evident, he had traversed this tunnel as many times as all the cells in his body had split. Jane imagined that the tunnel couldn't be too long, or it would cut through into some other building, but it seemed like the place was bigger on the inside.

They walked for all but two minutes, but in these conditions, it had felt like the best part of an hour. Without any form of time to go by, or a naturally spinning world, it was hard to get a basic idea of time here. At the end of the short trek, Brax had taken a quick jerk of a turn, and they were immediately greeted with a great deal of beaming halogen lights. It was as if the doorway to this dungeon like hideout was some sort of entrance to a form of heaven. In this world however, such a thing was only in a fool's imagination. A heaven in a damned world such as this was like wishing for eternal sunlight in the boy's world. It seemed these ideas had switched places when things like the portal were taken into account.

By spending the short period of time through the tunnel, the boy's eyes had already adjusted to dark surroundings, and the bright light shocked them, and confused them, almost as much as the pink emanation from the portal which had brought them here. And for a second in Lupe's head, he thought this could have been another portal, back to the world he knew, and loved.

His hopes were ever crushed in this world.

* * *

Tailen was shocked at the weight of the sack, and couldn't quite get to grips that his brother, could weigh so little. It seemed apparent that his canine body did not quite adjust well to the factory made air in this world. Even so, Tailen pressed on at a pace of a dashing shadow. Regardless of the extra weight and strange adjustment to his centre of gravity that had been applied to his stance, he was still as agile as ever, almost leaping through the back alleys of the Cradle, like a hunter in the night. Only this time he wasn't hunting, he was hiding on the move, a scary prospect to someone who didn't know quite what to do, or where to stop, if they ever could.

He had to do something soon, or someone would see him, and that someone could have been anyone inside the Union. He stole a glance at the sack, tearing desperate answers from his mind, begging for one of them to answer. But his heart tugged at him, and drowned all his logic, in hopes of a simple glance into the dark holder, to look at his brother's current situation. For all Tailen knew, the woman could have killed him in there, suffocated the animal, stealing what little life was left in him.

Tailen fought against himself, but found he was too wanting, begging to let his brother out. And as he slowed his pace, his decision seemed more evident. He began to slow further, until he had stopped altogether. He crept round yet another darker corner of the Cradle streets, a place where the unnatural sun did not shine. He lowered the carrier bag, and began to untie the binding at the top. In his anticipation, he couldn't get them undone, and almost found himself tightening them.

In his horror, he slowed himself, and fought back the shakes in his hands. His situation was becoming dire and unstable. At last the binding fell to the floor, and the opening lay limp, allowing a small tuft of dog hair to protrude out of the small opening. Tailen slowly pushed his hands into the hole, feeling the animals chest, trying to sense if there was life left. And in this one, there was. He found himself almost fighting the urge to open the bag further, even though the decision he had made could not be undone now. He pushed it apart, and folded it down until the dog looked as if it were asleep on some old worn sack, like a makeshift bed for a homeless one.

When Roland did not stir from his unconsciousness, Tailen almost found himself feeling like he wanted to give in to his hopes of brotherly redemption. Instead he desperately poked the dog with his palms, trying to wake Roland, like a child trying to wake its parents to comfort it after having a nightmare. Tailen felt like he would get no comfort this time. All hope of redemption was lost, especially after he had joined such a powerful state of force, which seemed to cause tyranny to everyone, other than the people who were under its rule. At last, at the very time Tailen gasped, Roland began to attempt to raise his head, but found his strength was weak, and found it difficult to raise himself.

He didn't fully understand what had happened or where he was, but after spending such a great deal of time trapped in the sack, breathing stale, hot, recycled air, his body begged for fresh air, but the processed air on this Cradle was something he had to accept as an alternative. Not quite remember his body was not human, Roland tried to get up without even opening his eyes, but found that as he stumbled, his sight was necessary for such a simple and basic task.

As he opened them, he found he wasn't on his own, he hadn't been taken and dumped, he had been taken yes, but led to a dark corner in one of these many streets. The person who had taken him however, was a shroud person, someone he had not even noticed in the crowd of the street he and his friends had walked. This was someone he did not expect.

Roland however, remained uneducated as to who this person was. The hood, the dark hood and shady attire hid every detail about the person body.

"Who are you?" He thought, then he realised, this human couldn't hear him, or his words of the mind. It seemed like the man before him was a reactor, not a psyche. He was unable to communicate in any way with this figure, and that could leave him in a very bad situation.

As if in some reply to Roland's mental question, the shadowy figure said 'Are you alright? Someone tried to take you . . . I . . . they are gone, can you understand me brother?'

In some mess of an understanding, things became much clearer to Roland. This wasn't the person that had kidnapped him. And as Roland saw the shine of a blade behind that cloak of trickery, he understood this person might have *dealt* with his captor in a rather brutal way. But there was no way of Roland to beg for his life, or at least negotiate his ending with this . . . new acquaintance. He hoped his useless begging through the mind wouldn't be necessary. Roland hoped he would not have to silently scream in his head as this psychotic shadow tore his entrails from his body with his efficient blade.

'I don't mean to hurt you, although I don't quite know what to do with you . . .' This made Roland relax a little, but what was it the man had called him earlier? "Brother?"

All of a sudden Roland's mind buzzed, and churned, and questioned itself, to try and make sense of the situation he had been dropped in, by two mysterious people, one killed, the other a killer. Then an unfortunate truth dawned on him and seemed to hit the side of his mind like a ten tonne weight of bricks.

This was *his* brother, Tailen.

It was an unlikely sight, but it *had* to be him. His attire proved that it was the man who had betrayed him for a life in the service of the man-demon, Sayre. He had gotten Roland into this mess, and if not for the small help from the canine whose body he took on now, he would have almost certainly been killed by Tailen's unlawful master. How Tailen had tried to tell him he had no choice, that his mind *pushed* him into doing it. But of course, he did in fact have a choice, he could have turned away, and perhaps paid his life for it, but the opt out option *was* there in the first place.

Roland couldn't speak to him, even if he tried, and had no idea how on earth to communicate to his brother. Worst of all, he had no idea how to get himself out of this situation. He needed to get back to the people that *could* understand him, wherever they might be.

The only thing Roland could do in this body was the typical thing any dog would do to a person. He let out a much unpractised, unexpected bark. This caught Tailen by surprise, as he jumped, just a little.

'I guess you can't talk to me, but I'm sure you can understand me, am I right?' The silence that reigned only made him fluster further, and his frustration grew. 'Uh . . . how about two barks yes, one bark no?'

And with no sign at all, Roland did as he heard, and barked twice. Tailen jumped once more, but this time a little less. It was the first time in an age since he had heard something like that, but it brought to him a sense of understanding. He tried to tax his mind of whatever option were left, searching for a solution to their current problem.

The one thing that upset Roland the most, was that his brother didn't even try to apologise for anything, when he had the chance in front of him, after all these years. Not once did it seem to cross his mind.

'Listen, I . . . I don't know quite how to solve this . . .' Tailen said. His ever diminishing resolve wearily went on. 'What can we do now?'

Roland felt worried about him, as if his brother was slowly breaking down as time went on. But there was only one thing Roland wanted to do at this point; something his brother did to him long ago. Walk away. He wasn't sure if that might anger Tailen, make him act rashly, and hurt or perhaps even kill Roland in blind anger. But he had no other choice. He couldn't stay with Tailen, and risk both of them getting killed. He had to return to Jane and Lupe, and try and find a solution for this decaying world.

He built up his courage as Tailen simply stared at him, as if searching for their answer on Roland's furry head. He began to turn, and slowly, walk away down the alley, waiting for Tailen to pounce on him, and restrain him. Roland stole one look behind himself to see what his brother intended on doing. As he glimpsed, all he saw was a man, now looking like a young child, stand there in shame as his only remaining family walked away from him. Still Tailen looked upon Roland's face, but found no answer to his questions.

Now they were even. But for the wrong reasons.

12

The Hidden White Belly

The immediate adjustment to the bright lights was quick, but nonetheless painful. Of all the high tech advancements this world seemed to have made, this underbelly hideout still remained lit by a modest advancement of lighting from the twenty first century. Some things, it seemed, were just too good to improve. As the boys wandered in to the vast lobby of the Independent's hideout, Brax veered off to one side to meet some compatriot of his with an ever remaining grim look on his face, and a frown on his brow. Jane and Lupe did not follow, instead walked straight to the middle of the bright room. It was a wonder that they could not see the room as they walked through the dark tunnel. They stood at the centre, bewildered by the sheer size of the room. The place must have cut and burrowed few dozens of buildings to maintain its diameter.

A few yards away, Brax formally shook hands with a more matured male, looking older and more experienced than anyone else in the room. To Jane, it was clear who he was. Behind the sham of conversation, this man was Pedley; his title however, remained unknown to them. They seemed to exchange some serious words, and like finely attuned clockwork, the both of them turned to face the boys, but the emotion on Brax's face had changed a little. Now the news was told to Pedley, perhaps he could be more laid back about the situation.

Lupe understood more clearly about Brax's feelings though. He knew that the loss, either lover or friend was something that would not go quietly. It was worse for Brax in this situation; he had seen the person dead, lying in her own blood. It was a vivid scene, something that could haunt to the bones, but perhaps for this short while, his mind could be at rest, while they discussed just what they could do next to resolve their situation, and make a difference to the corrupt standing of this Cradle.

'These, are the people from the other world, forced through the rift.' Brax said, and gestured for Pedley to go meet them. With a certain feeling of caution, the two men made their way to the boys; Pedley in particular looked a little weary of their presence here. It didn't take a genius to understand the danger they put on this place by just being here. Someone could easily have seen them come in here and never come out. Bt Pedley thought it was hardly likely, there were crowded streets everywhere. Keeping tabs on two people would be incredibly difficult to maintain. Sayre's hand however, did stretch far and wide about the Cradle.

'It's not often we get fugitives in here, so I apologise in advanced for everyone's . . . reluctance to share good wishes.' It was as if Pedley were trying to put good light on a negative matter. 'Brax has informed me that our plans did not go entirely as they should have, and for our carelessness, we've paid for it.' Both of them bowed their heads in respect to the dead, and Pedley continued. 'That is what we need to expect on this Cradle though, one slight slipup and we're done for, so you boys need to watch out and hold your tongues when you're out their.'

Lupe interrupted, 'Oh you got no problems with that, I don't think me or Jane would even attempt to talk to some of these people. Almost as if half of them were born with mechanical spoons up their-'

'We understand.' Jane intervened. 'But our concern right now is Roland, we need to find him.'

But the look on Pedley's face was not one of recognition, it looked as though he had already given up on that idea before it had chance to bloom in his mind.

'We'll see what we can do about that one.'

(No)

'In the meantime however, we need to focus on what you boys exactly intend to do in this world . . .' It seemed like Pedley had an idea of what the boys needed to do, even when they had no clue just exactly what their plans were. Coming here was their idea of inspiration, and a force to help with that task. However, as they heard the words from this man, they knew that perhaps some of their ideals and hopes of saving some of the people in this land were being dashed by the very man they had hopes in for help.

'You see, Pedley, Sir, we don't exactly know what we're planning on doing at all. Our current main concern is about Roland and helping him get back t how he was . . . turn him into something more . . . human.' Jane said. There was a tint of desperation in his voice, hoping that his attempts would change Pedley's mind about putting of the search for Roland. Then maybe they'd have a chance at helping their dog friend, and finding some answer to his and their problems on Cradle 1, if of course there were any way to safely traverse the place.

'Look here boys, I know this dog is a close friend of yours, but Sayre has eyes everywhere, perhaps even in our own hideout, something which we don't like to admit, but I believe he's lost on this vast Cradle somewhere, and in the worst case, your friend could be . . .' Pedley paused, attempting to try and not falter the boys' confidence.

'Dead . . . just like Sandra' Brax finished.

It was harsh, but it was more than possible. Roland may have escaped at first, but the agents of the Interior Union seemed efficient at their ways and dealings. The boys had to keep in mind that the worst scenario could possibly be the correct scenario.

'We'd at least like to try' Jane said

'Can't you put out some kind of "hit" but for missing people?' Lupe asked.

'You mean give the information to all our agents, and watch out for a dog? No offence young man, but I don't think something as unique as that would make itself remotely visible, if anything it . . . he, I mean . . . would try and make himself scarce on this Cradle.' Pedley seemed almost stubbornly negative about the situation. He had clearly made up his mind not to take any further action.

'I do believe, however, that we have some common interest.' Pedley began. 'There is a great deal of technology on that Science Cradle, which both you and me would like to get our hands on, and attempt to use it against Sayre's regimes. Getting there and getting *through* however, is the hard part.' Jane could already see Pedley's ulterior motive, at the very forefront of his mind. He wanted to use Jane's abilities against the monstrosities on Cradle 1, but he also found something about Lupe. Apparently there was something about Lupe too. Then Pedley began to talk again.

'We know you two have certain . . . abilities. When you came through that door, with the bright lights shining on you, our body scan picked them up.' When Pedley mentioned this, Jane had noticed that the lights were not as bright as they appeared on the outside. It as not just lighting, so it seemed, it was some sort of detector that scanned humans. The most puzzling thing however, was that he now told Jane and Lupe, that in fact Lupe had some sort of ability. Which was indeed, some good surprise.

'Uh, I'm sorry old man, I don't really think I follow you . . . I don't *feel* anything different about myself, there must be a-'. Lupe was instantly interrupted by Pedley's new found pride in scanning instruments.

'A mistake? Oh no, highly doubtful, these instruments are far too accurate, and highly thought of by most standards. You may not feel anything, but our machines say you're quite . . . well, *fast*.'

Lupe looked confused at first, and found it difficult to catch onto Pedley's drift of conversation. Lupe's self doubt seemed to blind him from the obvious answers. What he was now faced with was the lingering realisation, the only reason he had managed to get through to this place, was because there *was* something significantly special about him. What it was that was different, he didn't know, he felt just the same. He couldn't read minds, which was an obvious assumption, as he never could tell just want Jane and Roland were going on about at times, and had to catch the drift of a one sided conversation as Jane spoke. Instead, Lupe just stared at Pedley, waiting for the answer, in a look nothing short of great awe. The answer didn't come immediately, so Lupe felt the need to ask.

'I don't suppose you'd be a real *cool* guy and tell me just what the hell is different about me?!' Lupe's lack of understanding had initially made him frustrated. He didn't like not knowing what was going on with himself, nor did he like thee fact he wasn't in control of anything in this world, not even himself right now.

'You see we have two rather specialist qualities in a very select few human beings in this world' Pedley started, 'And those two things are what we call, "Psyches, and Reactors", I'm sure by the names you catch the general drift, albeit, a very shallow drift.' Pedley paused to let the first piece of information to sink in, and then continued. 'Your friend mister Jane here, is a Psyche, which everyone seems to be aware of already, but I highly doubt you fully understand his capabilities.'

'Yes yes yes, I understand that, but can you skip ahead to the part where I have become a freak of nature . . . well, whatever is classed as *nature* in this hellhole anyway.' Lupe said, and he could see that Pedley felt it a rude intrusion into his train of conversation. Lupe didn't care much for saving this mans feelings, especially when this man didn't care for saving *their* friend, who was malevolently taken and caught up in some awful situation. Lupe's impatience grew, but Jane's thirst for more knowledge only gagged for more. Whatever Lupe's advancement, it was sure to help them.

Pedley cleared his throat, but not due to the build up of phlegm, but to make a point of the fact that he was in charge here, and he was the person leading this talking.

'Alright, well we'll come back to your friend later if it matters to you that much. A reactor is simply someone who has a significantly heightened sense of reaction-'

'That wasn't self explanatory at all now was it . . . ?' Lupe interrupted, and his sarcasm shone through his impatience.

'*AND* your body is inevitably, faster, and more susceptible to reading notions a lot faster. For example, if a win bottle were to drop off a table-' Pedley was interrupted again, but this time, by Jane.

'He'd catch it in half the time at least . . .' He said, as if formulating some plan in his head. His face looked still, and full of inspiration.

In an obvious sign of frustration, Pedley continued.

'A-yesss . . .' Pedley said in a long exasperated tone. He was expecting another interrupting, but found the two both awe struck and speechless, as if it were some immense discovery. 'Of course we view Psyches a lot more useful than Reactors. They can almost kill with the mind; figure out what people are thinking, and so on, the possibilities are almost endless. Reactors can only just attempt to dodge things like a bullet, and are altogether more useful in removing themselves from situations. Psyches however, remove the situation itself.' Pedley smiled at this prospect, clearly wishing he could grasp that power. It was a scary unexpected face that only Brax picked up on. It was a face that he felt he needed to be weary about.

'Thanks for telling me I have some sort of awesome gift, but in actual fact that awesome gift is crap compared to some other more awesome gift. It does wonders for a guy's self esteem. "Hey, you are amazing! But there's someone more amazing and useful, so . . . yeah."' Lupe felt a little less fortunate, despite being a rare form of person.

'Well, I didn't mean it quite so largely, it's still an ability many people here would like to have for themselves . . .' Pedley stopped for a spit second, with a very puzzling face, which Jane now noticed too. Lupe however, remained disappointed with the way he had put things across. The way Pedley was trying to redeem himself was not working in Lupe's eyes. 'It's just your friend Jane here is essentially a lethal weapon through the mind, you however are a more physical weapon, and physical weapons are more temperamental . . .'

'Weapons?' Brax considered.

'Well, the ability, not the boys of course, they are after all only teenagers at best. More like gifted civilians.' Pedley said. It was at that point when Jane realised what he was before. Only a high ranked army officer referred non-fighting people as civilians. Here, the acting head of the hideout for the Independent Union, was some kind of headstrong sergeant or general.

"Some proud military leader . . . that's just what we need." Jane thought.

Pedley continued to explain to the boys what they were, and why they were so special. Jane, essentially capable of assaulting the mind, Lupe was something more physical. Jane immediately knew Lupe might have to save his ass, or was at least in charge of that job as of now. It could be a very important job after all.

* * *

As he started to walk away, looking like an average dog, simply going about his business, Roland did not feel like he was walking with no emotion. His canine heart was heavy, and his conscience was precariously eating away at him for his sudden choice to abandon his brother, the man who had saved him from being held captive. But Roland still did not know exactly why he had been taken. It was obvious it wasn't anything to do with Sayre, for Roland doubted his brother would go against his direction. Perhaps she had taken him as some sort of trophy, or had hopes of experimenting on him, either way that was not Roland's main concern. All he could think of doing at this point was finding Jane and Lupe again; they were the ones who could do with his knowledge of this place. But it was more than that; he *needed* them, especially Jane. It had been an age since he had successfully communicated with a human being, and the boys had been more of a breeze of fresh air, almost literally. They were different to everyone on this world; even the most pleasant of people from the more civilised Cradles had their minor downsides and slight hints of corruption.

His main issue was that the boys had no idea about the layout of the Cradle; all they had was a so called Independent spy leading them around. Roland knew his way around the Cradle, and had sought the aid of the Independents before; his only chance of meeting back with the boys now was to get back to the Independents. Though he doubted they would help him as they did before. Things had not gone so well. He would have to travel back to the White Belly, the hideout which the Independents thought of so highly, ran by that intolerably proud man Pedley. He had no other choice though, Jane and Lupe were sure to either be there, or been and gone. In any case, he had to go there and find answers.

He had since looked back on himself as he walked down these dark places, changing his direction to aim for his goal. As he looked behind, he somehow expected Tailen to be there, in a deep sense of rage, hurtling towards him swinging his blade. But there was never a single sound, no shadow or movement. Just the shadowy presence of nothing. He continued, only now quickening his pace. He did not feel like hanging around anymore. This Cradle was not short of its usual psychotic folk, if they had the right attributes of a higher human, they were allowed among the rest in the Glory Skies. Though this place clearly lacked its proclaimed glory.

As his mind frequently played tricks on him, turning meaningless objects into killer beasts, Roland kept up the pace in order to get to the hideout as quickly as he could. He was almost sure that Pedley would in some way use the boys for their abilities. He was almost certain that the White would have scanned Lupe, and Pedley would have been more than glad to tell him of his bodily advancements in this world. What he might use them for was what scared Roland. He knew that they were set on their goals, and perhaps a little blind faith in a leader they knew nothing of would have caused Pedley to . . . take advantage of their desperate nature. Particularly Lupe's, he was more than eager to try and get home, and Pedley would have gladly played on that eagerness.

Roland had no doubt Pedley was a corruptible man, given the right incentives. The Independents had on more than one occasion, tried to take over Cradle 1, no doubt to try and continue where the scientists of this world had left off, and seize control of the main technological advancements that never made it into circulation. The multiple occasions had been denied by many, and so few believed their excuses. But in this world, no one tried to question the Unions, the simply had the power over all, the power to take over, and the power to take away the high positions they had given to the countless civilians of this world.

He had to pick up his pace if he was to get to the hideout before any of the important members left. They would undoubtedly have information about where the boys had gone next. He didn't believe they'd stay there for long. All they wanted was to gain some information on how they should act next. But Pedley would have given them some sort of incentive to do some work for him. What kind of work, Roland could not say, but it would have almost certainly been something to utilise them for Pedley's own means. If he was lucky the people there would take him to the boys' whereabouts, but things didn't often go smoothly in this world. He had a feeling a little more diligent searching would be on the book this . . . what was it? Evening? Morning? Roland had no idea, he had no clue whether the boys would have taken the time of day as one to sleep, they were in a strange world, and had not yet gotten used to the unusual light. They might have misunderstood the climate; it was possible they might not have slept for almost a day. If they went on awake, they would feel like sleeping soon. If he were particularly lucky, they would be resting while he urgently made his way to them.

His quick dog-like canter sped up a bit, but he found that cornering took some consideration. He still had an hour or so worth of travelling to get through the always-busy main streets to get to the fake shop front, however he had no doubt he might get there unscathed. He may have disheartened his brother, but it was doubtful any of Sayre's minions were in search of him, and no other civilians would have wanted to draw the attention to themselves. That made him question what had happened.

"Just who was she?" he thought. The woman that now lay still touched by death, growing colder and dryer by the hour, who had smuggled him into her large carrier bag. She could not have simply been a citizen, though this place was filled with crazy folk, they would not have dared to get caught up with him, in fear for their own lives. They were absent minded, but not entirely without common sense. Even the simplest of minds had a good sense of self preservation in this world.

She couldn't have been one of Sayre's people; Roland had ruled that out the instant he knew Tailen had murdered her. Even after all this consideration whilst keeping his pace up, dodging various metallic objects on the streets, Roland could not possibly think of a viable reason for this act of kidnapping. It was almost *mindless.* She had obviously not expected anyone to have caught her, and she went about operation with the utmost precaution, and had almost gotten a full success. The idea that it had been staged had briefly touched his mind, but it did not stick, it would have been a careless plan, though it was one that no doubt Pedley would have thought of. This brought something up in his mind. Roland knew Pedley's past of susceptible considerations. Pedley would not have wanted the boys to be told of Pedley's previous dealing, it could have been purposeful for Roland to be kidnapped. It was a possible idea, but he could not prove anything until he could find the boys. Maybe Pedley's reaction would tell if he had thought up this plan of action.

If that was in fact the case, he had to warn the boys that Pedley's priorities would only lead them to a dangerous and difficult situation. Or possible a great deal of bad situations. Roland could not possibly tell if Pedley was mixed up in more complicated matters, and possibly in the control of Sayre himself. It was a bad thought indeed, but it was one that they had to take under consideration in these times. Everyone in this world had a price, and it seemed Sayre could pay any price. As bad as it seemed to consider Pedley's corruption, every possible situation just *had* to be considered. On this Cradle he just never could tell just what would happen, or even if the turnout of this situation was entirely dire.

Before Roland could acknowledge himself, his pace was fast as he turned a corner with a brighter feel to it, one that was under the visage of the ever burning unnatural sun. He had reached the main streets. He felt a sudden nervousness in his canine body, as if he had a similar feeling to butterflies, though it felt entirely different in his form. The feeling that his previous situation could rain down upon him again after his fortune with confronting his brother. People bustled, it was as if there was barrier between the shadowy streets and the more sunny ones, where people seemed almost *scared* of walking into the shadow, as if the very moment they took a step into it, their healthy spines would be immediately shattered or pierced by a preying agent. Their paranoia was their lifeline. Even as everyone seemingly walked around with a purpose to their actions, they all had a look, a strange psychic vibe in their heads that made them feel constantly out of control. As if someone was directing them and their needs.

Roland slowed. His alertness had become altogether more open to everything around him, swallowing up the situation. He felt like a naked man in front of millions, the irony was he knew he was no naked *man*. Even though he knew he would be blatantly ignored by all, the ones out of his eyesight would stare at him with their minds, filling their heads with babbling questions of fear and confusion. They knew not how what they saw was in front of them, so took according action to steer clear, and make out as if they had not noticed. If someone walked up to the dog and disembowelled the creature, there was no doubt that they would simply walk on by in hopes of removing themselves from the area.

As he trotted about the streets, he became all too aware of his lack of direction. He had not often been along these roads, and his mind knew little about what direction to go. It was the canine part of him that had kept its sense of direction, and told him which direction he should keep to. His body alone was directing him, but his human mind was defending him from invisible threats. He fully understood as he ran, slower than usual, that somewhere along the way, one of Sayre's men would see him and report back his situation and area, but he doubted they would make any active decision to rid the Cradle of him. No one would even consider helping him from this Cradle, let alone this world. But it had been people from another world that had quickly considered helping, and he would either be their inevitable downfall, like the previous men, or they would be his, and this Cradle's salvation.

The hours passed, and his pace had slowed considerably, but he was surrounded by familiarity. He knew he was close, and he had a feeling by heightened senses that there had been movement in places where there should not be. Luckily they would have seen him long before he even reached the centre of the Cradle, not knowing his direction was set towards the hideout of the Independents. He was but minutes away from the fake shop front, but possibly minutes too late to stop the boys from gallivanting into a situation Pedley would have pressured into their minds. He knew of the invaluable technologies on the Science Cradle, and that every Union wanted what was on there. But he questioned as to whether Pedley had the guts to make the boys do the dirty work of entering the place and extracting what so many desired. The thought could have crossed his mind on numerous occasions. Roland knew, deep down, that in his entrance to both boys' minds that they possessed immense amounts of ability and power. It could be within there abilities to assault the Science Cradle if they had control over the power, but it would be Pedley's control of that power that would cause them to go.

As his mind escaped him to think of the needs and desires of the boy's practices in Pedley's operations, Roland's body led him straight to the forefront of the shop through instinct. He took a sharp look around, and for once in this area, found himself alone in the street, looking somewhat abandoned of its population.

"There *is* rest for the wicked after all." He thought.

It had been an incredibly long time; his best guess was that it was indeed late night. With any luck, the boys would know this too and be sleeping within the hideout. But luck was never a luxury Roland had. He slowly strode into the shop, with its door still open, and found the familiar character behind the counter.

'You again? I thought we'd seen the last of you, I don't want no part of you're dealings, you're like a bad penny old boy, but go right through. I think you know where you're going.' It wasn't much of a greeting, but Roland considered it was a swift enough invite into the White Belly from the clerk.

As he wandered through the dark tunnels, his sight comparatively better than most humans, he quickly found the bright, almost holy looking entrance into the White Belly.

Though the sight he found was not a welcoming one, in fact it was essentially no sight at all. There were almost a quarter of the people that there used to be. Almost all the personnel had gone. Worry filled him instantly. It was not what he wanted to see. He searched the people that he saw, hoping one would reply with the powers so few possessed.

"Where are they? The boys . . . Pedley!"

There was almost nothing but silence within his mind, everyone looked at him, after having been called upon by him. But all looked stone faced, as if they felt no effort was required. Then a random sullen voice entered his head. That told news that he had gravely suspected.

"The larger portions of the personnel have gone out with Pedley and the boys . . ." a short silence ensued, before the replier realised he needed to explain the whereabouts of his friends.

" . . . To the Science Cradle . . ."

13

Landing in Fury

No matter how adept the technology of this time was, they still couldn't make a plane that didn't give you flight sickness.

Lupe had sat deliberately not facing any possible window or opening in the short range plane, but it hadn't helped. When they had first laid eyes on the craft, they had thought it was something that they had seen a movie of some sort. It almost reminded Jane of the aircraft flown in *Starship Troopers* except it was less rounded, and far less shiny. In fact, it was more like someone had taken the looks of that design, and then simply welded some scrap metal and some very precarious looking rotor blades on the sides. The ride wasn't particularly smooth either. Despite the fact that the atmosphere was entirely still (god knew how long there had been no wind or weather effect in this world), the plane lurched to the left and right, and had made a habit of frequently losing ten or twenty feet of altitude every few minutes. This routine the plane made was punishing Lupe, and it showed.

Jane looked across at the appalled face of Lupe, and not once did Lupe's head or eyes change the direction he was facing. His skin had gone a limestone colour, and he was almost as rigid as a seizure victim.

They were not the only plane however. There was a large number of remote areas on Cradle 11, where the Independents had managed to hide a great number of these machines. At this point of flight, they had poured in all their personnel to fit into the seven planes. There was about twelve to fifteen in each plane, armed to the teeth by the looks of things, and not one of them showed any sign or weariness of the impending danger that lay ahead of them.

Jane had been told of the remaining residents of the Science Cradle, their carnivorous ways and their brutal outlook on killing what lived. The thought clawed up and down his spine, and he could sense the same feeling in Lupe, though he had enough discomfort to focus on at this point. Pedley had shown a great deal of fearlessness in the current situation though, and the armed personnel in the craft seemed to be confident in this mission. But Brax had so often mentioned how it was almost classed as suicide to go to this Cradle.

And that was when the idea had hit him like a ten tonne bar. They had wanted him to come with them, as if he could change their fortune, change the tide of battle. But why? Although he had some amazing unnatural skill of the mind, he couldn't grasp why he and Lupe could possibly make the difference. Unless there was something Pedley was not telling them. Unless his powers reached further than the just mere communication with the mind, and Lupe was capable of tearing someone to pieces in a matter of milliseconds. He immediately thought it impossible at first. But everything impossible in his world had become a reality in this one. For all he knew him and Lupe could be the ultimate killing machines, the only ones people thought capable of bringing down Sayre and his corruption.

This hope however did not last long in his head. The plane lurched down again, leaving his bodily organs fifteen feet above him. That snapped him back into reality. No matter how powerful he was, he thought it impossible that he could bring himself to decimate the brain of a victim. But when confronted with your last breath, it was incredible what you would resolve to. He would dig deeper into his mind, if he had the chance, he would try. He would kill, if only to help his best friend whom he dragged into this situation to help him get back home, despite the ever increasing doubt of the matter.

"Lupe, when we get there, if we're attacked, don't hold back . . ."

Lupe looked up for the first time in the hours they were travelling. He had heard Jane, and looked confused. Jane's voice had sounded a little different in his head. A little too bold for his liking. He thought back at Jane, not knowing if his thoughts could reach him. He couldn't hear his own voice in his brain.

"Fight? We cant fight. That's for Pedley and his men-"

"Why do you think he brought us with him?" Jane thought, almost loudly, and he saw Lupe recognise the level of noise with a slight wince. Then Lupe looked back at him.

"I don't know what we're capable of, and I'm not sure id want to find out." Lupe was not renowned by his friends for any form of patriotism or boldness.

"When the time comes, I think our feelings might have to take a backseat. I don't trust Pedley, and I know you don't either, so lets just do as he says and keep our shadows on Brax, I think he's the most trustworthy." Jane replied

"Alright, but I'm following what you do, not what anyone else is telling me to do. I feel a bit lost without Roland, he needs our help more than these people. They're after power, not a revelation." His words wise, Jane was reminded why he was renowned as Wise-Old-Lupe.

"Alright, keep a hold of your stomach, I feel a drop coming in."

And as if they craft obeyed Jane's very command, it did its routine descent, but this time, Lupe was ready for it. The boys looked at each other, as if something odd had just happened.

"Hindsight, now that's something I'd like to see more of." Lupe sent to Jane

"Luck, and coincidence." Jane said

This world doesn't know the meaning of luck or coincidence. And Jane knew it. What he had just done had silently scared him, but he made a point of not showing it on his face. That was something Pedley either already knew about, or something he was best not told about. Jane's uncertainty of this whole situation was rising, and Roland's whereabouts was in his mind constantly. Part of him wished he was still alive somewhere and the other part of Jane *knew* he was alive. There was a band in Jane's head, and it had not yet been cut. That was enough to make him feel slightly certain about his hopes. But all the hope in the world couldn't tell him what they were about to face. Not even the grim but defiant look on Pedley's face, as he sat there near the front, could portray to anyone what the man had planned. But there was something going on in his brain, and he didn't want anyone to know what it was.

The craft lurched onward for what seemed hours. The continuous sun seemed to make every day a drag, making anyone believe that the day lasted forever. For all they knew, they could have been flying for days. The sun gave no information on how long they had been in this flying organ rearranging device. Even the land they looked down upon out of the dirty windows so many dozens of miles below them never seemed to change. It just looked arid and dead. The only change in scenery was the occasional rock, that looked as if it were eons old, and perhaps they were. It occurred to Jane, that if the plane failed, and started to plummet towards the ground, it could take them a few minutes to reach the ground, and there would be nothing to meet them but coarse, dusty discoloured desert. Not exactly a nice prospect to imagine, especially when his trust in the integrity of this craft was dwindling by every second.

Lupe had not moved an inch in the last few hours going on few years. In fact nothing about him had changed except his even paler complexion. He gripped onto his chair as if his life depended on it, every second of the journey, and had almost overcome the mental pain of every drop the craft made. To anyone sat around him who had taken the time to watch him, it would have made the journey's entertainment. If Lupe was ever threatened with torture, he would probably find he could withstand hours of it, as long as it was not in any way similar to his current situation.

It was at this point when they heard first word from the seemingly mute pilots about their position. But the news was both good, and yet grim for all at the same time.

'We have eye on our objective, and it's looking a little worse for wear.'

What the pilot meant was a small understatement of the Cradle's look. The thing looked battered, as if hit by hundreds of battery fire and something must have hit a sweet spot, because the entire Cradle was tilted. Not just a slight tilt. Almost as if the whole thing was at a thirty degree angle.

'Looks like someone came in a little hot and took out some all important stabilisers!' This came out as a mindless joke from Pedley's lips. He laughed as if this made no difference to their otherwise grim situation.

Homicidal ravagers and a Cradle that looked as if it could drop at any moment, was not what they could have hoped for. Either one of the two things would kill them, or it would make their mission a reconstruction of some horror ride.

Pedley looked over at Lupe and his slight smile broadened into a maniac's grin.

* * *

After spending some time staring at their destination, Jane soon realised that getting to Cradle 1 was a small feat, compared to the great task the pilot would have. Nobody really thought about it until a short while later. Not only did they have to explore around this broken city at an angle, but they had to land on it in the first place. It was simple to say, the plane was not designed to land off balance. A minor tilt would have been awkward enough, but now the pilot was beginning to get uneasy. These feelings were easily read, not by using psychic abilities, but by noticing that the plane wasn't flying in a straight line. The passengers found themselves weaving left and right a few metre at a time, and they were never going in one particular direction for more than three seconds. Pedley was growing impatient.

'Perhaps we should have a computer draw a straight line for you to follow? Or did you take a few too many quick swigs of your synthesised piss water?'

Again, as he spoke, the plane darted to the right at the same time as one of its reliable lurches, almost sending Lupe to his knees, begging for this hell ride to simply end his life.

'Apologies Sir, I just don't know which section I should be landing in . . . None of them . . . look suitable.'

Not once did he speak with any certainty, in fact, his speech was almost comparable to his flying.

'Alright, coming from somebody who has no experience with flying these things, I'll just have to tell you how to do your job. Try-'

But before Pedley could continue ripping the pilots dignity to shreds, Lupe broke in with his burst of wisdom.

'Take us in from the lower end of the Cradle, so we land nose up. You have to land nose up in a plane anyway, it just means we take a little jolt as we hit the tarmac . . . metal . . . whatever it is. I'm sure we can all handle one little extra bump. It'll be like climbing a sand dune after reaching the peak of Everest.'

The joke was not found by all. As a matter of fact, none of the people knew what Everest was until Jane added that small detail.

'A mountain, from our side of the world.'

Talk of the other world, their world, simply brought on more speechless travelling, and tensions were rising as they banked towards the dropping end of the Cradle. Hands were firmly on the arm rests, clutching the ends as if it offered some form of divine protection. It did not change the situation though, they were only a few minutes from landing on one of the most feared places on this rock. A place where the old world, the one of Jane and Lupe, was a mere playground compared to the atrocities that this world offered.

Pedley did not even argue with Lupe, he simply sat back, slouching, with no real recognition of the information that just might make the difference of saving their lives, and dying due to poor positioning. Nor did anyone expect the pilot to immediately take the order as if it were from Pedley himself. They proceeded, at no slow pace, directly toward what looked like a hanger, broken by age itself, and whatever form of rusting happened here. The doors hung loosely from the lower end of the opening. From afar, it looked no bigger than a garage door, but as they approached, Jane saw just how large other planes and ships must be. He had not seen anything that could fill enough of the open space that had been provided, but no doubt the other Unions with more combat able ships needed the room.

Dwarfed by the size of the opening, the pilot continued at full speed. Jane thought they would crash into the far end of the hanger, not realising how far back it went. So far back, "dwarfed" was not a word that easily described the size.

'A corner would be prudent pilot.' Pedley began.

'So we don't attract too much attention by landing smack bang in the middle of the place.'

There was no initial response from the person he addressed as "pilot", and it seemed he cared little for knowing any names. A man of ranks, and nothing else.

As Lupe had described, the plane began to lower, nose up. It was not as simple as it sounded.

Within seconds the nose touched too soon, there was a deafening sound of twisting metal, screaming as if dropped in a blast furnace, and the tilt was clearly greater than they had anticipated. Seconds passed as the plane continued to lower from the rear, and the horrifying sounds shattered through their ears. Jane's face was entirely rigid, and he felt even more touched by the sound that everyone else. It ran through his brain, yelling at him from the inside. The rear of the plane touched down at last, and everyone found themselves in a position like that of astronauts preparing for a take off.

'That has to be at least a forty five degree drop!' yelled the co-pilot in horror and disbelief. He looked frantic and scared, as if impending doom was upon his steps.

As he finished, there was more scraping noises. But it wasn't the nose of the plane. It was the entire underside of it. There was so little friction between the floor, that they found themselves sliding backwards from the far left corner of the hangar. No faster than the sliding started, they stopped dead on some kind of thick wedge metal panel covered in burn marks.

' . . . Sir, the afterburner panel just saved us.' Still solid in his seat like stone, the pilot said the words as if they were his last, despite them being miraculously held in place by something they had neither noticed, or needed.

'Calm! Stay . . . calm. I don't need anyone running rampant screaming of death and horrors. We landed, we're alive. Now let's focus before I start dismissing people.'

Jane had presumed that when Pedley spoke of dismissing officers, he did not mean it in a formal manner. They were on a semi-destroyed Cradle that reeked of death and blood. Now all formalities would be replaced by brutalities.

* * *

If it were possible to convert Roland's expression from canine to human, it would have been simple to describe: a disbelieving face of a man, standing there for hours without change. He sat there, hours after they had told him Jane and Lupe had left, completely confused, broken, and helpless. They were the only human companions he had had in a long time, and no one else could possibly want to make an effort of standing by him. His presence was far too dangerous, probably something the boys had overlooked initially. He had no other choice but to wait. He could not leave the place, for fear of being taken once more by unknown forces. And he couldn't risk confronting his brother again. That was a bulging nerve, that lacked the final gram of pressure to make it burst into chaos. His brother may have shown mercy in his surprise of Roland's refusal to have anything more to do with him. But Roland doubted he would have any more good will gestures from a member of his family. Now Tailen knew that Roland no longer counted him as family. Bonds were broken, and now they were irreparable. Roland had not meant to show such blunt feelings towards his brother. However he had no given choice. It was either a precarious standing with his brother, stuck between the wrath of Sayre, or worse: getting them both slain by agents of darkness.

Darkness. That was just the word Roland had been looking for to describe the Interior Union. They were not just simply bad men trying to convert others to their cause. No. that was just politics plain and simple. But this . . . this was homicidal oppression. Roland couldn't fathom the amount of terror and disarray the Interior Union had caused. This world was much older than his own. So old, nobody really knew what was here in the beginning. That was something both worlds had in common. Roland knew though, that there was always a presence of darkness. There would have been an Interior Union before the great destruction of the world's surface. Most likely, it was that darkness that caused the scarring, the decimation of a beautiful world.

Jane and Lupe had known a world of far more natural life. They had lived in his world for the same amount of time he had before he was dragged by the heels to this brother of Earth. He thought that perhaps their time in their world was more peaceful, and more prosperous than his own. Twenty years could have made a lot of difference. Little did he know the world had moved on, but never really changed. A phrase he knew well briefly crossed his mind when he compared this world to his own.

"Same shit, different toilet paper . . ."

And to some degree, it was most likely true. He knew things about this world long before Jane and Lupe had come. He had found what he was looking for in Cradle 1, just as they would in due time. The difference was that it was far safer back in his day of youthful living as a canine. Back when people were less unsettled by the sight of the only animal on this cursed shrunken excuse for an Earth. One thing he regretted though, was ever finding it all out. Bringing that information back to his supposed friends, the Independents. A grave mistake he had made. He was lucky however. He brought information back with him, but nothing else. He never took anyone with him. They had no chance of taking technology like they did now, provided they could escape with it without being torn to pieces by ruined men.

There was little difference between those ruined ones and the Interior Union. Just the washed faces, unscathed and impeccable. The ruined however, were a different story. Words could not describe the faces. The epitome of horror and despair mixed in one.

Shortly after his return, the inexplicable accident happened, where ordinary scientists and innocents became the endless rage and fury of the ruined. Nobody dared return, except the reckless. Pedley had tried before. Roland had no doubt that he had missed out that minor detail to the boys. Pedley had no intention of telling anyone that he had led a team to that place, and returned with no one but himself. His ship had looked battered to the extreme, and blood was spread across the entrance to the place where the men would have sat as they did now, in the ship that took Jane and Lupe to the final resting place of many. The wrong part of that statement was that they never really rested. Deep in their fragile minds, they were tormented by images forevermore.

Roland could only hope that the two boys' abilities would save them. They needed to find out what they wanted. They needed to know about this world, about their future, and about the greater problem this world had to offer them. Until their return, he could not do a thing otherwise. He could only sit, and wait. Sit and pray.

14

Vicious Encounters

There is no delaying the inevitable. They had to get out, regardless of whether their death was imminent, or to come in hours from now. Pedley had made his points quite clear. There were things here he wanted, and things here that Jane and Lupe wanted too. Pedley however, carried a higher state of priority. For now, he was the wing they hid under.

'You know, I'm told in some countries, the most highly considered person in a group of people enters last. And I do believe I'm of the highest rank in this rig.' His ignorance was pressing and grinding Lupe's gears.

For a short instance, Lupe felt a fury from nowhere. Sensibility soon shorted it. Raging at this point would cause more trouble than they could handle. And they didn't yet know how much trouble they were in by simply setting foot in this place either. Pedley did.

'That means that the lowest rank goes first, and you boys don't event have a rank.' Pedley's smile soon faded to show his serious expression. But Jane did not need the mere change in facial expression. He read Pedley like a list of items.

Pedley wanted to be the one alive at the end of it. And he wanted things from this place he could never have gotten before the boys showed up. But their deaths were sacrifice enough if it meant Pedley could have one last little breath of this stale empty air. Choices were not given. Jane and Lupe *would* be the first out, even if it meant throwing them out. That was evident in Pedley's eyes. The deepest, sharpest eyes of a bombardier. Unwilling to die for his country, unless it was with an explosive and destructive outcome. That just about summed up his personality. It made Lupe feel like Pedley was more of an Interior Union sort of guy. He lacked a certain self control that they had though. They enjoyed their silence and shadowy presence. They needed nothing from a man willing to cause a mess for his own ends.

Jane and Lupe exchanged brief glances. As Jane went immediately towards the exit, Lupe had pushed in front of him in lightening timing. Almost an ungodly timing. Jane showed confusion, but his expression was only half through when Lupe had made it outside, with no hesitation of what could be out their. His reaction and movement was something that puzzled Jane almost to insanity.

'Never liked that plane. Glad to be the first off the thing.' He made a fake smile as if that were the sole reason he left so fast. Jane knew though, that it wasn't just the frequent lurching that made Lupe so eager to remove himself from the craft. He could dig inside his friends head; he found essence of distaste towards Pedley, but also selflessness towards Jane. He wanted to be away from Pedley, which was evident enough. But it seemed he wanted Jane out of harms way before considering himself. An admirable quality of a friend, but Jane didn't want Lupe to be the one to lose his life in this world. Jane had nothing else. He knew that Lupe felt the same way about his presence in this world. He had nothing left but a friend who had been so far away all these years. Now that friend was all he had left. That single friend didn't quite cover his losses of love back home. Back in their world. It was Lupe who seemed to still hold irrational hope of returning home. Jane knew everyone's feelings about that matter. Everybody seemed to burst with the information of their situation. They weren't going to get home, back to their world. Even if they did, everybody seemed to think they weren't going to like what they'd find. What they'd be left with at the end of it all.

Jane made no haste to rush out the craft as fast as Lupe. He thought it impossible to match such speed. But he made no falter as he leapt the short drop from the plane to the floor. He almost fell as his mind forgot about the large angle at which the Cradle had sloped. Lupe had either known this would happen, or his reflexes had gotten the better of him, and he was quick to grab Jane by the under arms. He surprised himself sometimes; Jane could see it on the face. He would just shrug it off as a lucky time frequently. Now, however, he seemed to accept it as his own gift.

'Thanks . . .' Jane said, showing genuine surprise and gratitude to his friend.

'It's the least-'

'Out the way girls, let my men and I out before they start shedding tears of Love . . .' Pedley interrupted, before the boys shared the speech of friendship.

As if it were an order, Pedley's men immediately made out of the craft, instantly in combat faces and stances, as if they would be confronted by doom the instant their military boots touched the metal. Pedley was last, and made it out a little slower, simply stepping down the large gap rather than leaping like the rest of the party. As he stood and looked around, everyone seemed to relax a little, as if realising there was no immediate threat at hand.

Then they heard the most terrible wailing, so sharp it pierced the ears. To Jane, it was not just wailing. It was cutting deep into his mind. He could feel the terror and rage behind the voice. So much screaming and pain. Pure anger. For no reason at all.

'What the fu-' One of the men began, as Pedley grabbed him by the collar and shook him firmly and briefly to make the man stop talking.

'Say nothing you fool.' He whispered. 'They know we're here, but they aren't here right now, and I don't *want* them to be here right now, because of some man who could NOT keep his mouth shut at an inopportune time.'

'S-s-sorry sir . . .' The man whispered back.

On high alert, everybody stood their, waiting to be overrun in a matter of seconds. But minutes passed, and they were still standing with no noises to terrify them.

'We need to press on, now I think.' Jane said.

Pedley rolled his eyes. 'If you say so captain' He replied sarcastically.

'You are regrettably correct however. Now as you boys seemed so eager to jump out first, we'll give you the layout plans, and you can lead us onward. Get to it!' He raised his voice, and then seemed to retract his body, as if he had done something so horrifically wrong. Waiting to be jumped upon for his sin of breaking the silence. Too bad his sins were unnoticed by any nearby local, hungry for killing. A thought both Jane, Lupe, and most of the others seemed to share.

The pilot seemed to be the one holding the map of the area, and made no hesitation to hand it over, as if passing on the burden that made his life nothing but a boot-lick. With strength and seemingly solid servitude, Jane took the tablet, cold metal, like everything else in this world; dull, grey, and heartless. He expected nothing more from these so called "area plans" Pedley spoke of. Not geographically noted paper or anything of the like, but a technology based tablet, that sprang to life as the brush of Jane's fingertips. It appeared to have no immediate interface, just a simplified map, with a brief LED blink of where they were.

'The angle of the Cradle might mess things up a bit, but the general locations will be close enough.' The pilot began, and quickly hushed his voice soon afterwards, not due to the fierce glance of fear Pedley had shown at the pilot's need to make Jane aware of any difficulties.

'Nothing quite like surety in this world is there. How do you people get by . . .' Lupe said, and drew off in a mumble.

'We "people" get by just fine surviving in a world not thought to be survivable in its current climate.' Pedley muttered. But Jane held no notice to his words. He took a short breath, silently, as if to not show people of his digression to the matter at hand. He began to walk off in the direction that seemed to be the only exit to the hangar, unaware of exactly where they were going in the first place. There was no avoiding it, unless they fancied a trip through a ventilation system so typically seen in movies. He saw nothing of the sort though at a glance. Everything looked like it had been torn to pieces by some huge iron-skinned beast, and few explosions dotted here and there, marked with scorched carbon across the otherwise dull surfaces.

The few dozen yards between the craft and the entrance door to the halls that lay behind, creating a maze of a floating city, seemed to take an eternity to get to. With tensions on high, and no clear understanding of just what they were here for, Jane could feel an unfathomable amount of disarray as he moved closer to the door. It reminded him of the time him and Lupe were confronted with a similar object. The door with no handles.

With some thought of believing the door was automatic, unlike the other one, he walked towards it, jolting slightly as it failed to open on account of his movement.

'Careful now boy, you might knock that important mind of yours into oblivion.' Pedley said.

'Right, not automatic, I expected more from a highly advanced Cradle.' Jane replied.

'Highly advanced, yet half blown to pieces and possibly on its way out, I might hasten to add.' Lupe's reply was fair enough in their situation. It did look somewhat grim if the doors weren't even operational. There must be hundreds between them and their imaginary goal.

'Not just anyone is allowed through these doors.' one of the crewmen began. 'I don't believe they wanted people to walk in, feeling invited by a door opening to their every movement. These ones are password protected, just like the ones on every other Cradle.'

As the outspoken man began to utter what he believed would solve Jane's minor problem, Jane made haste in speaking it in earnest.

'Eleven.'

Like clockwork, the door opened. Obeying Jane's command without request of identification. The knowledge of that number's importance was evident enough.

'How in the hell did you know that?' Pedley showed some signs of disgust on his face, that Jane quickly melted through.

'How do you think we got *in* your damned world?' Lupe asked. 'We sure didn't walk into it like Jane was about to; else we'd be a few piles of mincemeat on the floor by now. We may be young, but we are not without wits.'

Pedley didn't show immediate anger; he just looked shocked and surprised to be put in his place by a young man, clearly speaking broken English with an unidentifiable accent. Everybody seemed to stare at this little dispute that had appeared from simply opening a door, which as yet, nobody had noticed it standing broadly open, leaving them all vulnerable to surprise attacks by the ruined men.

It was then that something caught Jane's eye. Not his actual eye, but his *mind's* eye. As if something had just darted across the halls beyond the door, but not physically. He felt he was being stalked by a mind without body. The anger of a damaged mind flooded into his. His balance faltered.

'Woah now, Psycho Jane, now's not the time to go all limp on me. I can't hold my own against these guys.' Lupe grabbed at Jane, though he knew he wouldn't entirely lose all sense of balance.

'I think it'd be an educated guess to say we're being watched already.' Jane remarked.

No words were said; the men just looked at each other, shortly followed by a brief nod forward by Pedley. They entered the corridor looking both ways, as if children all over again, watching out for the oncoming traffic. It wasn't the traffic they were worried about. As the last man, Pedley, crossed the line where the door was based, it shut behind them, with a large deep *click*. Emphasising the false sense of being trapped in such a large place. Jane looked up from the tablet computer, as if asking the question of which way to go. "Left, or Right?" he thought. But before anyone answered, he found the answer in the pilot's mind. A truly useful tool his mind had become.

'Left it is . . .' Jane mumbled. And they followed him in silence. Constantly peering beyond their backs. That was when Lupe noticed a short, low whirring noise above their heads. A sort of electronic motor noise of a small toy. But he saw nothing, and soon went back to checking the obvious paths for a man, or woman, exceedingly tempted to tear his head off at the blink of an eye.

The part that most haunted Lupe, was the thought of the ruined people here, not considering the torturing pain they might cause to their victims as they released their anger through tearing what they could grab away from the body. He could only imagine himself being disembowelled, an organ at a time, as those fiery flaring eyes stared at his horror stricken face, almost unaware of the pain, too drowned in shock. He thought he was imagining it, until he saw the face of that person in front of him. Staring him down, just as he believed. Blackened eyes, broken bones, charred flesh painted with the blood of innocents. The demon-figure reached at him with such unexpected desire, and he pulled back.

'The hell!?' Pedley roared as he saw the older of the two boys leap back as if for no reason, scared by the sight of the back of his friends head.

'What's the matter?' Jane asked.

'This hell, it's making me see things I wish I could un-see.' Lupe said, with a still face.

The men got jittery at his statement. They hadn't said a word since they got *on* the craft, as if bound by silence. The only ones who had spoken had been Pedley and the pilot. It was almost as if they feared for their lives, long before they landed, and were now eternally haunted by that echoing scream they had first heard. As if an awaiting death held more priority than sharing a few brief words with the people they now travelled with.

'*Move.*' Pedley said. 'And please refrain from making the only people protecting you, decide to change their minds and blow their skulls to pieces.' This man clearly lacked compassion, and now seemed driven by selfish will itself.

Jane led on, walking slower than a normal walking pace, slightly shaken by his friend's short terror experience. Then he noticed a noise above him, that wasn't human, but it was a noise from something tiny. Like a mini engine, or a computer driving, clicking quietly away. As if by reflex, he reached out with his mind, and found something *with* a mind, but at the same time, it wasn't living. He was sure the people on this Cradle were living. This was not a world for cliché horror pickups. He hadn't noticed himself stopping as he looked up towards the bare piping above him. Something shiny, moving, at least until it was aware of being watched. Then it stopped, like it was a child caught creeping downstairs at night time.

Everybody looked up to see what the stop was all about. They had chosen a bad time for themselves. Especially the man standing outside the darkened room they now passed. He was directly in the middle of the line, standing their, dumbfounded at what the party was looking at, not noticing those hateful eyes upon his innocent soul. One quick grab of an inhuman hand grappled onto the soldier's clothes, digging through into skin. The man was ripped into the room, and only briefly managed a short scream before it became filled with bloody gargling noises. The ruined one had tried to rip his throat to pieces to make good silence. Cunning ruined people they were, it seemed. Being at the back, Pedley had noticed far sooner than the men either side of the now large gap between the two halves of the group.

His voice almost lost inside his body, he finally managed a yell and the blood flowed out like pressurised water, and the gargling continued, as a ravaged groan escaped the ruined one's mouth. Releasing his anger on his new ragdoll.

'The man was grabbed!' He screamed, in such a high pitched voice, almost impossible to come from a man's mouth. 'Kill it! KILL. IT!' he yelled again and again. As if he was feeling so helpless despite his possession of a firearm himself.

With no real recognition, the men obeyed. Without aiming, they all sprayed a hail of lead through the door, not considered the fellow man they now fired upon as well. He was likely dead from immense pain, but humans were known to live through strange and horrific circumstances.

As soon as the firing had started, that wailing scream of a man filled with hate beyond comparison broke out. It did not stay so loud for long. It died out, slowly, as the life slowly slipped from the man's ill-possessed body. As they stopped firing upon the blackened room, unable to see any sign of movement, all they saw was blood flowing through the doorway, enough of a sign to say that *someone* was dead in there.

'Young man, Jane, is he dead? Are they both dead?' One soldier finally whispered. 'Do you feel them alive in your head?'

Jane just shook his head, and Lupe immediately returned his gaze to the pipes above.

'That was possibly my fault my friends. Though I could have made more of an attempt at stalking you silently, it would have been more efficient if only a small portion of your expedition turned their eyes from unsafe places.' A voice called from above. It sounded like a well spoken man, but it was all too perfect. Like a fake voice. A computer generated sound.

'What is that?!' Another man shrieked, readying his weapon.

With his eyes still fixed on the roof, his expression never changing, Lupe said a few brief words.

'A snail . . . a small, metal snail.'

Thought it sounded like complete mad talk to Pedley, he did find himself seeing a similar thing. A tiny robotic snail perched atop one of the pipes, with big eyes, staring at the group, now one man down.

'That is regrettably correct, scientists can be quite mad in their times of genius.' The snail stated. 'Though I do have a name, or rather, an abbreviation of my purpose upon this Cradle. In short, you can call me PETE, but do bear in mind that that stands for Personal Extrinsic Technical Escort.'

'A robot filled with data and information . . . in the form of a fucking *snail*?!' Pedley yelled, so overcome with grief and confusion, he had forgotten the code of silence they had mentally taken when they stepped foot upon Cradle 1.

'Like he said, scientists may be smart, but they sure are damned crazy in their times of intelligence.' Lupe remarked, almost untouched by the difficulty of their situation.

'If I may, I can escort you to the place you want to be. If it's information on technology and answers you need. I have built in life form detection, if that is of any help towards your safety on Cradle 1.'

'That'd be mighty handy Pete.' Jane said.

'Yes, yes it would be extremely handy.' Pedley finished. Greed almost overcoming the horror in his eyes of what just happened. The promise of information and technology had hit the right spot in his scheming mind. Now he was on top of things. Now he was going to get what he wanted.

PETE did something extraordinary then. He has some kind of spider web like rappelling tool on his underside, and slowing whirred down to the floor, and snapped the wire back into himself.

'I may seem a small device, but I assure you, I can move at a good human pace.' PETE said.

With surprise, they did actually follow him, no questions asked. Pedley seemed to assure that by glaring at every man in the party as he pushed passed everyone. Now they were on to something, *he* wanted to lead. He was to be the first to get what he wanted. It seemed like the front was somehow now safer with the addition of what looked like a shiny snail, weighing no more than a few hundred grams, if that. On they followed, however, because they had no choice but to trust this rather eccentric robot, he had, after all, the ability to make them aware of any more dangers. Biological ones, at least. It would be no surprise to find some kind of defence system integrated to protect people from the deranged men that now took up residency in this forsaken Cradle. Though if systems were as broken as the place looked, the party might find themselves against more dangerous things.

* * *

He walked like a man who had found himself. A man who had been built up with self doubt and lack of trust towards anything but his own judgement, which in itself seemed impaired in the current situation. That had quickly changed, perhaps for the better. He walked with pride in his stride, a small bounce to his now longer steps, and a seemingly lighter load on his shoulders. All of this, taken from the trust of something so trivial and odd, it almost seemed like the madness of a man so close to giving up hope, which he found ample supply in whatever he chose. Something drove him to it. Madness, desperation? Nobody really knew exactly what he was after, what it did, or if it even existed. Maybe it was indeed something in his fantasies, something that gave him false hope in this tainted world, filled with everything that felt wrong, and seemed on the brink of losing all its naturalness. Yet now he found hope, and the rest, seemed to share his sentiments. It was truly a blessing, in a world so far from religious belief, so adept in their trust of technology and power through people. It seemed like people here believed in anything they could, to give themselves an excuse to feel like their life was worth something, had some purpose. That is, after all, the reason so many religions in Jane and Lupe's world were so popular. People needed to feel importance, in whatever they may have done, regardless of its true worth. Sentimental value in otherwise odd items and objects was something that held great value, in both worlds, it seemed. This struck Jane as something the two worlds shared. Pedley, being the source of all this insight. Walking like a man who found his worth. Or found a way for his fantasies to become almost realistic, at least.

Seeing PETE drive himself at what looked like incredibly speeds gave Lupe ample reason to smile most of their journey down these identical corridors, which showed no direction to go by. Pete went on though, followed intently by a now at peace Pedley. Thought the thing seemed to be going at a mere two or so miles per hour in Jane's perception, the group felt it was a quick pace. Possibly due to their slow pace when alarm was high in their brains' priorities. Granted, alarm was still high, but PETE showed no possibility of slowing down. If it weren't for such a fast speed, Jane imagined they might have taken days to reach the epicentre of supposed knowledge on this Cradle. A place with Which PETE would no doubt be based. It could well be possible that PETE contained a vast amount of information himself. Despite his size, his memory banks must have been huge, due to the technological advancements in this world.

Lupe had problems of his own. Things were buzzing around his brain, mainly questions about himself. He started noticing things about the group, which were dissimilar to his own feelings at the time. Not emotional feelings, but *bodily* ones. Everybody was breathing, that slightest amount more, in conjunction with the pace that PETE upheld so aptly, yet Lupe remained concise in his breathing. Almost as if he was relaxing. He felt his heart beat staying steady. He had questioned himself when he cut in front of Jane earlier on with the situation of Pedley not wanting to be the first to be torn apart, still alive. He noticed these changes in his body, and yet at the same time, condemned them as tricks of the minds.

"Adrenaline." He thought. "Just excitement". No, that was the wrong word. The situation they were in wasn't excitement, just another form of the 'Fight or Flight' theory. Yes, that was it. But further questions entered his mind. The others would have experienced similar feelings of fear and horror, yet here they were, walking briskly, occasionally taking one or two drawn out breaths. His mind was cut off. He didn't want to think of himself as a changed man. Yet the signs were brutally apparent. His body was *better.* In movement at least. He recalled something in his memory about only special people being able to come through in this world. Sayre had almost drilled it into his mind as they ran through the warm pink light.

"You boys . . . special . . ." it echoed.

Then he was thrown off his train of thought by PETE's eccentric voice.

'We are here my friends, the databank central. In more common words, the place where all the know-it-all's kept their info!'

An overly cheery disposition that snail had. It made Pedley's skin crawl. The other soldiers however, seemed to be emotionless. Almost empty headed, they barely said a word. There was one short statement, which seemed of no urgency to PETE, that the small robotic snail mentioned, which put them instantly in a state of shock. Something they didn't want to hear.

'Oh, deary me, they appear to be coming to this very place. Most of them I believe. They do make such a mess of things.'

'They? What do you mean, those savages are coming? They know their way to this place?' Pedley would have shook PETE by the shoulders, if he was a human.

'Indeed, but they won't make it here for another twenty minutes or so. Even if they were at optimum pace.' Said like a true relaxed salesman. As if terror itself was nothing to fear.

'We need to get what we can and leave!' The pilot shouted.

'We will leave when we have what I . . . We came for. And only then. They have hands. We however, have bullets. Good odds by any means.' Pedley spoke, still calm. He was where he wanted to be, nobody was going to ruin his place of fantasy now. He turned and talked to PETE, who now found himself aboard a console, appearing to dock with a large panel.

'We need to know where the Biological Transfer device is.' What Pedley now asked, was something nobody in the room had even heard of. He asked it in a desperate undertone. This was what he came for, and it meant the world to him. *Both* worlds even.

'Ah, well, that is right through those doors, possibly the most prided possession the scientists ever created. What exactly do you plan on transferring to yourself? May I ask? This process requires two willing subjects. One of which, will undoubtedly resemble a mothball afterwards.' Pete chuckled to himself, in an arrogant computerised sort of way.

'That's where these boys come in. Men, let's get them through, they have a purpose to serve in this world.' The soldiers obeyed him like robots, still almost expressionless. They still showed fear of this place, yet Pedley seemed to hold sway over them somehow.

Two men on each boy, the held Jane and Lupe under the arms, and dragged them behind Pedley through a door on the very opposite side of the small room where PETE was now fully docked in, looking like a snug addition to the computer systems.

'What is this? Why are you taking us?' Lupe shouted, feeling more desperation than Pedley initially felt.

'You my young man are gifted in body.' He turned to Jane. 'And you, in mind.' He tapped the side of his head and smiled. 'I think I need both of these evidently amazing gifts to prove myself a worthy leader of Cradle 11. Sayre will have no choice but to resign to my power.' He now turned back to Jane and paused for a short while. Considering him closely.

'What is it with me? I know I have strange control over the mind, something I never asked for. But what is it I have that makes me such a useful tool?'

'You, Jane, can do more than you think. It's not all about reading minds. That's just a little aspect of your ability. Hell, I find it lucky you haven't realised how to obliterate mine, or any of my men's minds. You could, you know . . .' Pedley said. Totally certainty now showed. His pride was in full bloom.

'Now, men, place Jane first in the dock over there.' He pointed to a contraption that looked close to a device of torture. Straps and belts hung loosely like skin off the metal bars, needles the size of six inch drill pieces aimed at its centre, ready to sap the host of its every force.

For reasons unknown, it wasn't Jane who was struggling while being rammed into the right hand side of the device. He found no fight in himself. It was Lupe, who screamed almost nonsense to his friend, almost brought to tears and he fought without prevail against the soldiers who now held him like unbreakable chains. Jane thought it was Bulgarian, something about Fate.

Still, in peaceful calm, Pedley loaded himself into the left dock, looking slightly more humane than the side that Jane was now being strapped into. These men knew the device, and knew how to lock up a person in it. Clearly there was more to their current situation than they were originally told. Pedley strapped himself in, locking the metal restraints himself, and requesting assistance for his other arm. Jane, now safely locked in, with a face of stone, stared out into space.

The room itself was dark. It seemed like the lights had been blown on one side of it, and it was a large room indeed. But that was almost unnoticeable in this light. What else the room held was a mystery nobody cared to notice. PETE had said the place was safe for a good twenty minutes. How much they could trust him, was another matter.

'Now PETE my friend, if you'd care to turn on this machine and help me get my tricky business over and done with, I would be most grateful.' The men stood behind Pedley's chamber he was now held, half of the backs were touched by the darkness. A mistake, they now unknowingly made.

'I'm sorry.' The now more human voice of PETE uttered through an invisible speaker system embedded into the roof said.

'What?' Fantasy voice, gone.

'It was twenty minutes for the *main* group to get here. Your men are gone. I had no intention of simply letting you take power, you never rightly deserved.' If PETE had a face, a mischievous smile would have no doubt been pasted on it.

That was when Lupe felt it. Except, he felt nothing. That was the problem. The men that were holding him were gone, in silence. Without notice. Jane looked over his shoulder behind Pedley in his contraption. Also, those two men gone. Vanished, as if for no reason. Then Lupe turned to Jane, who now stood there still staring, almost rigid in his bonds that still held him. But he wasn't staring at nothing. He was looking in Lupe's direction, behind him.

'We're here.' It whispered in his ear. Some foreign liquid now falling on Lupe's shoulder. Saliva, not that of the guards who once held him.

'THEY'RE IN HERE!' Pedley screamed, then his shouting was cut off as he finished his sentence. Lupe saw it all, and yet heard nothing of it. Within a blink of human eyes, his throat was torn away from him, by hands, charred and red and raw with age and decimation. They had learned how to silently kill with great prowess. It made them feel *good*.

"Lupe, get over here and let me out." Jane said calmly inside Lupe's head. "You can make it over here faster than anyone can think."

It wasn't a time calculable by blinks, or milliseconds. It was such a short time. The only way anyone could have described the speed at which Lupe darted at Jane, his hands ready to remove the straps that held his friends locked limbs, would have been to say the ruined one, and had only just begun to reach to tear off his flesh. It—*he,* had lurched for Lupe's spine, and found nothing, before it could think.

'Worm!' It shouted, and began to leap forward at Lupe, its small party of three now tearing gristle and muscle away from Pedley's stripped, limp corpse. They were like savages in a frenzy of blood, tearing away skin as if it were some pain they were relieving themselves of.

The leap was not fast enough, at least by Lupe's standards. By the time the ruined one had made it half the distance between its jumping point and its prey, Lupe had already removed most of the straps from Jane, and was tugging him free of the machination the scientists of this once thriving Cradle had created.

'Slaughterrr himmm!' It hissed, now reaching out at the boys, scraping Lupe's arm as they dodged the attack, mainly down to Lupe's insane force.

Jane immediately went for the door back to the room PETE was docked in, hoping that the snail hadn't locked them out, to face their barbaric deaths. Alone, Jane could never have made the distance at full sprinting speed. But Lupe seemed to drive them forward at a maddening rate.

The ruined one, now almost accepting its loss in great fury yelled both at the boys and its hunting part.

'Foolsss, the hunt is getting awaaay . . .' Its voice now a husky crackling version, of what it may have sounded like when it was still considered as a man.

In half a second of dazing movement and confusing, Jane found himself being thrown through the door, that was a mere blur to his vision. He thought he was halfway to passing out, but he found he remained conscious throughout. He wasn't losing touch of consciousness, his eyes were losing track of a realistic perspective of *time*. Lupe had traversed a few meters in less than a tenth of a second, and Jane's brain wasn't keeping up with it. He heard a voice, almost relieved.

'Thank god! I shall lock the door, it will never be opened again!' PETE proposed.

'W-what-' was all Jane could manage in his confusion.

Before he could think twice, the metal door shut with a mind blowing thud. Bolting in at least seven different areas, slammed through the walls my hidden machinery. Some kind of security door that appeared normal to the human eye.

'You have a great deal of explaining to do to us before we crush you like a *real* snail, like we do in our world. Only this time it won't be by accident.' Lupe said wit fury, as his lungs now caught up with his activities. He felt instant exhaustion, and he collapsed with Jane against his side. Both sat there, eyes closed far what felt like eternity; in a room neither of them cared perceived to be dangerous. Right now, they were relieved to not have been ripped asunder by madmen, or have themselves drained and injected into another madman, affected by his own insane plots.

* * *

'I say, young men, you should really consider waking yourselves, this is no place to be lingering for much longer.' PETE urged, reminding of Jane in his empty daze of the rabbit from Alice in Wonderland, eager to make good time to his 'very important date'.

'Please, I implore you to get up and listen to me. I know you're not of this world, I know the answers to questions you do not yet know you seek!' PETE seemed desperate now, his true personality burning through.

Jane managed a groan.

'Why-why is it you sound so real? So human?'

'As I said before, scientists can be quite eccentric in their times of genius. To put it bluntly, I designed myself.'

All in an instant, Jane's fuzziness cleared, and he showed a face of utter confusion as he looked up a PETE, still neatly perched in his dock, allowing him to interface with the computer. He seemed to be accessing something at the same time.

'A computer designed itself a unit wander in?' Lupe asked, far more clearly than Jane could.

'No, no no-' PETE was cut off by Lupe again.

'Why a *snail* of all things. Computers should be more intelligent than that.'

'I am—I was not, a computer before. I, was the scientist who created this conduit of knowledge, this computer with answers to all that needed to be known by travellers. Unfortunately, in my hour of success, the men went rampant after an unclassified experiment went wrong. Some believe it was purposefully put in the air by an undercover Union-'

'You put your consciousness into a robot, a snail, so as not to arouse any unwanted attention. I could feel your consciousness when we got here.' Jane said, slowly gathering his wit again.

'That *is* extraordinary. I've never known anyone to notice that deep before.' PETE replied.

'Carry on with the part about answers. And that other bit about the Union's involvement.' Lupe was eager to cut to the chase, unlike Jane, who was still finding his bearings in his mind.

'The Interior Union. Undoubtedly you know of their presence in the world. It's like a parasite that cannot, and will not die. They believe they did this, to stop the other Unions ever gaining a technological advantage. They purposefully blasted Cradle 1 half to hell. I'm afraid it won't last much longer in its current state. You came by a little late.'

'How late?' Jane asked.

'The Cradle's dispersion systems have been failing for months, going on years now. This large tilt has been getting worse. Once it reaches critical degree, it will fall from the sky.' PETE appeared quite distressed, as if his *life* was in danger.

'*How late?*' Jane asked again.

'Your timing really was quite awkward . . . twenty seven minutes . . .'

'You gotta be screwin with us here.' Lupe said. just as he reached the end of his words, they could hear a terrible cry outside the doors they had escaped from.

'They are here boys, they've reached us. You *must* leave soon.' PETE's distress grew and grew, he looked left and right with his ocular devices.

'Not until you tell us everything we need.' Jane said, with utmost clarity, his brain was recovered and in top shape, the presence of raging emotions were high all around them, he could feel it.

'You came from the other side of this world. A world much like this. Identical to this in fact, only you don't fully understand why. The portal you entered, how you got here, it is *perfect*. Mathematically of course. Everything that goes in, comes out solved. You boys, a student of psychology, enhanced his skills with brain function; you can do far more with your brain. As for you Lupe, you're what we like to call a 'Reactor'. You move with reflexes of a creature unlike what we've seen. We don't know why the portal does this. It just does. It has no reason to.

'The link between these two worlds, yours and mine, is that they maintain balance. Without one world, the other would not exist. What happens in one happens in the other, to keep in equilibrium. We are told by travellers about the Cold War. That happened here, only many, many centuries later. Things turned out a little different, as you can tell.'

'Tell me why we can't get back.' Lupe's eyes glazed with moisture. His feelings for the rest of his life would be based on the answer to this question.

'The portals, they are one way, even if you could go back, if you found a way, I don't believe you'd want to . . .'

'Why not?' Jane seemed to know they would be stuck here, but the why was what always dig at his brain. What made the people in this world want to stay here?

'Time. For reasons unknown, time here is a little different. The portals, they're all over the world, they make the world seem to stand still permanently. The sun you notice is always out. Whatever timescale there is here, months go past in your world, in mere hours in this one. A day in this crooked world, is a year in your own.

'If you found a way to get back, you'd be returning to a world that is long gone from your era, it will have moved on. The world you'd return to, just wouldn't be your own anymore.' As PETE finished his explanation, the ground made squeals of ripping metal. The floor was shuddering, and the ruined ones seemed to make shrills of fear, more than ones of rage.

'You *must* go no, the Cradle is nearly at critical position, it will begin to descend, with us in it!'

'Why can't we take you with us?' Jane asked desperately, he wanted to know more, he needed to know more about the world that he was now stuck in. 'There is too much more we need to know!'

'I am afraid my life was spent on this Cradle, and my work is done. The rest is up to you. There is one thing, young Jane Abra'am.' PETE called him by his biological father's real surname. 'You hold a great key to the protection of this world. What is in one world *is* in another. Now there is an imbalance.' Before PETE could finish the ground shook, and both boys, now with the true looks of young men in their time of importance, were brought to their knees again, but the crying out of the Cradle. It sounded like it was dying, and was going to take everything in it, all those years of research, down with it. Safer broken, than in the hands of the Interior Union.

The boys now made it for the exit door they had come in, when PETE had led them to this room for the first time, and made haste out of it, this time Lupe keeping normal running pace to stay behind with Jane.

'And remember Jane, you can do far more damaging things with your brain than you think!' PETE cried, just as the door was shut, and he was left to his fate, to be buried with his own work.

Now with alarm bells ringing in their ears, and the emergency lighting flashing away at their faces, Jane and Lupe ran the way they came from through what their memory would allow. Now under the threat of falling dozens of miles toward the ground, and being torn apart by ruined men now in their last minutes of life, they hurried along the once dim and grey corridors, now brightened by hypnotic colours. There was no time to think, they were forced to run whatever direction they could manage at a fast pace. Jane could feel them coming in behind at speed, willing themselves on to get revenge on their hunt that got away. The ruined wanted their last hour to be filled with the ecstasy of murder, to bask in the blood of young men, only months before their twenties. Young, prime blood, to warm their faces, before they made their final trip to hell.

'Behind—they are behind us, and we're not going to outrun them.' Jane said to Lupe, already losing his breath, trying desperately to talk without sacrificing their already slow running pace.

'If we don't thin them out, or get rid of them somehow, we might never make it to the ship. Even if we did make it, I cant *fly* the thing!' Lupe replied, with no signs of being out of breath. 'They said you can do things with your brain, *damaging* things.'

Jane looked reluctant. He didn't know anything about what he could do, or even how he could do it. It was one simple task to read a brain, but to crush one; it required some form of experience. He had read somewhere in one of his psychological books, that whatever the brain interprets, the body will make it real. He needed to cause pain to those ruined ones; he needed to make their brain *think* their bodies were being hurt in some way. The only thing that crossed his mind was memories of the man he had seen on the unwelcoming concrete floor, after jumping for no good reason. His head was a picture to be forgotten. All he could think of now, was to transfer that memory into as many of the ruined men that now pursued him and Lupe.

A skull shattering crack, the feeling of the head being pounded by solid floor. The brain hitting the inside of the fractured skull so hard, it haemorrhaged and exploded within the skull, seeping through the fractures that now became cracks as the impact gave its full force. His head was filled with brutal images, of cranial liquids, and he tried to send it out.

At first he felt it might backfire, and go into his own brain. Then he noticed cries of pain from behind. The ruined ones were closer than he could have imagined, and Lupe showed fear in his face, that meant he had slowed down because of Jane focusing on thinking rather than running. Then came the sounds: Not of screaming, not of crying out in pain—but the crack of bone. The impact a block of cement would have if it was dropped on the head of someone from a great high.

Over and over they heard the rip of bone, tearing away at their chasers heads, until Jane felt them no more, not one of them still running behind. For now, prime blood would stay in their bodies, ready to be spilled in other sinister ways this world had to offer.

The tilt of the floor made it incredibly hard to run; walking behind PETE when they initially made it on board was easy compared to this. The simple task was now becoming ever more precarious as the Cradle cried out in squealing metal, almost as if it was trying to tear itself apart, but was it was built too strongly, and simply made its cries as it began its slow decent towards the lower angled side where the stabilisers had begun to fail. Now at over forty five degrees, Jane found himself constantly bumping into the right hand side wall, carefully watching so he wouldn't inadvertently find himself drifting into an open door, greeting him with its wide mouth, perhaps filled with more gnarled living bodies of once civilised scientists. Lupe on the other hand, found no difficulty in remaining fairly central. He ran directly behind Jane, believing that Jane's mind would contain the memory of exactly where the main hanger they had arrived in was based. Of course, flying back would be another matter.

It had taken them the best part of half an hour at brisk walking pace to get from the place the met PETE to the databank room, and at their current speed, the boys hoped to make it there in a little under half the time. Time was of the essence now, as just a few minutes could be the difference of miraculous escape, and plummeting to their death miles below, joining the hundreds of other men who did not deserve their quick deaths.

Jane could feel no presence about these halls as he ran crookedly through the flashing walls, looking as though they would close in on them at any time. He half expected this Cradle to be part of the living chaotic bodies that had desecrated the soldier's bodies with such skill. Jane could feel the thing speaking to him, begging him to stay, to keep it company while it fell from heaven, fell from the so called Glory Skies. But it was too late now. The degree the Cradle was tilted at was so severe; it had already dropped considerable distance, as Jane could feel the pressure go in his ears. If they did not come across the large hanger soon, the Cradle would have its wish. Eventually the gargantuan beast would fall so rapidly, the boys would have found themselves in lessened gravity. That would be the time when they could consider themselves taken by this world.

Brief minutes had passed in what seemed like seconds to Lupe. He was feeling the grind in his ears, the mysteriously human wails of a thing made of pure metal. He found no falter in his own step, and his lungs were holding out nicely, but he was well aware of Jane growing tired. He had acted not by choice earlier, but by impulse. His body had driven him hard, moved him where his brain willed him to be, and in doing so, had saved both of their lives. Here he ran, trusting in Jane's judgement, and was so caught up in maintaining the pace, that he almost fell over his own heels as Jane stopped abruptly at a place that he felt he didn't recognise.

'We passed it.' Jane said, now out of breath. 'It's that door there!' He pointed to a door they were only meters away from, and had passed without notice due to the emergency lighting not revealing its whereabouts unless intently looked for. They were lucky, the Cradle had almost purposely concealed it from them, however this time, it had not been successful in its desperate attempts.

They walked to the door, Lupe now uttering the password in an urgent Natural voice.

'Eleven! Eleven for the love od god!' Almost reluctantly, the door shafted itself open with apparent strain. Power systems were shutting down.

They ran through the door, half expecting an army to be waiting for them behind the door, to shut off their escape path. The room was as empty as they had left it, only this time, they found the craft in an incredibly awkward place, almost balancing on the afterburner panel they had first landed against.

They both looked outside the huge mouth of the hangar, staring at the desolate dry air outside, now filled with debris and sand, as it rushed past held in wind that Cradle now created through displacement. Getting out would be a problem. But taking off in the first place was the bigger one on their minds.

'I can't fly this thing, and I'd be willing to bet my life that you couldn't either.' Lupe said.

'You are quite right there my young friends, but I can!' The friendly voice shouted. In their fear and confusion, they had forgotten of their greatest ally. Brax.

He had stayed in the craft, feeling weary of the flying, and he woke realising the party had gone forgetting of his very existence. Jane himself didn't even remember to shadow Brax as the two boys had agreed. They had been lost in a new environment.

'How could we have forgotten about you?' Lupe asked, not aware that they should have been feeling great distrust to the Independents now.

'It seems in this day and age, I'm more easily looked over. Now we must leave, this place seems to be dropping from the sky like a rock.' Brax smiled, and offered a welcoming gesture onto the ship.

'Don't you think you should be asking about everyone else's whereabouts?' Jane now raised his suspicion. 'You are an Independent, and Pedley seemed to have been-'

'A corrupt man, driven by his desires for power. I, am not Pedley, I cannot convince you of my innocence in this situation, but you need to trust me here, I want to get off this metal beast as much as you do. Roland is in just as much trouble as we are, it would seem. The Independents have obviously been conferring with the Interior Union, without my knowledge.'

Jane could not disagree with Brax, and Lupe showed great hope in his thoughts of Brax, that was evident enough with reading his mind, but his face showed it as well. Hope was seldom seen on Lupe's face in the past few days. Well, past few *years* it seemed. As if realising his thoughts were being read, he turned to Jane in silent questioning.

'All right, we have no other choice.' Jane finally agreed.

'Jump in, we have no time, and out take off is going to more difficult than I could ever imagine.' Brax jumped in, not waiting for confirmation from the boys' decision.

"Let's trust him, I'm no psychic, but the guy seems genuinely choked up about his faction being dirty." Lupe thought, knowing Jane would be hearing.

"It seems that way. We must get back to Roland. We need to save him, wherever he may be." And on that last thought they both leapt up into the craft, almost rolling to the far side of the ships inner panels due to the angle.

Brax flicked switches on all sides of his as he strapped himself in, and an unsure expression filled his brow. Take off would be unimaginably difficult indeed. He went to flip more, seemingly important ones, highlighted with white boxes drawn around them. He had had a bright idea. He hesitated and flipped about half of them, and the craft began to shudder and rattle, as if it were a smaller scale version of the Cradle that was now emulating the movement.

'I'm going to lift half the craft up!' He shouted towards the back where the boys now strapped themselves in. 'We'll be throwing ourselves out that door, and fall. It's gonna get uncomfortable. Twisty is all I can say to describe it.' He turned back and clutched the controls the pilot once held, but this time, with the skin on his fingers going bright white. He was clutching them like a madman holding onto his beliefs.

The engines roared uncontrollably, and the scraping noise of the nose rubbing against the floor began again, this time heard faintly over the noises that now surrounded them. The ship was now levelling out, and slowly moving towards its left, towards the mouth of the hanger a few hundred meters away. It now gained momentum, and they passengers now found themselves thrown against the left of the seats they were strapped into, and the scraping began again as the moved off of the panel they had been jammed on.

Closer and closer the exit came, and the closer they got, the worse the shaking was. It felt like the craft would simply break apart under the stress it was having on its right where the engine was located, now whirring away for its life. Lupe and Jane did not expect anything as worse to come, yet this was the easiest part of exiting the Cradle. Brax had not told them of the small issue they had to maintain some stability once they got out. The right engine was on full throttle, and the left one had been off this whole time. He needed to reengage it as they left the Cradle, but even then, they would be free falling until they engines created enough power to fight against the velocity, and the spinning they would experience once they were dropped out.

It was Lupe who now stared into space, clutching the armrests with his life. The lurches on the way here were nothing compared to the rollercoaster he now anticipated. Jane however, closed his eyes gently, and held on to his senses, making sure not to tense himself too much when holding on, or else the intense shudders could break his bones, the vibrations already rattling his body. The haze he felt when Lupe was pushing his body out of the room where Pedley had almost stripped him of his life force was returning. Just as the craft tipped off the edge.

* * *

The faces of every citizen was nothing of importance, they held the same expression since they had begun their life on this sordid planet. Once education was over, everything became repetitive, a simple means to an end. Different jobs, different routines, families were never alike. But it all came together in the same fashion. Everybody had no idea why they were living, or what purpose they had in this life, in this world. Yet on they lived, on they worked, in hopes of answers to questions that simply didn't exist to pass them by like a refreshing breeze. Day in, day out, these answers would never come, and the world forgot their most important unanswered question that defined them. Yet, on they lived.

People turned to different means of escaping their troubles. Some turned to religions, large and small, with differing beliefs that were essentially the same; give up your ordinary life, and add another repetitive action in it. "Oh, and while you're at it, you're contributions would be most *appreciated."*

Religions, were based largely on the monetary gain. That was where others would change belief.

Medicine was the next form of relief. Slowly overcome by their doubts, the people would turn to medicine to offer tablets, which would make them feel happier. Some took legitimate ones, often making only a small amount of difference, making the good times better, and the bad times almost unbearable. Others chose the illegitimate forms, which were developed again for the money. Some could argue that drugs and religion were largely the same. Only sometimes the drugs drove you over the edge. Sometimes over the edge meant quite literally.

Things had not gone well for him. He noticed the solemn faces of everyone around them, the permanent pain of living they all must have surely felt. Living in an imperfect broken world, filled with corruption and hate. Wars and tribulations. He thought he was the only person who could see the pain on the day to day faces of this world's common-folk. He didn't turn to religion, he had tried it once before, and found the hypocrisy too frustrating. Then he turned to the doctors, offering medicine, to treat his disease they called "depression". *Nothing of these initially helped, until a friend of old had run across him. He could barely recognise the man, yet in his face he could see familiarity.*

This man had shown him alternative drugs, in various different forms, powder, liquid, some more expensive than others. He found that at first, they helped, in only small amounts. It became evident afterwards, that it would take more and more to cure his sadness he felt for this world and its inhabitants. Thrown into vagrancy, his addiction to the cure of sadness, he found that like all the rest of the so called solutions this world had to offer, he wound up in the same place he began in. Only this time, he had thrown himself into a self destructive state.

He couldn't take this state of mind for much longer, and eventually resorted to his first act of theft. But it did not end in thievery; it ended in murder, and suicide.

He saw the same feeling on that woman's face that he had seen all these years. She was lost in her life, unable to comprehend her dislike to the life she lead. He could see that very clearly. The money she had on her, would no doubt cause her more pain, like he himself had caused. He thought of it as an act of mercy, to relieve her of this burden, to fuel his last moment of drug enhanced happiness. He simply walked up to her, with a warm face a mother would show to a child. He put his arm out to her bag she carried, and her face screwed up into horror. But he acted quickly in snatching it, and her grip was easily removed from her possessions. Like an automatic reaction, she swung away at him like a flailing bird, in free fall in the sky.

Her attachment to her bag of sadness amused him, and he simply swatted her blows away, suddenly realising they were becoming more and more forceful. She now began to scream to whoever may be in the vicinity. He could see now, she had become irreversibly attached to her sadness, probably unable to live without it now she was so far under its hold. Better that she lost everything now, he thought.

Instead of deflecting away her random blows to his midsection, he grabbed at her arms, gaining hold of her immediately. He pulled her into the nearest corner he could find, and removed his grip from one arm to her neck. His other, moved to the top of her skull.

He had never taken a life before, but was well aware of the way to snap a neck, as he grew up as child on a farm with chickens, and regularly broke their necks. How different could this situation be? She continued to scream, now flailing, trying in earnest to escape from him. Her efforts fell short. He began to put pressure on her head to one side, and pushed her chin in the other direction. The tension was there, all he had to do was push just a little further, and her misery would be over. She flailed more, no longer screaming, but making desperate throaty noises, that he could not understand.

He pushed until he heard it. Until he felt *it. Her body immediately went limp as her neck snapped, just as the chickens' had. He had ended her pain, and she had helped him gain his happiness. Her soul would be in peace in whatever world she entered next, he was sure.*

He made his way to where he scored usually, the shifty looking character seeing him, and smiling. He was about to become richer today it seemed. His favourite addict was on his way to him, with a purse in his hand. How amusing. The mad guy he had sold drugs to had stolen just to get jacked. But the dealer didn't care. Money was money to him. The exchange was over as fast as the life his customer had just taken. A simple nod was all he got from his business for today.

Finally, his happiness would welcome him with open arms. He just needed to get back to his place, a mere block away. The journey seemed shorter than usual, as if time was on his side. The streets weren't busy, but there were people about. He walked like a man at peace himself, on his way to a very important date indeed. He pulled out his flat key; he lived in a very shoddy block of flats, mostly brown from age and weather. Putting it into the lock, the door opened with a creak of old bones and he drifted inside like a spectre. Making his way up, he didn't jump up two stairs at a time today, he walked patiently to his top floor flat, and floated into his flat, ready for his time to come.

The time between getting through the door and finding himself on his shredded chair, perhaps aeons old, was gone in his memory. He sat there with his head swaying, his mind clear, his thoughts gone, and his soul at rest. All of a sudden, he remembered the feeling of drifting. How it would make him so happy to drift in the open air. He was high up after all, and the view would be spectacular. Yes. He was in the mood for flying.

He staggered up out of his low set chair, giggling to himself as he stumbled towards the window, opening it and looking upon the depressed world he now lived for the last time. The wind brushed his cheek like a lover, caressing him, asking him to join her. He took his step onto the ledge, and felt himself truly drifting in the open air.

"Don't! Stop yourself!' *A voice in his head cried, and he looked down at a young kid looking up at him as he drifted forward. Only now he felt it. He was drifting, his lover had lied to him, led him on. Slowly he fell with that boy's image being the last in his eyes. The kid would probably remember it for the rest of his life. Another thing on top of his list of sad things he had to carry with him. How unfortunate for the young boy.*

Wind now rushing through his hair, he whispered to himself, as if feeling at peace for all the trouble he had once felt.

'Goodbye my son, goodbye my Jane . . .'

* * *

There was no breeze—just the flashing scene of the sky flying around his head at unfathomable speeds. Jane found himself being pressed against the side of the craft as he regained what little consciousness he could spare. Brax had battered the console in front of him in hopes of getting the other engine to work harder, he himself being held to one side by the g-force. He screamed and screamed, his mouth moving, but the sounds never making it over the roar of two engines, now at the brink of overdrive. Jane couldn't see focus on any object through what little visibility there was through the front window of the cockpit, he could barely turn his head to ensure Lupe's safety. He could feel his mind slipping again, but fought against it. He wanted to be conscious to witness his own death at the very least.

He felt it fight against the dancing. The craft struggling away, trying to prevent itself from continuing in one direction, but it fought with little avail. On and on, the now hoarse voice of Brax went unheard as he slammed the craft, now pleading for it to save them from the unwelcome ground that would greet them miles below. Like a metal bird, it plummeted down and down, roaring in its fight against gravity, now slowing its spinning speed, the ship needed to start gaining some up thrust. Even if they managed to stop the spinning, they were already at terminal velocity now. They needed to gain air, and despite the many miles above ground they had fell from, they were being eaten away fast.

Brax now held both hands against the handles that seemed to be fully turned in the opposite direction the wind had them swirling in, almost trying to tear it off the main console. Almost as if being beaten into submission by his attempts, the bird did indeed begin to slow the spin considerably. Within seconds they found themselves now being lifted off their seats as they were falling, this time at a more natural angle. To Lupe it felt like the fair rides he had so often seen, and all but refused flatly to go on, until just once he plucked up the courage do partake in the entertainment. It tore apart his stomach from the rest of his body, and now, he felt a similar torture.

Brax had the controls levelled now, sweat forming on his brow, his body completely stiff as he reached over to push up more switches. They caused sounds from the engine that sounded like air being pressurised. Then came the true roar of a lion from the engines, which they had been holding back for all this time, as they went into over-burn, almost toppling the threshold of falling. All of sudden the boys found themselves being pushed back down on their seats with such force; it could have crushed their spines. The bird was fighting back against the pull of the earth, and its very own rage broke out.

To Jane, it seemed like technology in this world had its own feeling of being alive. As if all the machines in the world were actually animals of burden, who unleashed their very own anger and fury when faced with dire consequences. Without the primal fury of such things, perhaps they would not be alive for as long as they had been.

Blood flowed from Lupe's nose as the pressure got to his brain, and he managed the strain of whipping it away with his arm that he had to tear off from his armrest, after being locked in place by fright. It did little to help, as more came, now from both nostrils. The forces were reaching far into their bodies, and would wreak havoc until they were finally taken in with open arms by the harsh ground, or until the lover that was the wind, would allow them safe flight, and at least an extra day in this world to live on and make a difference. Perhaps answers to questions they themselves had forgotten.

Slowly the craft pressed upward with untold rage, never ceasing to maintain the pressure it held, fighting against the gravity of the floor that lay beneath them. Brax was still full of fright, his mind still considering the possibility of it simply not being enough of a push. The ship had unleashed a storm alright, but he wasn't sure if it would be enough, until he found his body feeling more normal than it had the past few minutes. He felt gravity more naturally, and looked out the cockpit window to find a sight fit for untold relief.

Onwards, and upwards the engines pushed hard, bursting upwards, leaving the ground to its lonely state, preparing its imminent welcome of a floating city on its way shortly.

'We need to get further out in case the Cradle comes down on us!' Lupe shouted at Brax, who turned and nodded with urgency.

Instead of making height, he now let the engines relax a little, removing the strain from them, requesting them for their help in pushing their souls a little further out, to prevent the life hungry Cradle from collapsing upon them.

They remained silent, despite the fact that they would be able to hear each other. The engines quieted, now under less stress, and made considerably less noise. Brax turned the craft to one side and began to climb up towards where they had fallen from.

'I think I'd like to see a monstrous city fall from the sky, the way the rogue angels did those thousands of years ago. At least that's what some old book said.' Brax said, turning his ear to the boys in case they had something to add.

'It'd be a sight for the ages.' Lupe eventually replied, and turned his attention to the upper area of the window.

They had actually made a great deal of distance between the point where the Cradle was. In their sights was a desert, and a huge object, looking as if it were floating down, trailing a cloud of dust behind it, cutting through the air as it went nose down towards the earth. It looked as though it would take an age to finally meet its rest, but they flew closer, showing the true size of the Cradle from a distance. They could see more clearly now, as more spires, grey buildings, broke off and joined the gathering debris above the main structure.

It was almost a heavenly sight. Granted, it was a place of death by all standards. It had brought this world pain, and trouble. To see it now falling from its home in the Glory Skies was almost . . . beautiful. They braced themselves as it cut through the last few thousand feet through the air, in preparation for some horrifying crash as it hit the floor.

They felt nothing, and for some time, they heard nothing. The sound soon reached them as it caught up to speed, and they heard a faint crash of thunder. It must have been vaporised as it hit the floor, but it churned up so much dust from the ground, it was hidden from sight. Back to the dust it returned. The technology—gone. The horrors were gone. Yet this world remained so dangerous in its present state. The Cradle, despite its size, was but a pawn in an otherwise complex world.

'Let's get back. It's over now. We need to find Roland.' Jane said, holding back his tears. The Cradle, in its madness, reminded him of the person he lost. The sadness was falling in the wind, and met a happy ending for everyone but itself.

15

On the Mend

The silence they held on their return was one of respect. Silence in remembrance of the ones who had passed. Thought none of them truly knew any of them men on that Cradle. Each of them no doubt had lives. PETE was among that last with any form of humane thoughts. He had gone down with the ship, acting as its last captain. This world had lived in fear of Cradle 1 all this time. Now it was gone, perhaps for the greater good, and the world would move on. Some would forget about its loss, but others would remember it for what it was. Perhaps even others would remember it as something else—A place of knowledge, as opposed to death.

Lupe had found himself some cloth to wipe his nose with. The bleeding hadn't persisted. He held it there for most of the journey back to Cradle 11, even though it probably stopped long before they would arrive back at the Independent's base. That was another issue the boys would have to fight their way through. Something seemed amiss about them all though. Almost as if there wasn't much to them. Though Pedley had showed that they had secrets, and kept them well. Brax could have been doing the same. But there was something about him that struck the boys as trustworthy, almost as if he was more *human* than the rest of them. Having feelings didn't make him any more human than the rest. That was just a viewpoint. Jane was well aware that certain people showed feelings in different ways. Psychotics generally showed little at all. It was impossible to say that the entire Independent Union was comprised of psychotics though. The world was crazy, but not that crazy.

Jane could find no false thoughts in Brax's immediate thoughts. He genuinely seemed like somebody they could trust. Yet why the Independents had hidden so much, and why they had converged with the Interior Union confused Jane. He knew power could make a man bend. But this world couldn't take anymore corruption. It would end in more destruction, like the so called "cold war" of this future.

They remained on course, Jane had deemed it safe to fall asleep, albeit in an awkward position, but his body was tired.

Lupe on the other hand, remained well awake. He kept looking out the front window of the craft, waiting for their destination to appear. And, like a bad penny, it did indeed come into sight. Lupe hadn't noticed how different both Cradles had looked compared to each other. Cradle 1 had far fewer spires, and was altogether more flat, despite the angle at which it once hung. Cradle 11 however, seemed far more prominent. Like a magical city of old, only monotone in colour. Everything was that formal grey, other than the areas of the city which remained in the constant shadow of its higher walls.

Lupe looked onto the centre spire, which rose thousands of feet higher than the very base of the Cradle. As they got closer, its features became more apparent. The main spire itself seemed more adorned than its far smaller counterparts. He presumed he knew who resided there. Sayre was a man of image. He needed not be anywhere to give people the image of supremacy. They just needed to look up to remind who was always watching them. There must have been hundreds of people in that tower. Agents of the Interior Union, keeping watch on the insects below.

Brax flew lower to where they had set off from, aiming towards the East Arm, now cutting off half the city from view. They were now under the eye of Sayre. Even the White Belly was a place his eyes now wandered. It was here they began their search for Roland, and their quest for a place of safety.

Jane woke the second the ship touched down in the makeshift hanger, one considerably smaller than the one they had landed in on Cradle 1. He tried to make a vow to himself never to get in such a craft again, as it had led him to a place he couldn't have forgotten, but it had also saved them. Brax was the first to get out his seat and unstrap himself, offering a helping hand to the two boys fumbling with their own seats as their hands shook due to the remnants of stress in their brains.

'Steady now, I've got it.' He said, as he carefully removed Jane's safety belt.

'What do we do once we get in there?' Lupe asked Brax, only half concentrating on setting himself free of the spring locked straps across his waist.

'I have a feeling there will be almost certainly no one there. Sayre's arms have reached far enough. He will have presumed Pedley's job was done. Or at the very least we were all killed on that Cradle. There'd be no need for anyone to still be in there.' He replied, now focusing his attention on getting Lupe out.

They opened the side cockpit door, this time able to step out on solid level floor. The tiny compact hangar was indeed empty, but what lay in the white room ahead could bring surprise. They only had to hope that escaping the fall of Cradle 1 would not have been a means to an altogether pointless death.

Brax gestured silence to them both, tucking in a service pistol neither of the boys had seen before into the rear of his trousers, letting it stick out over his shirt. He opened the door, this one being a manual one, letting in a white haze as they walked through. What he said about nobody being inside was almost true. With one exception.

'May I enquire as to the location of the rest of the party?' The lady asked. No welcome, no "thank goodness you're alive". As Jane had thought, they lacked some kind of emotion.

'They were killed, but we escaped, Cradle 1, it's been-' Lupe began before the lady cut him off.

'Destroyed. Yes, I am well aware of that fact. Most unacceptable-' This time it was Jane who interrupted, with an idea in his eyes.

'There is only one reason somebody shows emotion, at least one other reason that doesn't involve being a psychopath.'

The woman kept babbling on about it 'Not doing, no. It was not at all acceptable.' Yet Jane went on.

'You've been hypnotised.' He said. As he did so, she stopped, almost frozen in times.

'How could that be?' Brax asked.

'Pupil dilation?' Lupe asked. He had heard of it before in a book of psychology he once studied himself. 'Her pupils are dilated.'

As if being discovered and given no other choice, she raised her right hand, in it, clutched a pistol much like the one that Brax had hidden behind him.

'Unwise.' She said, but before she could continue, a shot was fired.

Surprise was shown on her face. It was not from her own weapon. Almost as fast as Lupe had moved on the Cradle, Brax himself had slung his weapon out and planted a shot into the lower abdomen of the woman. He then felt threatened as she looked down at the hole she now earned, and anger took over her face. He buried two more into her chest, with not an inch gap between the two entry wounds. There came another noise, not one of weapons fire though. One this world had only one of. It was the bark of a dog trapped somewhere.

Together the three of them scuffled around the room, searching for the source of Roland's cry for help, and Jane used his mind to siphon where the activity was from. He found it to be *inside* the woman's desk, in what seemed to be a large frontal compartment, big enough to fit a great deal more than a dog.

'No key.' Brax said, holding up the gun.

"Roland, move back and to the right, Brax is going to blow off the lock." Jane's thoughts were met with a scuffling noise from inside Roland's prison. Brax took no time, and obliterated the lock in a second, and the door swung forward, with a ragged looking Roland limping out on his three legs.

'Now how is it that you wound up here?' The apparent surprise appeared on Brax's face, who half expected another journey to search out what had become of their old friend Roland. Finding him here was something they had not expected, and even now, they had not truly accepted it.

"Through some rather unfortunate events, my brother had confronted my kidnapper, and watched me as I walked away from him. I came here as quickly as my partial body would take me, yet I was too late. You boys had already left to find your answers on that Cradle." Jane relayed Roland's thoughts to Brax and Lupe.

'Your brother? He freed you? That woman was one of the independents . . . Brax told us it was part of a plan to get you here safely.' Lupe said.

'Though I have doubts about the Independent's true actions behind that kidnapping. It may have been lucky that your brother helped you out. By the way, who is he?' Brax asked Roland, awaiting his thoughts from Roland.

"Regrettably, my brother, Tailen, is an agent of Sayre. He followed the woman you said was one of yours. I believe he didn't want to see me hurt, though I feared for my life as I left him behind me in those dark streets." Like a statue he stood, as Roland relayed his thoughts, despite the lack of one leg, he looked more proud now to be reunited with the few people he now trusted.

'That . . . I did not know. That might make things slightly more difficult if we were to run into him again. Either he would fall under us, or help us.' Brax said, soon finished by Lupe.

'Or we fall under him. There were no other wounds on that woman you knew. He killed her with little or no interruptions.'

"He is right, though. Sayre may be our altogether greatest threat, but I have a feeling my brother will be seeking me out. He'll perhaps even go out of his way to make sure he does run into me again. And he doesn't tend to stop to ask for details either." Roland conferred.

'Even though everything appears to be on the other side of our aims, we have nothing else to do. We have to do something about Sayre. His hands reach further than most could have imagined. Even in other *Unions!* Regardless of what is needed from me, we're the only people that would make the attempts.' Jane spoke.

'You're right about us being the only ones. We can expect no help from the other Unions. Not just because Sayre might be dug into them somehow, but out of pure knowledge, nobody has dared face him and his unseen force.' Brax replied.

'What if his force is just that . . . unseen, non-existent?' Lupe said.

'Well, that's impossible-' Brax began.

'Why is it?' Jane said. 'Roland says he might have a point.'

'What if the Interior Union is like the Independents—just a force that caused a little bit of a problem, and made important use of rarely being seen. It gives people the impression that they are some massive chaotic force, when in actual fact it's just a few select skilled men, capable of great things . . .' Lupe continued.

Indeed, it was a viable thought. Though it was almost impossible to consider, after all the corruption and hardship the Interior Union had caused. They stood there and considered the fact, until Jane finally found an idea deep inside his head.

'There would be one way for me to find out . . . though it could be reckless and dangerous.'

'We've had our fair share of dangerous, I'm sure your bright idea won't get us too deep in the proverbial shit.' Lupe said. 'Go on, shoot.'

'I can read minds, deeper now than I ever thought I could before. What if we grabbed ourselves hold of an Interior operative? All we'd have to do is ask the question. That'd get his mind going in the place we wanted.'

"A good idea, my friend, but finding an operative might be a lot harder than you think. We'd need to cook up ourselves an issue, something they'd want to get at us for." Jane said what Roland had thought to him.

'That is, unless we get somebody a little more . . . desperate to get to us.' Brax said, now all the pieces were falling into his consideration.

"I'm no psychic." Roland started. "But I know what you're thinking, and I find the idea almost psychotic. Tailen no longer feels himself loved by his own brother. Him going out of his way to find me isn't a feeling of yearning. My brother wants to kill me, it is Sayre's will, and he's not stupid enough to fight against *that* kind of will."

'We have ourselves enough manpower, not to mention me and Jane perfect capable of keeping ourselves alive on a city filled with the damned. I think we could have a chance.' Lupe said.

It did seem that way at glance. It was two boys with great ability, a spy himself, able to protect them in more physical ways, against what they perceived to be a lost brother. They did not know of Tailen's destructive attitude towards everything. He had so far acted out of compassion, and partly confusion. His feelings had gotten in his own way countless times, and no doubt Sayre knew about it. By now, his errors would have caught up to him, and Sayre would be eager to set things right. They could not afford to mess this idea up, they were after all, the only people in this world that cared about the future of this world. It was one full of sadness, but people lived on, wanting to fulfil their lives. These two boys, a brother lost on his own, and a spy who was now Union-less, had only themselves. Loss among them could be catastrophic for their resolve. Yet this idea was the only one that seemed feasible. It was the easiest solution they could find, but among the most dangerous. This world was based on risks, and so far, they had overcome them all.

'Occam's Razor. The simplest solution is always the best.' Jane said. It was a theory he had read about in his countless information searches.

"If indeed you believe this to be the simplest solution. By the looks of your faces, you have set your minds on it. I guess I have to go along in this situation, I am aware that we have little other choice. Do not think Tailen would be easy to trick or capture. He could be one of few agents, or possibly, one of hundreds if you are wrong. But if he is one of few, then he is one of the few that shaped the way people in this world see the Interior Union. He has helped cause this mass terror." He waited for Jane to speak his thoughts, and waited further as everyone considered what he had just made clear to them.

Their idea was decided, yet the danger was something to be considered, something to ponder for a long period of time. They had their basic foundation for a plan, now they needed to work out the details.

'As far as I see, the White Belly is entirely abandoned. We can draw up our plans here; it seems moderately safe for the time being. However I don't think it will be long before they come and bulldoze the place, replace it with something more useful.'

Brax gestured them towards a door to a room with huge panes of glass, allowing sight inside and outside of it. It appeared to be a meeting room of some sort, only the chairs were overturned, and it looked empty and abandoned. The whole place looked the same, and they now saw its true scale. The White Belly was actually fairly small. It made them believe it was possible for the Independent Union to have been a sham. Just another object for people to consider as a group that caused unrest in the balance of the Interior Unions processes. Though perhaps Sayre had only commissioned such a place to be in existent to eventually bend to his desire, and seek out the things he had wanted. And he had almost done just that.

'Come to think of it, I never did see many people around, just the same few, all of them kind of distant looking . . .' Brax said, as he walked them to the door, grasping the handle, and pushing it open, pushing a chair away from the entrance.

They put 4 chairs in upright positions, one being placed diagonally so Roland was able to jump onto it, and they sat their and looked at one another. Hoping for some plan to dart between their minds.

*   *   *

One of his few personnel came in to fill him in on the situation. A Cradle didn't fall from the sky, holding all the technology this world had been designing for no good reason. It was evident Pedley had done as he was asked, and the woman he had "commissioned" to relieve him of his duty never reported back. Things had gone wrong on that Cradle, things that he did not plan for. When his plans failed, Sayre did not accept them with any bitterness. He didn't accept them at all; rather, he chose to destroy what had caused the mess. His Union had control over a great deal, but his master could not stop a Cradle from falling from the skies. His master did however have the power to remove Sayre from his now precarious position as overseer of this world's domination. Sayre needed to absolve the situation, and fast.

It was obvious that these young travellers he had tempted into this world had something to do with it. It was the boys and their old friend, the dog. This seemed like a test for his rising protégé, Tailen. It was clear Tailen was hiding his resentment for his brother who had come back to cause much more irritation. Now he felt it a fitting plan to send Tailen and his skilled blade to deal with the mess makers of Sayre's master's perfect rule. He was a reliable agent, a good killer, and he was one of the few that had helped shape the image of the Interior Union to what it was in the minds of the people today.

'Call in Tailen.' He gently whispered to his protégé, who now stood currently silent in the corner of Sayre's door. 'I have need of his services once more.' He said little else, and the young man now exited the room without word, or sound in his step. What was strange was Tailen's punctuality, or rather, lack of it.

'Where is that damned man?' Sayre said to himself.

'Here. Always here . . .' The voice said from behind him.

'Of course you are.' Sayre said, not acting at all surprised, but smiling to himself all the same. 'Something went wrong.'

'Seldom does that happen Sir, was it to do with those travellers you brought here?' Tailen asked.

Sayre did not immediately answer. He was considering the statement Tailen had made, as if it was Sayre's fault that they were here, ruining the plans of the one higher up.

'You are aware, that our master told me that if I were to come across these two boys, I was to bring them. For what purpose, is not for me to ask.' Sayre said, seeing fit that his words were well heard as he looked to where he believed Tailen's eyes to be. The people in this Union rarely showed large areas of their faces. It was best to keep people guessing about details. It was, after all, one of the factors that made this Union so successful in its deeds. Keeping the people unaware of just what was behind the veil.

'I would not question his needs, or requests. If I am allowed to presume your wishes-' Tailen started to say, as Sayre answered his question with no pause.

'In this case, I believe your presumptions may be correct. But voice it in any case, that we may be clear.'

'You wish for me to "remove" their presence from this Cradle, from this world?' Tailen finally finished.

'That, is correct. And your brother-'

'I will make no hesitation if he is to get in my way.' Tailen said, all rather too defensively for Sayre's liking.

'I am aware of you failings; make no mistake in perceiving otherwise. In this case, I *need* you to set aside your mind for this issue of ours. However, these travellers need to be removed from this world, but that is not your primary objective. Our master is more willing to do that himself. He needs you to bring them here, to him.' Sayre said this simply, and concisely, as if it were some easy task despite its awkward nature.

'The details of how you try to do so are of your own thoughts, I need not know, just get the job done. I expect to see you back here with them. We will take them to him by force once they are here.' Sayre continued.

'Very well.' Tailen said, seeing Sayre turn, as if to end the conversation by act. Now was Tailen's time to leave as miraculously as he had entered. Now was his time to plan, he would do so on his way to the East Arm. These troublesome people would no doubt remain in the place they found familiar.

Exiting the main spire took little time. For an ordinary person taking more usual means of transport, it would have taken the best part of a morning. Tailen however, removed himself from the spire from the outside. He leapt down great heights at a time, until eventually he reached the bottom, in streets as dead as night, having the great shadows cast on them by the central monument of the Cradle. He chose to stick to a slower pace towards his goal, he needed the time to strategize how to trick untrusting people into following him without question. Or at least give them a false sense of trust. With his brother with them, he had a great feat to prove to himself.

* * *

A basic foundation. That was what they started with. And that was what they were now still stuck with. Between the four of them, not a single word was uttered to aid their problem. As far as drawing attention was concerned, bringing a Cradle down to the ground was as best it got, and if that didn't get Sayre's attention, then what in god's name would? Brax would have expected, the boys too, by now, that Sayre would have heard the news of late, and sent an envoy to assess the situation of the White Belly. Desolate as it was, the bright white haze still remained.

All of them had considered in their mind of the fact that nobody could have heard about Cradle 1 and its gruesome inhabitants dropping from the sky. But it had been made quite clear to all on this world, that Cradle 1 held great importance. Word must have got out to the other Unions at least. No doubt some would try and attend to the wreckage, and salvage what they could, if they felt like baring the barren wastes for days on end. The technology was like broken beyond repair after falling dozens of miles.

No, Sayre must have known. It was just a matter of time before they were sought after by him. The way in which they were sought after mattered a great deal though. They needed to know when, and remain on their guard. It was important they were alive to gain the information about the true background of the Interior Union, not to simply come across it as their limp bodies were thrown to the ground.

Hours had passed, though none of them had noticed how long the silence had gone on for. Each of them in deep though, all of them sharing similar sentiments of the obviously imminent defeat they now faced. They would have to hide in an unwelcoming world that none of them felt at home in. Constantly haunted by the prospect of being watched as prey. There was no real use for this hideout anymore, the place had been torn to pieces, and stripped of its possessions. All it now had was space and light—something in ample supply in this world, albeit in undesirable forms.

'I can't . . .' Lupe began, running his hands through his now straggled hair.

'We know. We all know. This plan is getting harder the more I think through it. We just can't sit and wait here for much longer, somebody will come.' Brax said, and instantly realised what he had just said.

'Somebody will come . . .' Lupe repeated.

"The answer was in our actions, it seems." Roland transferred to Jane.

'It seems to me like an awkward plan, though it may work. What could we do in the meantime? And who will they send?' Jane asked. It wasn't just who they'd send, it was how the person would come. Like a shadow, but with guns a-blazing, little or no time to think.

'Yeah, that is kinda tedious, we might want to set up fort here, so we don't get sliced to holy hell as we politely ask "'Scuse me, mind tellin' us if your little party up in the fancy spire is nothing but a five man conference?"' Lupe said, always the sarcastic in an otherwise grim situation.

Waiting was a truly hard thing to do, especially with how long the days seemed to feel in this world. But on the other side of things, if and when somebody came to check on the vacancy of this old hideout, they had nothing to hide behind other than a pane of glass and some chairs. At this current time, they weren't even able to see the entrance way. This became evident as Lupe took a glance over at the general direction, and everyone else's nervous eyes followed.

'Kid's got a point. I can't even make out the doorway entrance, and it's highly doubtful those Interior guys make much noise. I'd rather not get slaughtered with my thumb stuck up my own ass.' Brax said, getting up out of the chair and heading for the door.

The rest of them followed closely, Roland being the last to hop down from his chair and wander over towards the boys. More apprehensive than usual, Brax opened the door and made a few steps into the main room while looking around for uninvited visitors. All clear. For now.

The idea of having themselves ready for when someone came was a sensible one, but how they could prepare was another matter. There was nothing here, only the lifeless body of the woman that had tried to stop them.

'I think I'd feel better if we tucked her away someplace else.' Jane said, drawing Brax's attention to her with his eyes. 'I've had my fair share of death at sight, not so sure I want the smell of it for very long.'

Without word, Brax carefully lifted the corpse by her under arms, and tried to stuff her in the place where Roland had been kept. It was a little harder than he initially thought, as she had stiffened up in the past few hours. Her weapon dropped out, and he quickly scooped it up and tucked it in his waistband. He closed the door as best he could, but after having blown off the locking mechanism, the door wouldn't fully shut. Finally he found some form of tape—that was at least the best description for the stuff. It wasn't clear or brown, or even silver like duct tape, but it looked about right all the same, just a little thicker.

'Thanks.' Jane uttered, as Brax made it back over to where Jane and Lupe were standing.

"We do still have that craft." Roland sent to Jane.

'He's right.' Jane said.

'What did he say?' Brax asked, Jane hadn't remembered to forward on Roland's thoughts this time.

'The ship in the hangar, what can we use from it?' Jane asked, shaking his head and blinking his eyes after he had realised he had forgotten to share Roland's thoughts. It was beginning to become tiresome.

'Ah, yes, what if we need to use it again to fly off this Cradle?' Brax asked.

'Doubtful.' Lupe said. 'If we're alive and kicking by the end of the week, however long that is in this place, I don't think we'd have need of it.' He was half right. They'd either be killed in that time, or have made the smallest bit of difference by then to the problems they now had.

'Ok, the way I see it, it'd be good for me and your friend Lupe here to help me strip the bird of its wings.' Brax said to Jane. 'You can call us with this.' He tapped his forehead. 'Roland can keep watch with you. Doggy senses are pretty good so I've heard.'

'Oh, and now we know your mind is all powerful and all, can you try opening a permanent connection between our minds and Roland's? That'd give us a little more help in the way of sharing ideas, don't you think?' Lupe asked, as he walked away towards the door to the hangar, not waiting for Brax. His impatience for this world was growing, even though he knew full well that curing the disease that was the Interior Union, would not bring his life and his love back.

'I guess I could try . . . it might take me some time to figure-'

'You got plenty of time. I think me and Mr Brax here will be tearing all we can make use of off that rickety ride out there.' And Lupe walked through the door. Brax followed him shortly after, offering a glance of sympathy for Lupe towards Jane. Everybody knew how badly he was taking it. This world had hit Lupe the hardest for some reason. He was in the same situation they all felt stuck in, but he seemed to have the least resolve. It was just the fact about people handling things differently. Quite differently. He would just have to come to terms with it in his own time.

"I believe we should get to work on this link he spoke of. He's quite right, it is making things difficult, but our minds need to work together." Roland said, in his inner voice.

'We need to maintain our senses as well. We don't want to get caught unaware.' Jane replied. It was something Brax had mentioned earlier, only with less "thumbs in asses". 'What should we start with?'

"Something quite simple, a small thought, only you need to open your mind to theirs, and pass it rather than listen and speak it. Like forwarding a message, but without such a long delay." Roland said in his mind, his bright blue husky eyes staring into Jane's.

Jane went back into the meeting room they had spent so long in, and grabbed two of the chairs, almost underestimating their weight as he tried to make his way through the door with one in each hand. He almost bashed the wall with quite a force, but managed to counterbalance the weight he didn't account for. His cheeks went red with slight embarrassment, though Roland paid no noticed to this minor overlook. He pulled the chairs to the centre of the bright but messy room they now stood in, and cat down on one of them. Roland hopped on one soon afterwards, both of them facing the entranceway they had entered all that time ago, and met Pedley for the first time.

"We'll try something basic first; pass it onto them in the next room. I'm sure we'll eventually get the passing on to a fine art, though I believe they might get irritated about the constant utterances going on inside their head." Roland said.

'Don't want them thinking they're going insane now do we.' Jane smiled. At the prospect of causing a little humorous irritation. Then his face straightened again. He felt it was no time for messing around; funny things could have turned serious, especially in Lupe's case.

'How about a little hello?' Jane asked.

"A good start, try and get yourself an open link between us all as I speak my words." Roland replied.

Jane looked down, concentrating on his now folded palms, in hopes he would find focus there. At first, he heard nothing from Roland's thoughts. And thought he had lost the connection with him.

Brax and Lupe had been looking over the craft, realising there was in fact very little they could do to the thing. It was apparent during their exit of Cradle 1 that the ship was built solidity, even in the greatest of forces, it held strong. The only things of use would be whatever weapons were left insides. Brax did however manage to tear out a few of the radio transmitters from inside. At least that way they could talk over large distances without difficulty. Then he had second thoughts about the use of the radios. If Jane got his little mind tricks working, they would barely need to talk, he could do all the transmitting.

Lupe was busy struggling with a loose panel on the inside, when he immediately lost his grip and fell off balance, landing on his back inside the craft.

'Everything alright in there?' Brax asked.

'Damn psychics!' Was all he got in reply.

'What's on your mind?' Brax asked, still lacking understanding.

'The dog is in my head saying hi . . . guess they're getting somewhere with that task.' Lupe explained. The thing he had asked of them both was now the thing that bothered him the most.

"Sorry." The both of them heard in their heads. It was a voice they hadn't heard before. Was that Roland's?

Almost shocked at the immediate process, Roland's canine head lifted in surprise to Jane. He had sent the first message only to Lupe by accident, but he had almost instantly shared everyone's speech and thoughts between them all.

"Well, uh . . . no problem Roland." Brax sent between them. The feeling was one they were not familiar with, but all the same, they managed to send what they wanted with no real concentration at all. Jane was actually doing all the work, his mind was making the entire space around them like a little conversation in the air. Progress none of them had expected quite so quickly. Jane was indeed a truly gifted individual.

Although he knew well of his achievement, Jane still sat there staring down at his hands, focused entirely on the people around him. Still no one around that shouldn't be. Though he could feel something he didn't want to—the scent of decay in his brain. Not only was he picking up the people alive, he was also feeling the dead woman in the cupboard. It haunted his mind, and yet he couldn't get rid of it, he needed to keep the whole area in his channel.

"Alright, great, you managed it, but try and use your brain to warn me what you're doing next time. At a time when I don't have heavy objects in my grasp." Lupe said, complacently. Jane could feel the fiery core of Lupe's emotions crashing around like a wind swept sea. Lupe didn't expect an answer, but carried on his tugging all the same.

It appeared he would be largely unsuccessful in pulling the panel off, and it was questionable as to what they would be using it for. It was more likely he was just trying to tear it off to release some stress. That's what Brax thought of it anyway. He just sat there in the pilot seat checking over the small radio devices he had salvaged, occasionally looking up to see Lupe's progress, or lack of it.

'Might be an idea to use your rage on something that we *need* tearing off.' Brax said, hoping he wouldn't experience the full brunt of Lupe's frustration. Surprisingly, he was greeted by an apologetic face.

"Sorry guys. It's just not been my week." He said over Jane's mental network. "Surprisingly enough, I did actually have a life back on my world, more than what you'd think of your average geek."

Despite his apparent intellect, he didn't actually fit the stereotypical look of a geek. Since he had come through the portal to this world, he had looked more mature, more of a man than ever. Maybe it wasn't just the other world that time affected. It had made more of a man out of both the boys than they had first looked. Both had come in at the end of their teens, almost breaking into the twenties, but now they appeared to be pushing beyond that stage. It was possible it could be the length of the days. The sun never went down, and they couldn't remember the last time they had rested since they first met Brax. Their faces must have showed intense exhaustion after the past few days they had had. Roland's however, showed very little, he was always on the edge of everything.

Nobody chose to continue toe conversation about what they had left behind; it would only make their situation feel direr. They couldn't afford to lose their drive now; they had an aim to keep to, an almost impossible aim that the world may have depended on. If they found out the true facts behind the Interior Union, exactly what they had done and how, people all over this Cradle may have their fears and anxieties lifted. They could live out their long lives without a heavy shadow upon their backs, threatening their existence at the sight of a falter of integrity.

Lupe now stood looking around him, looking for something more constructive to do. There really was nothing in this craft, or so it appeared. Just seats that they had be sat in, and a few odd box shapes scattered about, most of them empty.

'You boys got luggage bays above your heads?' He asked Brax.

'You mean like, compartments above the seats? Just give 'em a bash and they'll swing right open.'

'Thanks.' He said, and turned his attention to the tiniest little gaps he could see in the metal above his head. He gave one of them a forceful jab with him fist, and a mountain of bags fell upon his, as the entire rows compartments flooded open. Lupe was instantly knocked on the head by a case, and half buried in a daze.

To this, Brax let out a truly hearty laugh, something none of them had done in a great deal of time. Lupe regained what little consciousness he lost, and fought against the weight that lay upon him, almost tripping as he made his way out of the mess.

'Swing right on my head more like, last time I take your advice with trust.' He said, with a little less irritation. He turned his main attention to what he had bundled onto the floor in such a destructive fashion when he heard word from Jane.

"Everything alright in there? Sounded like you dropped something. A lot of somethings.'

"Your friend is fine." Brax said back. "He just found himself some thing to go through." He turned his attention to everything on the floor, and assisted Lupe into looking into it. It appeared to be a small gold mine of fresh clothing, mainly military greys and navy coloured attire. They had been wearing the same clothes for a while now, and it would be a refreshing change to put something else less sticky on.

Brax handed Lupe some of it, ones he felt might fit Lupe and Jane, and Lupe left the room to hand some of it over. For the first time as Lupe entered the room, Jane looked up from his place in his seat to find Lupe already throwing over some combats and a grey shirt, with less of a sad attitude written across his face. He appeared to have lightened up a little by now.

'Thanks, I feel like a trash can on a humid day. But, where do I change?' Jane asked. Lupe just shrugged his shoulders and looked around the room as if to say "Anywhere". Jane just sighed and walked over to one of the desks nearer the back of the room to remove his dank sweaty clothing. It began to smell like death to him already, possibly the idea of his own. These clothes had witnessed the death of many; no doubt they had clung onto him like a disease.

He slipped on the combats without problem, and they felt like they had slowly adjusted to his waist size, like an elastic waistline, only more of an unnatural feeling. He pulled the grey shirt over his head, and felt immediate relief. He vouched to simply leave his close over at the back of the room. They could stay here and be destroyed along with this place, he was eager to leave them behind. The first of many things he felt he would need to let go of. Luckily clothes were easily replaced. People, memories, were not.

Lupe had already slipped out and back into the hanger to change himself, Brax was still fiddling with other devices he had torn out, looking grim about their eventual purpose in their mission.

'I don't think I'd worry about those things man, all the technology worthwhile was dead an' buried a few hours ago.' Lupe said to Brax, who was now getting restless with his tinkering.

'You're probably right, but this is keeping me sane, we got nothing else to help us out other than these two guns crammed into my pants. I guess you're the only one more worthwhile with a gun in his hand.' Brax pulled out the one he had taken from the woman, and held it out handle first to Lupe.

He just stood there staring at it, like some foreign object of mistrust. Until the last few days, he had never seen a firearm in person, only ever on the media in his world. Then Brax said something that Lupe found quite odd.

'I think you're quite the mover.'

'I have a funny feeling you are too.' He replied, without thinking.

'Haha. It appears young Jane's psychic abilities rubbed off a little. But you're quite right. I couldn't have killed that woman without having a little help from the body.' He said, and dropped the gun he held out down a bit to get a more detailed looked at it. He spoke, as if remembering from what the gun told him.

'Like you, I wasn't originally from this world. It changed me into a similar state as you when I was younger, I came here a long time ago, longer than you could imagine.' He held it out once more, this time Lupe gripped it softly, and pulled it away in his hand, considering the weapon. These things were heavier than he imagined. 'Point and shoot, just don't lock your arm, leave it loose or your shoulder will be six inches further back than it usually would.'

Lupe pointed it forward, and felt instant reluctance. He had not killed before, just ran, though in the last few hours he had been in a particularly defensive state. He wanted to protect Jane, it was his instinct, as if his body had ordered him to do it. He protected Jane as best he could, kept him out of harms way, while Jane did the other work with his mind.

'I pray I won't need to use it. War isn't a strong point of mine.' He said, and to this, Brax smiled. He had no doubt felt the same in his life, but this world had pulled him into the destructive circle.

'War does funny things to us. Makes us do things we didn't set out to do. We can only hope our side wins.' He said to Lupe.

'We can also hope our side is about the same size as theirs, though I doubt it somewhat.' Lupe said, feeling doubts about their original idea of the Union not being as body strong as people thought.

'We can use those things you fell over.' Brax said, pointing to some strap looking devices beneath Lupe's feat. He picked them up, and saw what they were in an instant. Gun straps. He threw one to Brax, and held one for himself, completely unaware of how to adorn himself with it. Though Brax made quick work of it, strapping it around his left arm, leaving the small pocket facing frontwards for his right hand to holster the gun. Lupe had tried to do the same, only ended up with half of it hanging off his left shoulder. Brax walked up to him and set the thing straight, as if taming it like a wild beast.

Lupe holstered his own gun, feeling the small weight go down on his left side. He didn't feel manly, the presence of a gun on his body only made him feel . . . more accountable. Now he held more responsibility for the group's protection, and he wasn't all too eager to accept it.

'What's in it is all we have; we'll find no ammunition where we're going.' Brax said.

'Where's that?'

'Half to hell.'

They made their way back into the bright white room where Roland and Jane now sat, a little more relaxed, paying attention to the surroundings, awaiting any change in person count. And there they sat waiting, for what was a minute to them. Days elsewhere.

* * *

He had wandered through the streets finding relatively no one to sneak by. His slow walk had become a brisk one, as his patience was wearing thin. He was about to in and do something he had never done before, and he had little time to consider what he was doing. The task they had set him, to find his brother and his companions, was difficult. He could not subdue them or capture them. He needed to lead them there like sheep. The only thing on his side was family relations, and that was what he needed to work with. He knew the hideout had been abandoned. Sayre had made short work of removing the people he had used as tools there; they had made their own way to the ground from the Cradle. Sayre, or rather his master had done something to their minds, they appeared to be empty husks. The people he was after were no doubt somewhere in that vicinity. They would probably be waiting for someone to come too.

He couldn't simply walk in, confess his regretful actions to his brother, and then expect them to follow him into a furnace; they'd surely try to kill him on sight, and not know who they were dealing with. He had no intention of making them aware of his presence that blatantly. He never removed his hooded cloak, it was what kept his actions hidden, and the Interior Union had its own figurative cloak, to hide its true form from the eyes of the citizens on this Cradle.

If they tried to attack him, he would have no choice but to fight back, that was evident enough. If he killed one of them however, he would experience a far more painful death from his unseen master. He had no doubt of that. His actions in the next few hours, days perhaps, would be of utmost importance. He needed to plan concisely, and work the travellers with his brother the way he saw necessary. They needed to trust him, through Roland, if not from first judgement. He had promised to himself now, that no matter what his brother did, he would no longer falter in his desire to fulfil Sayre's needs and remove Roland from this world. But now he was being asked to do the very opposite, and try and bring trust to his brothers eyes, and possibly him own. It would become a particularly confusing time for him, but he had to make do. His objective was now his life, he had be trained to look at things that way. He needed to trick his brother and his friends, no matter how guilty he felt for doing so. His future depended on it. In the coming times, his master might reveal himself to the travellers, and Tailen. That would be an interesting outcome indeed.

Until that time, he needed to focus. He had been getting all to relaxed walking through empty streets, but he would soon fall upon the more populated streets of the East Arm, and he needed to make it through those places without being seen. The Interior Unions presence was best felt, but never seen. Tailen intended to keep it that way. Revolt was unlikely, though some of these people may have deep lying thoughts about making an attempt on a shady looking character such as Tailen. They'd fail undoubtedly, but he was not here to draw attention to himself. The matter of getting the travellers and Roland back to the spire was a difficult one, but he'd have to come to that later. Concentration on the matter at hand was imperative. He began to increase his pace as he came towards the East Arm Causeway. Things were about to get busy, even at this time of night. However non-existent the night was, the body still felt it.

The first sight of a person appeared in his keen vision, and he quickly leapt to the less looked upon rooftops of the dull grey buildings. The roofs were flat, which made his stealthy approach easier. Houses in his old world were far more awkward to run across, and you were likely to kill yourself in trying to run across them. He felt more at home at this height, out of the immediate vision of the people. Loneliness bothered him on very few occasions, but in these times it never clung to his mind. He felt at peace not being looked upon. He kept up his brisk jog, often dropping down a foot or two due to the differences in height of the buildings.

Though the sun shone upon him, his dark clothing still kept him almost natural with the mechanical grey colouring of the buildings. It was largely a darker place in the East Arm, due to the central spire casting an eternal shadow on half of it. It certainly made sneaking around easier, but only for half of Tailen's journey. The White Belly was placed behind one of the corners of a largely open square. He would have to go right in the front door, the false front, to get in. Once he was in, he would have to tread lightly, and be intensely watchful of his senses. He was to be expected. He had made it into the lighter area of the streets, now sticking further to the centre of the rooftops to avoid being spotted and made haste towards the square where his targets laid in wait.

The odd thing about these streets was not the lack of vehicles and the like, but the noise. It was odd to be in a place where there was a genuine bustle of noise, people walking in tight spaces, talking amongst themselves in what they believed to be a quiet tone. Altogether, it was like a hymn being sung by too many different tones. Not one of the conversations was he able to make out. He was not entirely sure he wanted to. As he glanced over the edge of the rooftop he was darting across, he stole a glance to the crowd below, scouring the crowd for anyone of interest. Then a set of eyes locked onto his, rather, his entire person.

He quickly veered back to the central part of the building where he was nicely kept out of sight. He had been seen. It was a dubious mistake to have made, but he was sure the person couldn't have made him out. No doubt they recognised him for what he was, and they would make short conversation amongst themselves at what they had seen. He hoped his curiosity would not cost him dearly in the future. He came to a where he would have to cross over a street to further rooftops, something he had done countless times before, yet he hesitated. He slowed as he reached the edge, and looked over at the rest of the buildings he was due to traverse. He saw he was only minutes away. He stood there and thought to himself. He would have to now earnestly sell himself as genuine. He needed his highest wits about him.

He took a few steps back and rushed forward; leaping to the final stint he would now have to make it across, before he made it to the hideout.

* * *

Lupe had constantly shifted in his place, showing his apparent discomfort with the weapon he now wore. Brax and Lupe had gone and fetched their own chairs from where they had previously been sat, and took seats near Roland and Jane. The four of them sat there, with nothing to do, for a great amount of time. It was impossible to say exactly how long they had been waiting. Tracking time felt so hard, and there was nothing left around them to tell them whether it was day or night. Their bodies told them it was night, at least.

On numerous occasions one or two of them had tried to start up a conversation, but tensions were high, and sleep was lacking, causing all attempts at talking to falls hort. They sat in a semi circle, a few yards away from where the entrance lay, now open. They were counting on the fact that the white room had almost blinded them as the walked in, their expected guest would not have the upper hand. Roland hadn't even taken the chance to lie down, as an ordinary dog would, but none of them had actually ever seen him do so. It was almost as if he had too much pride in being a human, he tried not to give in to his canine instincts.

'If it makes you uncomfortable, then just hold it in your hands; just be sure not to set it off into any of our legs.' Brax said to Lupe, as he shifted his balance to the other side, allowing the gun to dangle from its holster. But instead of replying, Lupe just sat up straight, like the rest of them, in apparent discomfort.

"Feel anyone moving out of the ordinary?" Roland asked. The rest of them now getting used to him speaking through their heads.

'Nothing . . . just the crowds outside. But somebody did act a little strange, as if they saw something.' Jane said.

'There's a lot of strange stuff in this world. Wouldn't count on it being what we're after.' Lupe said, dismissing the fact that people had lived here for a long time. Whatever was considered odd at the time would be a norm by now.

"Don't count on that Lupe; it may be a small warning for us to keep to our senses." Roland wisely advised.

Waiting was difficult enough; it was the anticipation that killed the nerves the most. They were essentially waiting for a time to come where they had no idea what the possible outcome would be. It was possible for something to go wrong, somebody to get injured, or killed. They felt the need to stick to their advantages in whatever shape or form they came. Right now, they hoped they would outnumber a single person. They didn't even stop to think about the possibilities of it being more than one person. Or the very idea that the Interior Union might have considered burying them with the building. After all, appearances meant very little to them.

Then it came to him.

"The roof." Jane whispered. All of them instantly looking up. "He's on it."

'There is only one entrance; he has to come through the front shop, as we did, ready yourselves.' Brax said, nodding for Lupe to be prepared.

* * *

He was above the place he was told to investigate first. He had never actually been to the White Belly, though he knew it existed. It was one of the things that were not one of his concerns, and Sayre had not considered it high enough priority to send Tailen there to investigate at any time. But times changed. He knelt to the floor of the roof and looked over the edge at where the entrance was. The door would be open, despite the fact the shop looked closed, and that much was true. The difficulty was getting down without drawing any attention to himself. He couldn't afford anyone becoming curious, and following him in, ruining his entire operation. When fear was on high, anything could happen if a little too much pressure was applied. He was also told to be aware of his mind, the young boy Sayre and his master cared most about was apparently quite a prodigy with his mind. He needed to tell the closest to the truth he could, or his deeper plans would be found out, and ruined. He might not count on his brother killing him, but the others might not share the same sentiments, and not hesitate to kill if they found they were being lured places they didn't want to go.

He paid close attention to the crowd, trying to make out every single set of eyes at once, slowly counting down to the time he would decide to drop like a shadowy veil.

One.

They were wandering around; some of them he noticed were walking as if in circles. He could swear that they were walking places without purpose.

Two.

It was actually puzzling his subconscious, the way they walked. As if they were projections, made to look as if they were real people. But really, they were people. Just lost people.

Three.

He dropped, his cloak flapping silently as the air displaced around him, and bent his knees as he felt the brisk touch of the ground against his toes, and rushed through the door almost without any sound, but the latch of the door. He turned around, in the darkened front room of the shop he now stood in, to check to see if anyone had turned to see the short spectacle. He had timed it impeccably. Not a soul was awakened to his presence. He turned, and found the long, dark tunnel to the Independent's hideout was already welcoming him. Darkness. The type of tunnel he would feel most at home in.

He ducked his head, appearing to be of quite a high stature compared to the height of the passageway he know silently walked in. His boots were of a soft leathery material, which offered him both grip, and an utterly deadly silence with every step. Almost as if his every movement was but a ghost, causing no sound. He would have to be sure not to startle them, though he expected them to be waiting for him. He was told to be expected, information passed down to him by his master above Sayre. He never questioned information passed to him, it was always correct, though the source of the information was one to be bewildered about.

He crept slowly at first down the long dark tunnel, not wanting to raise any immediate suspicion. Him charging headfirst wasn't a viable option. He vouched to go as close to the entrance as he could without a sound, then he would decide how to make his entrance. He was meters away from what appeared to be the opening; his eyes could now see a gentle haze of white glowing from out a hole on the right. It reminded him of the way he got into this world, only the light was more comforting back then. Now it was like a bad omen.

He found himself noticing his breathing, trying desperately to keep it under his control, so it would make anymore noise than his heartbeat, which by now, was pounding, and crying out to be freed from his chest. Slower and slower he walked as he moved closer to what was now a brighter haze of unnatural white. Then he heard the faint sound of a mechanical *click*.

'We are fully aware of your being there mister. Our friend Jane here could smell you from a mile off.' It was a voice unknown to Tailen, one of a particularly older man, which belonged to neither Roland, nor either of the younger men, still boys of their world.

He did something he hadn't done for quite some time now, even when he slept, he kept him hood over the main portion of his face, yet now, he found himself pulling it back off his head, and raising his arms out wide. Then he made his first mistake, he went to walk into the door without warning them first. Tension was not an animal to be played with.

It nearly cost him his life, and perhaps more, as the first to pounce, quite literally, was his brother. He had stepped out into the entrance, and been instantly blinded by the white as his eyes screamed for adjustment. At the same time he almost clamoured backwards, making an erratic jerking gesture with his arms. Roland leapt, unaware of the face he now saw in mid air. Fangs bared—eyes sharp. Then it was his own mistake this time. He all of a sudden came to understand who the person he was about to land on was. Tailen was too blinded at this point to see clearly, but like a reflex, he saw the shadow in front of his eyes, now coming upon him, and swung wildly in front of him, planting his fore arm directly into Roland's muzzle. Roland flung to one side, partially dazed by what had happened.

During all of this, Jane had sat there staring, horrified at what the outcome had become. Time was going slow for him, and yet he still hadn't noticed Lupe preparing himself for his own share of action. He had acted upon what he thought was a situation turning sour, and had tugged his gun out of its pouch with horrifying speed, and without thought, pressed hard down on the trigger. The sound, coming only feet away from Jane, snapped them all into shock.

Lupe had never fired a gun before, and it showed. Tailen's face was pale with fright, his hands now high in the air with devout enthusiasm, for the sake of his own safety. His attention turned to the noise, and the funny feeling he had in his leg. Warm, numb, and slowly becoming foreign to his body. It was the same limb that was completely missing on Roland's body.

'I . . . I didn't expect to startle . . . you . . .' And with a short breath, he collapsed on the floor. Plans were all well and good down on paper, even in the mind. But they were human, most of them at least, and mistakes were made on the most part. Their hopes were hanging by a thread of existence now.

* * *

All dangers aside, their compassion acted on the forefront of their minds, as opposed to their fear of what this killer was capable of doing. Rather than go over and help Roland, Jane and Brax found themselves rushing over to crouch at Tailen, who was now looking all too pale, and Lupe stood their, the gun in his hand steady as a rock, with little thought going on inside his head. He had clearly shocked himself more than anyone else, and his mind had almost completely shut down.

Roland made haste at shaking off his wooziness, and stood back up on all three legs to see at what had happened during his time of carelessness. He was surprised to see the scene of his friends helping his brother, talking to him, asking him questions he couldn't make out, the blow to the head had knocked his hearing off course, and everything sounded like he was underwater. He tried to shake it off, and it made a small amount of difference. Trying to walk over to where they were turned out to be more difficult than he first imagined. With his ears acting up, his balance was degrading. He looked down, as if he were a drunkard trying to find an illogical sense of focus from the ground. Looking up again, he tried once more to press forward, to attend to his own brother.

Brax stood up; noticing Lupe's frozen stature, and put his hand on Lupe's. It was warm, sweaty, and frozen solid. He felt the stone cold grip Lupe had on the gun, almost like a clamp made of steel, locked in position. He pressed harder on Lupe's knuckle behind his thumb—an old trick he had learnt about disarming opponents, only in this case, the situation was a little less dangerous.

'You did what I would have, given the time. I feel my reactions are not quite as tuned as yours are, at your young age.' He said, trying to comfort Lupe. Only what he said was true, he was about to fire, until Lupe had startled him. It made him feel uneasy at Lupe's ability to react so fast. It was beyond even this world.

Lupe's eyes gently flickered as his mind tried so hard to process exactly what had just gone on. His brain was catching up with events, and it almost forgot to take care of his legs. He felt himself almost crumple under an invisible weight. It was the gun; he was so sure of it in his temporary madness. He loosened his grip, and in doing so, Brax gently slid the gun out of his hands. Blood slowly started to flow back into his hand and face, but he still felt just as dizzy as he had only seconds ago. He felt the hot flush come over his face, as he turned toward Brax with a sullen guilty look on his face.

'You're just saying that, to make my fuck up look a lot less worse.'

'I wish I was . . .' Brax replied, still weary, still considering the scared boy in front of him, who had little comprehension of his own power. All he understood was the downsides of it, and that wouldn't help his already decaying attitude towards his future life here.

Brax turned, realising he was unable to further put Lupe to rest, and paid close attention to their guest, who was now bleeding out his leg onto the floor at an alarmingly fast rate. It wasn't their actions alone that had caused their ill fate. It was this *room* as well, the whole stench of the Independents had left a chaotic mark of its own on this world, though little of the outside world would ever realise of its existence. Roland had now made it over to the floor area where Tailen now laid, looking more tired than he ever looked. He was concerned about his brother, regardless of what had just happened. Family ties had bound deep. Jane had his hand on the leg, pressing over the deep wound, completely unaware of how drenched his hand was with blood. It would hit him sooner than he could expect, such gruesome truths always did. For now, Brax had to make the most of the shock everyone was in, and try to tend to the wound while he had the attention.

Roland looked like he felt incredibly awkward, if he were a human, he could have comforted his brother, with the simple touch of the hands. In his present state, he was evidently frustrated with his boundaries, but at the same time, the show of deep regret pulsed in his face like any other human. That was something that would be there for an age, the blatant human characteristics on a canine face, which were almost impossible to miss.

'Your hand, press harder.' Brax said to Jane, hoping his request wouldn't run too deep in Jane's mind. The boy had great power over his mind, but while he was in intense confusion, he was as conformable as any other.

'Lupe, I need you to take off his fatigues, if we want the bleeding to stop, I need a clear sight of the entry wound.' Lupe's reactions were not quite as quick and as sure as they were before, but he nevertheless did the best he could to attend with what was left of his mind to the situation. He tried to pull down Tailen's strangely fabricated trousers, realising they would catch on his shoes. He turned his attention to them, and fumbled as he tried to take them off, constantly slipping between his moist hands.

Eventually, in his blind panic, he threw off the shoes and pulled off Tailen's trousers, falling back himself as they flew loose, leaving his chest area dank with blood. Under these garments, Tailen wore a tight pair of what looked to be long length boxers, which came down just above where the bloody, half clotted wound was. It was a sight to make anyone sick, the skin half torched black, now surrounded by half congealed blood.

'Sorry young man, this knife here is going in, and it ain't comin' out til the lead comes with it.' Brax said to Tailen, who was now half awake, yet still caught in his daze. The pain would soon wake him up, with or without his attentive senses.

Brax took no time in preparing a thing, and simple moved Jane's hands towards the upper thigh to cut off the blood as best he could. He allowed his hands to be moved, and the remaining clean skin on his arms was white, due to the amount of pressure he was putting through his arms. Brax gritted his teeth, and slowly slipped in the knife as smoothly as he could. Screaming broke out, and pain rattled through Tailen's mind, blowing his sanity to its limits.

Through he pushed; he had stabbed a man before, but with less guilt than he felt now. The man had come to kill them, to rid the world of them, yet here he was now, trying to help the man with as little pain involved as possible. He felt the knife scrape minutely on what felt like a metal, and tried to scoop as it, but the tissue around it had swelled, making a clean removal impossible.

'Five seconds of unimaginable pain, I guarantee you.' Brax said finally. Roland now lying down with his head stooped low. Lupe had remained standing, and Jane had his eyes fixed on the blood all around him. It was like being surrounded by demons, only they were there in his mind only. His wits were slowly escaping him, and Brax noticed the slight increase in blood flow as Jane's pressure was slowly releasing.

He made his time, and pushed harder against the inside of the wound, getting a substantial length of leeway behind the bullet, and tried to scoop it up with the pen knife he had kept with him always. At first, he though he had let it slip as he brought the knife up as fast as he dared. His promises of only five seconds could have been a mistake, but he carried on despite his doubts. Jane's eyes widened as he saw the clotted bullet ooze out of the wound his eyes were fixed on. He turned, and heaved his guts out, harder than he could remember, and laid next to the fetid mass his stomach had created, unaware of the blood flow now pulsing through Tailen's leg.

Lupe had gathered his senses far faster than the rest, and removed his shirt as fast as his hand-eye coordination would allow, throwing the grey military shirt under the leg, and wrapping it uncomfortably tight over the leg. The blood stained through it almost instantly, but it was all they had to make a makeshift bandage.

'Good thinking. Quick as usual.' Brax said, hoping this would ease Lupe's mind. No such luck. He was the only one speaking, the rest of them feeling the true meaning of being helpless. Their time was running out now, their only hope of success lay in the time that Tailen was given by whatever god was left. Without medical attention he would, eventually, die of severe blood loss. But nobody on this Cradle would see to him willingly, such things were not common amenities in this world.

Brax grabbed Tailen by his shoulders, and heaved him onto a chair, he needed him to sit upright, and it would help him stay in consciousness if he wasn't lying down. Lupe stood there; bear chested, his eyes begging for a way he could assist. They noticed Jane's eyes squinting in what appeared to be discomfort, the way someone would if sound was too loud.

'Jane? Open the channel between us all?' Lupe asked, wanting to be connected with Roland.

'You don't want to hear it . . .' He said. Roland wasn't just sobbing in his head; he was practically tearing his inner voice to pieces in rage and agony. He was likely well aware of how dire Tailen's next few hours would be.

'Everyone take five minutes to sit, and relax.' Brax announced, still staying close to Tailen to monitor his situation. This time, they all sat on the floor, staring at Tailen as he swayed in his painful dream, reflecting on what had just happened to them. Now things were desperate, and they didn't know the half of it.

'They . . . he sent me to kill you . . . Roland . . .' He uttered, behind his slurred words of semi-consciousness. 'Now I cant . . . I won't.' He finished, now finding some strength to hold his head up, and look to his brother, this time, as an equal.

'Jane.' Brax nodded towards him. 'Let us all in.'

In their heads they could sense the bottled up sorrow from Roland's part, as he watched and held his gaze on his brother. He was just as guilty as the rest of them for the errors here, but this was more to him. This was family. No prior rejections could hold anger over his agony for Tailen.

"Better perhaps, for the both of us, that you did . . ." He solemnly cried through their heads.

Tailen had made up his mind in his words. His task was over; this had decided it for him. No further order from Sayre, no promise of agony from their master would worry his frail heart now. He was a man on a timescale, and he resolved to do what he could in the little time he had left.

'They sent me here to kill you all. But now . . . now I find it in myself to do what I can to aid you. It's the least I can do to make up for my decisions. For the chaos I have caused in this world.' His head swaying again to one side, as he fought through his urge to sleep through the throbbing of his leg.

"You need not make atonement for your actions." Roland replied, now with more force in his voice, but it was one not full of resentment or condemnation. It was vigilance. "You did what you felt necessary to live. Nothing that we have not been guilty of." That much was true, however philosophical, however light minded it was. They were all guilty of simply trying to survive, in an otherwise unforgiving harsh world.

'Nevertheless, we would be incredible grateful for your help. Our final task is one we can only do with your aid.' Brax uttered, trying to put little stress on their urgency at this time.

"In my state . . .' He swallowed, finding it harder every second to do arbitrary tasks. ' . . . I fear I may not be as useful as I once was.' He smiled, albeit extremely awkwardly, but there was honesty in his voice.

'Information is just as useful as actions.' Jane said, now feeling more attached to the situation. His mind was letting its thoughts out freely, as if it had given up on holding back a single thing. 'There is a-plenty we need to know.'

"I would feel obliged to answer your questions, at least for my brother's sake, to get back his respect.'

"You need not feel like you need to earn it. In these times, forgiveness seems to come easy. It's a shame it had to come to this for us to find that out.' Roland said, so quickly in reply, to ensure Tailen felt as little guilt as possible.

'Then, please . . . make haste in your questions. I may have hours ahead, but my answers would be best said in clarity of mind.' Tailen said, moving his body forward in apparent discomfort, directing as much of his hearing toward whoever spoke first. Lupe however remained silent, and showed no signs of breaking his silence until his mind laid at rest. Though the guilt would run deep through him, far past the time of Tailen's eventual demise. It was his fault, after all.

'What is most important, to us at this time, is the true nature behind the Interior Union.' Brax began. 'More to the point, just who's part of it? To this Tailen smiled, at least a little.

'That . . . that was the beauty of it all. There was essentially one man behind it all, though I don't know of him. Sayre is beneath him, and I beneath Sayre. There are . . . others, just pawns in the game Sayre's master is playing, who mean almost nothing. They wander like the people of this world, but with a few more orders.' Tailen said, now finding less struggle in his words. The pain was alleviating, at least for the short term.

What they really needed to know had been told, and it proved their curiosities true. The Interior Union had been based on only a few. A select few men, capable of instilling a false presence into the minds of millions of people on this Cradle. It wasn't just the Cradle though. Unions all over the planet, in their own Cradle's, had partially feared the Interior Union for their shadowy rule. The Interior Union had power over people's minds, and far more than anyone could ever realise. Tailen's master was entirely a secret, which nobody, save possibly Sayre could know. Whether the group found those secrets or not, it wasn't their main concern. Stopping the Interior Union, and showing the people of its true form, was what they really aimed to do, through trials and tribulations. They had been through many already, to save a small part of a world they hardly knew.

'What else?' Tailen asked, as if expecting so much more.

'We . . . we have nothing else to ask . . .' Jane said, almost feeling guilty for using so little of Tailen's knowledge of the Interior Union. After all this time, all these mistakes, for what was otherwise a simple question to answer.

'Ha . . . it seems like the solutions to most problems and questions are always the easy ones.' Tailen replied, in his more satirical dying man's tone, whatever that felt like. Though his words did make Jane look slightly more intently at him, as if he had taken one of Jane's thoughts from his head.

'These past few days, that's been the case.' He said to Tailen, as if hinting at the idea of there being a link. But Tailen showed no sign of recognition. He just nodded grimly.

"There is of course, the small objective of getting into the spire." Roland said, searching for more from Tailen. He thought it might help him feel like his actions were still of great use to them.

'I can't walk out there like this.' He said, gesturing to his bare blood stained leg. 'These clothes, this hood, they'll know from what I'm from.'

'That is, unless we dress you up in these.' Lupe said, surprising all of them. He had somehow walked out of the room and grabbed an extra set of clothing, including another shirt for himself to cover his blood patched chest. 'You'd look like an average guy. Almost.' It was the leg that was the problem.

'What if we dressed up the leg so tightly, with as much as we can? Then it'd just like he had a limp, as long as they don't see the blood.' Jane suggested. 'Then he could walk with us, without having to avoid people too often. Nobody has seen your face have they?' Jane asked.

Instead of replying, Tailen just shook his head. It was a well suited plan, though he wasn't too fixed on walking so far on his leg, it would drain what little energy he had left. Though he had no other choice, he felt. He needed to help his brother and his companions do what they set out to. He had no doubt they were going to press forward with good intentions, regardless of the measurement of their failure. It was clear to him; they'd not stop until the last of them was dead or dying.

'Are you up for that my man?' Brax asked, offering out a hand, to make the deal.

'There is little else I'd care to do in these times.' He replied, and shook his hand with a light grip. Soon, he'd be unable to do much more than that.

"You need not strain yourself, going to these ends to see us to our goal. We could wait to find another way." Roland said.

'I see no other, brother. It is this or nothing . . . I know you can see that. Let me do this final deed, so I may rest easy when all is said and done.' And at that last word, he tried his best to move out of his chair. With little avail, he eventually managed to get up, with the help of Brax' iron will. Tailen grabbed the clothes from Lupe as he held them out.

'Despite my body, I will manage to change myself, I owe myself them much.' He said, offering a good will smile at Lupe. He held nothing against the boy for doing what he did. He thought that if he were in a similar situation, he would have no doubt done something similar. Though if it had been Tailen, the person would be dead long before now. The boy's incompetence had been a minor blessing, if that was at all how it could be described.

He made his way through the closest door to the hangar, and removed what clothing he had on, including the shirt that was strapped around his leg. The blood was still flowing, slower now, but still, it showed no sign of holding up. He grabbed what he could, and folded it as neatly as he could, wiping the leg at first, which stung like hell's fury. Then he wrapped it back over with a few torn pieces of what was close to cloth in this world. For the first time, he put on an outfit that had never suited him, at least he felt that way. He looked more . . . ordinary now. Dressed in a deep green shirt and navy trousers, he thought he'd pass the brief inspection the citizens' eyes would cast on passers by. Even his limp showed no immediate attention to the bullet wound that caused a writhing pain in his body. Just a main that had seen the wars, at a glance. Nobody was ever intent on searching deeper through their curiosities. It was healthier for them that way. They were more likely not to be "removed" from existence by the people they should not have been sizing up.

He hobbled back in, slowly getting used to not dragging his feet, instead placing all his weight up on one leg as he walked. The pain was there, sure and true. It was not going to let him forget about it anytime soon, it was a parasite, slowly wearing down his life force. He looked at the two young men that stood in front of him, the causes of all the distress on this Cradle, and then glanced past Brax to Roland.

'Last hours, better spent with a brother.' He said. 'Shall we leave? There is of course no time like the present.'

'True enough.' Brax said, taking the hint to make lead at least until Tailen felt it was his time to bring them toward the spire, and through it when that time came. Jane and Lupe looked slightly down towards the floor, avoiding prolonged eye contact with Tailen, as if in respect of the dead. His words and feelings would now be for Roland alone, even if they had to go through Jane's channel and into everyone else's mind. They would give him that much.

With little said, and already an awkwardly slow pace, they made their way into the tunnel, leaving the White Belly, for the last time. Of that they were sure.

16

The Last Trail

The first steps into the square from the false shop front were ones of great anticipation. Not only did they feel like they were being eyed from all over, but they had sense of being all too vulnerable to everyone around them. The change from electric created light, to a now more sharp sunlight burned at the back of their eyes, like a migraine doing its worst for a few brief seconds. The sun was never out in blue skies, it was always partially filtered through sandy looking clouds, which seemed never to move. There was no wind on this world. There was in fact little left of the natural climate, but like resourceful things they are, humans thrived nonetheless.

Without any hesitation, Brax moved forward, ensuring the rest were at his side, or closely behind as they walked, catering for Tailen's slow pace. He hid his discomfort well; they couldn't imagine the pain he was putting himself through to see that they made it to where they needed to go. Jane and Lupe walked side by side, with Brax, while Roland and Tailen walked behind, for what felt like their last miles together. The rest of them had no intention of making a great deal of conversation with Tailen until the time came for them to request for further assistance. Instead, the boys now looked towards Brax for guidance, instead of Roland. Right now he was the one in control; he was now the impartial one.

They wandered, uncomfortably closely to the main part of the crowds in this square, walking towards the narrow streets where Tailen had come from, only from greater heights. It was probably for the best, to walk amongst the people, it was less likely that they would be spotted as odd. If they walked in the open spaces, people were more likely to have their attention brought to Roland's odd presence, along with the limping man they saw walking beside him. Right now, their safety was in the depths of danger. It seemed their entire time in this world had been under such conditions. Though if they had done any of it, any other way, their situation may not have been quite so fortunate.

They wandered into the street that was an almost direct path the to spire that they could see between the rooftops, aside from one slight turn they needed to make; the turn that spelled the leap of judgement from Tailen. Though that was farther away in timescale than originally, they had to keep to a comfortable pace. But no doubt, even the slowest of speeds would become a pain to a fragile condition. It was something they would just have to fight through when the time came. The problem with their plans now, was that they were depending on going forward, and dealing with things as they came. Eventually, things would become overwhelming as the problems piled up. They had no other choice as of now. There was no more planning to be done, no more consultations. What came before them, would spell disaster or miracle. Either of which, they had to accept graciously. It was all they had left to do. Their lives, their futures depended on it.

It was easy to consider, that somebody never really remembers just how much pain they were in, when an accident happened, physical, or emotional. In this case, it was likely the last things they would experience, and moreover, the things they would never have memories of. Living past the greatest trials of their lives would not bring an easy life, only memories of pain and oppression. The revolutionaries of Jane and Lupe's world had suffered immense difficulty in their trials, for the sake of others. Now it was their turn to do such a thing, so selflessly, in a world that was not their own. Though in some years, they would have no choice but to call it their own. They had forgotten all hopes of ever returning to their world. Too much had been said and done, they had to make what they could of their time here. They had to make the most of Tailen's conformation, so brief and partial that it was.

People eyes drifted towards Roland, as they passed in close quarters through the streets. It was almost impossible to stay out of the way of everyone. Regardless of daily time, the streets were always busy with the people that had slept previously. No doubt there were two separate crowds in this world, ones that were awake during the first half of the days, and the people of the other half. There was no real difference in appearance that the boys could tell. Everyone looked to be in a similar mood, almost identical to common citizens on their Earth. PETE had spoken of some form of balance between the two worlds. These balances were perhaps the reason there were so many fundamental similarities between the people. There were the happy and the sad, the violent and corrupt, all seen in both worlds. The only difference was the environment they were in. Chaos was known to run amok in Jane and Lupe's world, in countries they had never been in. This Cradle was no doubt the mirror of those places, but with what appeared to be a far more formidable force.

Jane had never really considered the jobs people filled, what they did, day in and day out. They had shops, ones the boys had never been in, and other such buildings, close to those of the other world offices. It was almost impossible to tell exactly *what* the people did, though they obviously did something. It wasn't high on Jane's priorities, but it scratched at his mind nonetheless. They were just lost people. As the group walked down the street, gazing around them in silence, each of them considered different parts of the world they had never truly paid attention to before; the people, the true nature of the buildings, the severity of just how strict the attitude was. It was a sad sight from many directions, many viewpoints, and yet, the people lived without disdain. They had lived with the way things were for so long, their minds had gotten used to it becoming a normality, what was considered wrong, was soon found to be acceptable. It was like a trend, only their lives were the main affected, the Unions being the benefactors.

They had made their way towards the chicane in the street, a brief turn in both directions, which altered their course from a road permanently radiated by the sun, to one in full dim shadow, of their target destination. It was a might sight now, the shadow it created, making it seem evermore decadent. This was why the people accepted their life changes. It wasn't just a literal shadow the spire casted upon them. It instilled a sense of fear for something they had never seen, or even fully understood. They turned, into what appeared to be a different world altogether, the once busy streets, now turning to seemingly vast empty walkways. It was doubtful they would see many more people on this section of the Cradle, it was probably widely considered as a road to ruin, the path of shadow, the last trail to uncertainty.

Tailen's brow was now sodden with perspiration, and his strength had weakened slowly to a point where he found himself running a marathon in mere half meter steps. He pushed himself on, well aware that the others saw his weak state, and tried to slower their pace to accommodate him.

'Do not slow on my account, I can keep up, your time is precious.' He said, and reluctantly, they sped up to their starting pace. All of them were extremely weary, particularly Roland, of his degrading state. He had no stick to put half his weight on as he strode forward, and he denied the exhaustion that his pain had brought to his heart. He felt no inclination to give in to his body's needs to shut down, and punished himself further to help his brother's friends. He felt his time coming to a brief end, and knew he was only hours away from slipping out completely. He had lots pints of blood now, and he saw the faint appearance of a bloody patch seeping through his trousers. He moved his hand their, covering it, and strode on.

Brax felt the weapons he had concealed underneath shirt, cooling down as they began to change to the temperature of the surrounding streets. The sun had shone here once perhaps, many years ago, but since the spire had been put in its place, these streets had lost their warmth. They would remain cold to their depths, as long as the spire remained. Even if they successfully removed the Interior Union from this Cradle, the spire would likely remain, the streets would still be considered of bad fortune. It was a rationale, the people would never forget, for years to come. Brax alone was now a man without any other purpose. The Union he had worked for, appeared to be of questionable roots, and he had no where else to turn after this ordeal. What happened in the coming hours would define him for the rest of his days, but he was unsure as to what he'd do for himself if he made it through alive.

It was a concept none of them had considered, particularly so as of now. If they did somehow make it through whatever they expected to fulfil, none of them had a clue what they might do afterwards. They would just have to make a life for themselves, and fit in with the rest of society as best they could. For Roland, it would no doubt be particularly difficult. It was obvious he would have to remain close to Jane for communications sake, though his life would be lead in a depressive mood. Nobody ever expected him to get over what would eventually become of Tailen. He had proven to be a brother worthy of Roland's respect now, even in light of his previous dealings, he had fought for what meant most in the end.

The best part of an hour passed, and they found themselves only minutes away from the very base of the spire. Tailen's pale face was now a far more ghostly white than it was before. They had come a long way, and the journey had been a slow one so far. The chills had reached deep into them, as there was no heat from any particular source to insulate them as they walked. Lupe had his arms crossed over his chest, as his body let out an involuntary shiver. This was possibly their easiest challenge, walking towards their goal, but the anticipation was the fear that dug deep, and the cold didn't help alleviate it. Their faces were grim, Tailen's more than most, though Jane had a certain drive hidden deep beneath it. He had something to prove to himself, he wanted to use his abilities to their limit as best he could; to finish what he felt was his final duty to this world.

They each had a certain duty to withhold; this was going to become their grave or their home, for the rest of their lives. Though he had nothing to back up the fears deep in the rear of his mind, Jane felt a certain doubt, almost as if he knew what the root of the Interior Union was. He had no idea what made his mind think this, though he felt a certain link with the idea, as if he shared a bond. He swept away the idea, deep into his mind as an absurdity, but really, it *scared* him to think he could have anything to do with the chaos that ensued around them. When he and Lupe had first ran through the portal, they had been told of a certain disaster and of their apparent abilities at the time. It was possible they were the very people that could help, or that having them in this world, meant the Interior Union's success over in the other world. They had clear connections in the other world, and had come through the way Jane and Lupe had.

That was something they questioned themselves about when PETE had told them of the impossibility of getting back to their world. How exactly did the Interior Union communicate with their members between the two worlds? How was it possible for all of this to be planned for not only them, but Roland and his brother as well? There were questions that still remained unanswered, and they were the ones that would now mean the importance of their actions. If they could get back, and the Interior Unions real leader knew how, Jane and Lupe would want to know. Though it would quite possibly cost them something they could not afford. Their own desires of home were dangerously outweighing the choice of ending the Union's chaos. The one factor giving Jane the resolve to stand by his action to help this world, was that both worlds remained in balance. They couldn't simply run away from this world's problems, as they would slowly creep into their own. Jane couldn't bear to see such things happen in his own world. He had seen things he wished others had not, and had done things that would forever be imprinted into his conscience.

Lupe however, would be a more difficult character to consider. His moods were ever changing, and it was clear to them all, that he would almost jump at the chance of going home to the life he missed so much, regardless of what it may cost this world, of what it may cost them. He felt he had caused a large part of what had happened to Tailen. He had blamed himself so fiercely for what was an unfortunate but honest mistake to make, and now he had to walk a watch the outcome of his actions. He had to watch someone's brother die slowly, in pain, walking miles, because of his particularly fast abilities. He resented the speed he had been anonymously gifted since he pulled the trigger. In his mind he had screamed for himself to hold back, yet his body and gone ahead. He had soon forgotten that he had saved Jane's life on countless occasions due to his speed, but he clearly felt his mistake outweighed his achievements. He walked by Jane's side, occasionally stealing a glance behind him to inform himself of how Tailen was holding out. His condition was nothing short of imminent failure, but every time he looked, Lupe found himself believing that Tailen had gotten severely worse after ever passing minute.

They only had a short few minutes before they reached the innermost sanctum of the shadow casting Union of this Cradle. Their emotions were at peak, almost as temperamental as the world itself. They couldn't handle any more failures. They had been lucky enough to make it far enough with ill situations, but the last one would be fatal.

They could not afford to make any form of mistake when confronted by Sayre, and his master. Tailen knew well of Sayre's mental powers, and could only imagine the danger of his master's. Half of this battle would be Jane's. His mind had to hold out, and his peace of mind was already entirely shattered.

Brax had taken out one of his guns, and held it out again to Lupe.

'What is done is done. We need you more than ever to be on full alert. If you still blame yourself for what happened, then consider this your pardon. But you *must not* hold back now.'

They had stopped now, allowing for Tailen to take a break, as Brax now faced Lupe head on, backed up by the look of hope from Jane. Instead of arguing, or debating his actions, Lupe simple took hold of the gun from Brax, in a gentle and sorrowful movement.

'I'll do what I can . . .' He said quietly, and turned to continue walking; now stuffing it into his pocket. Jane could see Lupe was becoming a new character now. He had given up on hope, and faith, and the only thing that drove him onward, was the lack of any alternative. He would die doing what he could, or die a lost soul on this Cradle, stuck in this world he had rejected, swearing it would never become his home.

The rest followed with some hesitation, but soon restructured their shape. They didn't want to go in as a broken unit. They needed all the strength they could muster. They found themselves at the foot of the spire, a great towering wonder of the world. It was a desire to know what exactly was held at the top of the spire, a room no doubt, filled with something of interest, eternally guarded by the master of the Interior Union.

They walked to what appeared to be a large entrance, no windows, just a great door, that looked almost stone-like. Tailen now made an effort to get ahead of them, to face the door with his full bodice, and uttered a few brief words that were incoherent to the rest of the group. With a heaving groan from deep behind the walls of the spire, the doors edged open, revealing an entirely empty ground floor, comprised of stone and what looked to Jane like slate. Without warning, the doors closed behind them, their actions chosen, their fate sealed within these dark doors.

The ground floor was only partially warmer than the street they had just entered from, and offered no luxuries. It was a room with nothing of interest, other than a wide set of winding cold steps that led to the countless floors above, slowly getting narrower as they increased in height. The walls were adorned in stone carvings, similar to winding vines, and the floor had patterns Jane had never seen before, almost ancient. Tailen considered the stairs with apprehension, though he had little choice but to follow the people he had led here. He waited for them to make a decision to climb the stairs, though it didn't come immediately.

"How could something so empty bring about such fear and control . . ." Roland said with awe and grief.

'The mind . . . it does all the work . . .' Tailen replied; now finding it a struggle to make his speech audible. He felt himself slipping further into his sleepy state. He could barely feel the clothes on his skin.

'We must go on, we must go up.' Jane finally said, and Tailen made first to go up the stairs. He noticed that none of the rest of them had been quite so eager. He wanted to get it all over with, so he could have some chance of rest before passing his time. His expression showed some questions, which were soon laid to rest as Roland went before him, heading for the stairs, followed by Brax. Jane and Lupe stood their, and offered a brief glance at each other. It felt like a similar situation that had got them here in the first place, the inexplicable reasons why they had run into the world. They were faced with a similar decision, and found themselves answering the call accordingly. They made way towards the stooping Tailen, and the others, holding their breath in tentative nervousness. Now was the final stint of the journey. They perhaps had a huge effort ahead, climbing the hundreds of steps, and carrying Tailen along the way which would no doubt be necessary. They did not expect their misfortune to affect them at this point. Though the forces at work were far more informed than they could have known.

Tailen put his good leg on the first step, and like a fatal injection, their minds were blown away by a force so immense, they couldn't fight against it. Even with Jane's control of mind, he found himself fighting a losing battle to regain control over his own mind.

"You, travellers of the other world, have been expected, by me. I have long awaited your arrival, we have much to discuss, before I have need to remove you from this world. You have in your possession a great threat to our plans. You cannot interfere." Behind the madness that filled his mind, Jane noticed a slight undertone in the voice—something almost recognisable, but not apparent, as his brain slowly slipped into darkness. He fell to the floor, but felt nothing, not even the cold reception of the stone.

17

Mirrors of Other World

He had made the *journey several times before, now having the preparation down to a fine art within his mind, welcoming the strange things his senses felt every time he made the journey. He had a certain attachment to this world, as if it were like a young child to him, that he had tried so adamantly to bend to submission. He knew little about the sciences involved in the connections between the two worlds, but found them to be of massive importance. He had witnessed the Cold War of the second world, the damnation it had put itself through, and had survived through the worst part. He came back to this world, to feel a little more peace and harmony, to get away from the pressures he felt on his sanity everyday.*

He had made friends, Sayre had known of his skills and importance at the very first sight, recognising a great mind when he saw one. They had planned for what was almost an age for this world, they had immense thoughts for social overhaul, and had already dug deep into the other worlds political system. It was like a fine clock, and they now had control over the small cogs, seemingly insignificant, but important for the overall performance. What lay ahead were troubling times, but they were the ones behind it. They had created what they thought to be a perfect alternative for the worlds.

He slowly made his way out of the pink haze in the room, and stepped outside the warehouse door, into a largely barren field with weeds popping out from the ground in remote locations. The warehouse itself looked abandoned and out of use, but the local authorities had not shown any desire to get their hands dirty with it. It was the perfect place to hide something so important, so special, and so wondrous. This was his secret, his prodigy of the ages. Nobody was ever going to discover it, him and Sayre were the only ones that would ever use it to its full potential. And such vast potential it had. The world would never know what happened, neither of them.

He held a great deal of contempt for this world as he walked on its ground towards to main roads, which saw very little traffic of late. The ground, despite having little vegetation in this area, was far more healthy and natural than the ground of his world. It had been laid to waste by wars and destruction, yet his world was vastly superior in his state of mind, and he intended to ensure that imbalance was kept. He held his frustration back as he watched this world thrive around him, the people still held back by making use of just its ground, there was so much more above to be had. He had been here several times, each time he noticed a great deal of advancement in their technology, but it still fell short of the type he saw in his world. Here they had cities with buildings that reached to just a few thousand feet. He had seen far greater heights reached over in the other world, and the cities floated as if on nothing, miles and miles above. He had always declared he would build himself the tallest tower, in which he would lock away himself and his secrets of travel.

This world deserved nothing but the bitterness of his values, and he swore that it would soon see it, but first, he needed to clear through a few objectives in this world. He wanted to make sure his plans were carried through, and ensure there was no possibility of them failing, fragile as they were. He intended to do things, he would have felt contempt for, had they been acted on his own life, and it partly was his life he was destroying. It was a decision he would have to make. It had no direct effect on him, and as long as that remained the case, his conscience would remain steady as a rock. His heart had been torn of its compassion, long before the days his world became a wasteland. He could only blame himself for his own calamity.

He came to the metal fencing, inferior as it was; it couldn't stop a small car at slow speeds even on a good day, and opened the rusty makeshift gate, turned, and locked it with his electronic key. The lock itself, looked old and rusty like any other, but it was far denser than even the strongest metals in this world. It was quite possible for somebody to vault the fence had they the desire, but he doubted it quite surely. Nobody wanted to go into an abandoned barren field; the only suspects would be drunks in great need to let loose their bladders like an acidic torrent.

He had a place he needed to be; somewhere he needed to watch closely. There was a man he had been observing quite intently, with a sick passion on his visage, a quite self destructive mind. The man's ill state would make his tasks far easier. He found the best plan, was one that had been formulated for what seemed like years, though in his world, he could create and implement these tasks in a few days. The two worlds had their advantages in the scheme of things, and time was of the essence, though never in short supply. He'd been planning alright, and it was done to perfection. Even Sayre had applauded his ideas, claiming them to be of extreme ingenuity, which of course, they were.

He turned now in the direction of a single van, the only oncoming traffic that might pass this way for another few hours at least. He flagged it down with his right hand, and began to walk towards the place it was beginning to pull over to. The door opened ahead of him, and he pleasantly jumped inside, finding the ever welcome smile of Sayre at the wheel. Heaven knew where he'd got the van from this time, the man had serious ways of acquiring such items in deadly fashions, though Sayre's master cared little for his antics. He got the job done, ludicrously smoothly, that was all he wanted.

'It is a fine day for a scheme to be let loose, one might say?' Sayre said, still with his eyes on his master, and he pulled away from the lay by and began the journey down the road to the busy town that was in their first main interests.

'Of that, I have no doubt.' He said, in his implacable accent. 'Travelling burns the brain cells a little too much, I'd be greatly obliged if I could earn myself a little sleep.'

Sayre nodded at the request, and immediately focused his attention on the road, despite there being no immediate worries for miles to come. His master had requested sleep, but never found it. His mind was far too active at this point, and he found himself going over and over situations in his head, plotting as if it were a second nature to his subconscious. He thought he had every problem solved in every aspect, and that was what made him so dangerous. Through perfection, he struck fear. Through his mind, he caused death, in unimaginable ways. It had been one of the few qualities that brought him and Sayre together. The idea that their world was above this one they now travelled in. The idea that through shadow, a control could be instilled in people's minds was one of high complexities. Though Sayre's master had it down to a fine art now, it was only a matter of time before he had it on a large scale.

His head lay on the brittle glass of the van, and rumbled through his head like a drill over these roads. They were so poorly made; it was little wonder this world experience so many accidents involving these vehicles with wheels. He had noticed this world's technology eventually advanced to methods of flying, it had even come amazingly close to public travel at the speed of sound. It had been removed from existence for some reason. He had heard of many crashes happening all over the place. Little wonder they hadn't developed things like Cradle's. If the great minds of this world had tried, they'd have almost damned themselves from step one. Their Cradle's would have fallen from the sky. In his world, that was almost impossible, unless of course the correct type of pressure was applied. He remembered his time on Cradle 1, inserting neurotoxins this world had created, into the automated air systems. It had driven them mad. As it turned out, this world had been increasingly resourceful to him when it came to chaos. For that, he was grateful.

He found the seat in the van increasingly uncomfortable, every minute he ended up changing position slightly, after losing feeling in his legs and ass. These vehicles were supposed to be highly thought of around here, and yet they were so damned awful. They had a long way to go before they reached his standards of living. That was for sure. He couldn't sleep, and he knew Sayre was aware of this fact; he wasn't the only one with power of the mind. He was looking out the windows at the fields he passed, often seeing a few large metal structures keeping large cables off the ground, which ran for miles. Most likely power, he thought. They would do well to fathom how his world gathered its power from the Earth's surface. He found himself smiling as he considered the possibility that this world still got its energy from oil and other similar fuels.

Among the many fields he was so envious of, he noticed the blatant disrespect some people had for the countryside and structures around them. They had driven under countless bridges that went over the roads, with strange colourful letters written across them, often depicting odd objects, or the most pathetic of rude words that had died out long ago in his mind. The sides of the roads were filled with trash, paper, and bottles—mostly glass ones, and other waste material. Humans were a destructive race in any world; they could only hope that they never spread their disease onto other worlds.

He had wondered about the wars on many occasions, he had seen no visible evidence on this world of any wars, no desolate places. The people seemed altogether unhindered in their day to day lives by the political minds. They walked around, as if under no sense of control, which he thought to be most peculiar. What use were they if they weren't in some sort of control? They were far more productive when given clear directions and fearful incentives if they tried to do otherwise. He had once considered taking the world for himself; he could be a leader it had never seen. He quickly gave up the thought years, well, days ago, and just viewed this world as a lesser of two brothers. One would fall; all it needed was a brief push, or a little weight, to make the final tip. He turned to Sayre, who had spent a little extra time here to observe what his master had requested.

'Tell me; is there anything, I mean anything *at all worth taking? Does this world genuinely shoot itself in the foot with its idealistic rules?'*

'It's a funny observation, though mostly true. From what I can tell, the politics and way of life is almost madness. We are humans alike, but they live in such self destructive fashions. It's actually quite amusing to watch. You should try it.' Sayre said, showing his apparent amusement.

'I intend to, quite soon in fact.' He briefly said, then turned his attention back to the country.

It was a shame he couldn't bring a little of it with him. He would quite like natural soil, and some of these odd little plants that seemed to be everywhere. They grew in the worst of conditions, and still thrived. They reminded him of himself. He had a rule, that he would never bring anything from this tainted world to his own, so that he might not risk bringing the foul teachings of this world into his own. A fitting ideal to keep to, he thought at first, but he found himself ever keen to disobey his own order to satisfy his curiosity for what other forms of destruction this world had to offer. He was sure it had a great many. It would only take a small seed to grow into a tree of chaos, to bring this world down to its knees, where he believed it belonged.

He had almost forgotten the scene of the sun moving, here it rose up from behind the distance, and in a few hours to come, he might witness it coming down. He had seen this happen on a number of occasions before, and still it amazed him. It had been years since he'd seen such a spectacle in his world. Their world had stopped its usual course, and the world had made quite some distance, making the climate what it was. Nobody had ever travelled to the other side of their world; the place was eternally frozen; like the so called "North Pole" of this world, only it covered fifty percent of what remained a barren land. He had walked to the edge once, on his own. He had stood there on the ground, feeling the chill going from the floor through to his boots, and through his body. For once, it was possible to see some kind of sunset on his world, thought few ever bothered to make the trip to the frozen wastes. There was nothing but more ground to walk upon in an eternal night. No Cradles had been erected in that part of the world either; it had no rich resources of use, no thermal power to rely on.

He looked at the time on the radio transmitter that the vehicle had built in, and saw it was becoming past midday already. They had only a few hours to fit in what they needed to do, and then when the sun began to hide its face for another twelve hours, they would be long gone, having completed their preparations. Sayre had once tried to use the radio in the van once or twice, and found it to be senseless rabble rather than any form of knowledgeable material. Their world had long given up on musical entertainment, and similar talk shows. Life was too important to be wasted on such mindless activities. It was considered a waste of time by most of the people. With the immense amount of capabilities in their world, there was no time to stop and listen to something that would become obsolete within weeks.

Sayre had imminently lost patience with the radio all that while ago, however his master felt a distinct link between him and it, wanting to hear a little more. He had no taste for it, whatever it was considered, but he found it interesting in any case. Even though he felt a considerable amount of hatred towards this world, he often found himself yearning to see more from it, and hear the things it had to offer. It was an illogical thought, he knew it well. It was almost senseless for him to care, and yet he still did, he still felt a small curiosity. The world had made its small hold on him, in hopes of changing his mind—though it had no such luck. Once he had his plans set in place, it would take more than a world to stop him.

He had become ever more frustrated with the lack of comfort, and searched Sayre's understanding for more answers.

'How much longer must I wait?' His impatience was never audibly shown in his words, though Sayre was aware of it. He had trained himself to.

'I'm afraid your posterior will have to hold out for an hour more, at most. How about you treat yourself to that sleep you spoke of?' Sayre spoke more seriously now.

Without answer, his master agreed to his suggestion, and made a more mental attempt at resting. There was no other way out of his discomfort, other than death of course. He slowly searched his brain, asking for it to shut down its main processes. It obeyed willingly, and he found himself drifting against the oily window. It didn't particularly bother him a great deal, though he made a special effort to guard his brain from anything. He trusted Sayre, but he had no question of doubt about the mental abilities of people in this world. He was special, and there would most likely be other similar to himself. Perhaps some all too similar for his liking. He made haste about pushing that thought out of his mind, as he dropped his now heavy eyes.

Sayre made a few brief glances over at him during the journey, but swiftly pointed his concentration back to road, where sun now gleamed low in the distance. Their time was close now, and his master could read his very feelings, even in his sleepy state. Sayre had jealousies of his master's abilities, but had soon pushed them aside. He was better friend than a foe. Sayre had even proven extremely resourceful, and had agreed to a large point of his plans. When he found his master asking him to oversee the entire ordeal, to ensure this world found its end under his had, he had been more than honoured.

He himself had felt a similar sense of regret that this world existed. He didn't share his master's interest in the minor intricacies this world had. He viewed them as more of a problem than his master. To Sayre, they were burdens on an otherwise productive life. There was no sense in repetitive sounds, when there was fear to strike into people. That was Sayre's main source of entertainment. He enjoyed the evil he spread across his own world, and found even more interest in causing it in this world. In previous days, he had experienced an everlasting, brutal rain shower. He, like his master, had known weather to be similar to this in his own world, but not quite so ravenous. He found deep inside himself, gratitude towards the different Unions for causing the world to stop in its tracks, tearing down its natural cycle. They had saved themselves a lot of hard work and discomfort.

That was something in particular that this world clearly knew nothing of. He found no luxury or relaxation in this world. Everybody seemed to work around circumstances that were affecting their lives, and yet on they went working. In his past research during the short days he spent in this world, he had made note of the way the politics had changed. As a matter of fact, he found that it barely changed at all. The men the people looked up to for guidance, were men of weak minds, and had little scope for advancement. All in all, it was a bad world, run by people in the worst positions. Sayre's world was far better run by the military forces. It was what made things advance so far.

What did this world have in the manner of advancement? Nuclear weapons had been shortly adapted into forms of power—a laughable prospect indeed. The energy was minor, and the waste was massive. They had long gone past the nuclear stages in his world, finding its only use to be of massive power over minds. Here, in this world, they threatened with their weapons, instead of actually using them. He had read about the "Cold War" of this world. It was incomparable compared to the Cold war he had experienced. They had acted instead of talking, and torched the world they had. Some considered it a mistake, but most others just took it as it was, and continued with their lives. Over here, they had the power to destroy their own world, and Sayre begged *for them to do it. He and his master could have gotten on with more important matters in their own world, not having to share the balance between both worlds.*

It was a hindrance to them, nothing more. Whatever they did was done half fold. They had caused the global warming of this world by decimating their own. Here they blamed it on their forms of power. Little did they know they had little effect on their own climate. This world had been degrading to fit the standards of Sayre's, slowly increasing in heat, as they sun shone eternally in the other world. The North and South becoming ever colder as the frozen wastes of the other dropped below recognisable heats. For whatever reason, the people here had made journeys to walk across the cold places. Sayre had laughed to himself about that—such a waste of energy and time. What did they have to prove afterwards? They could walk for days at a time in the cold? They could survive in harsh places when provided with food beforehand. They would find it difficult to live that way forever. Therefore, they proved nothing in his sense of thinking.

Unfortunately, like the plague they were, the humans of this world had continued thriving in their worsening world. Their selfishness and pride had been of the biggest amusement to his master. While people lay dying in hostile areas, the others build up for themselves greater, richer empires. The Interior Union was a group for bad deeds, but this was like a false economy. While there were people unhappy with basic standards, unable to reach their full potential, they would be nothing more than a weight on the shoulders of the world. It would be better that they be given something useful to do. Sayre had ceased finding tangible reasons for that minor overlook of this world, but found none. They were just plain blind to the possibilities of genuine resourcefulness. They would have little more time to learn the ways of making use of their population.

To Sayre and his master, they would have only weeks to enjoy what little life they had. But for them, they had several years ahead of them. It would be a surprise to see how far they'd get in that time. Perhaps they might have developed better uses of power, or simply guts to use the weapons they hoarded so inexplicably badly. His master could only hope they began to slowly tear themselves apart. It would make his job far more enjoyable to do. At the very least, he could see things unwinding the way he wanted them to.

He came to a set of signs on the road, that still remained mostly straight aside from a few slight bends, which the van had taken harshly, which showed letters before numbers in certain directions, and what appeared to be the names of towns in others. He had little time to consider the names of any of these, he just made note of direction. He had been here before, gone along this road. He had been assigned to make note of certain people, and their daily routines. Sayre found this most disturbing, as the people showed a huge lack of scheduling. It had made his job hard, but he soon got the skill of understanding down to a tee.

This specific target was a man, who had shown weakness of mind. Sayre had felt his presence almost beyond psychotic. All he needed to receive was a little encouragement in one direction, and he and the people he was associated with would be in peril. That was the first part of their plan. The second was one that involved a little waiting. Relationships needed to be made, and they had to wait for a long time in this world, only hours in their own. Sayre had watched the relationship grow in a matter of hours, in this world, months. Both of the targets were of some relation, but Sayre knew little of what they had to do with his master's ideas. He rarely asked, knowing that if they needed to be removed, they were obviously of great danger.

He took the nearest turn after hours worth of seeing the same signs over and over, telling him he was only miles away at a time. He sent a short quick message over to his master through his mind. He had never beckoned his master by physical means, he found it all too personal, and was mentally fearful of what touch might do to him.

"We're here. The first time is now."

* * *

They had pulled into a small town that was nearer the middle of this country, a hundred miles from any ocean near the land. It felt cold every day they had come here, particularly this day. There was no rain, just grey, depressing looking skies, and a bitter chill in the wind, which broke through even the thickest of clothing. To Sayre's master, it was like a deathly knife coursing through his body. He had not been used to such bad days in this world, and had become increasingly hostile towards them. It fuelled his hatred further.

He had not been wearing the clothing of his world today; he had something more special planned. For the first time, he was going to become one of the many despicable citizens of this town. He had a mission to fulfil, and he intended to do it with precision. The man he was mimicking on this chilling winters day, was going to be taken care of, to ensure he didn't find himself in the same place where Sayre's master was. Sayre was in charge of making sure that didn't happen. And they both knew Sayre had little patience for keeping the man alive. He had brought along one of the weapons of their world, similar to the hand held guns of this world, but with far higher potency for death.

His master was wearing what appeared to be blue trousers, made of an odd material he had not seen on his world, but what in ample supply in this one. It was thick, almost too rough for the liking of the skin, and yet everybody here wore them. These ones were tattered beyond ordinary use, for some reason, the man his master was copying kept them that way. Above these he had a long green coat, of a similar condition. It had no holes unlike the trousers, but still offered little protection from the now blustering wind. This was all topped off by a low level hat, stained with whatever colourings they could find of similarity, so his master could cover the greater part of his face—an Interior Union custom.

They were now a short distance away from the van now, when Sayre had remembered the lack of security in this world. He turned, and pushed cheap plastic buttons on the key required for the vans initialisation. They saw the two lights flash at the rear of the van, signalling its useless locks. He turned back, and they began to walk towards their destination. The shady man they needed to impersonate would be here at any time now, he always was. He had clients of some sort, whom he saw regularly, most of them looking similar to the way Sayre's master was dressed. They sought something from him, which they paid a high price for, Sayre had no idea exactly what it was, but they had brought similar substances that would create a far more devastating effect on the brain.

They had taken their place on the corner, both of them crawling behind their skin due to the wind, which slowly bit through their hands and feet at first, then further into the core of their bodies. Sayre stood watch on one section of the streets, and his master on the other. Somebody had seen them, and immediately began to make his way towards Sayre's master. This was not the man they needed to hide from the world.

'Hey, you, I don't have enough for my usual, so I was like . . . er . . . wondering if I could get the same for what I got here in my hand . . .' The scraggly looking man now begged.

'Take it, and leave.' The master said, pulling out two of the vials he had stashed in the pockets of the coat, which offered little warmth to his blue hands.

'Thanks man!' The man said, running off, as he realised he owed no charge. Today was his lucky day. More than could be said of other men on this day.

"Handled like a master of his trade." Sayre said to his master through their minds.

"He looked desperate, and we have no time for interference. We have a seed to plant, and it will grow far quicker than any other.' He replied out loud. 'One we might view in a short while, I think.'

They stood there for another few minutes, and finally caught sight of the man they had been waiting for. He had been running towards the area his sales were usually made, and made no initial realisation of a man standing in his place, dressed almost identically to him—aside from his blackened shoes of unknown origin. The master had no intentions of changing his footwear. Sayre nodded towards the man to his master, and began to walk towards him. He had stopped jogging by this point, showing his evident lack of fitness.

Sayre maintained his steady striding towards the man, and stuffed his right hand deeper into his pocket, clutching the weapon that would end one small issue with their plans.

'What you want-' He began, before he was suddenly silenced, his eyes spreading wide. Sayre, put one hand on the man's shoulder, physically holding him up so he didn't slump onto the floor, like the corpse he now became.

Sayre continued to push the man back over across the street he had came from, making quick work of packing his body into the dark alley. Nobody had seen, everyone was far too concerned with keeping warm, holding their hair in place, and making it home in time for their evening's relaxation. He dropped the man into one of the waste bins that ere in abundance in this world. They made for excellent temporary hiding places, Sayre felt he could possibly hide an ample supply of bodies in one, and it would be days before anybody found them—time enough for him and his master to be back in their world.

He wandered back over to his master, looking in both directions, observing the few people and vehicles that passed by. The roads were dangerous places. The people had almost no control over their vehicles, and on multiple occasions, Sayre found himself daunted by the fact he had to cross them for the first time in his life. He had stuffed both hands into his pockets, now feeling the slight warmth in his right one, where there now appeared a small hole. It had been over as fast as they had seen him. He had been taken care of; now all that was left was the main target for this town.

Sayre had opted to place himself on the nearby seating, which was torture in itself compared to the seats they had in the van. It was made of some plastic type material, painted to look like wood, with numerous slats held together by poorly cast metal. Still, Sayre found it a better place to be. He was less likely to attract they eye so many meters away, sat there, watching. This time they had a little longer to wait, the man's clients were erratic people; largely self destructive and they appeared to have no sense of the life around them.

His master had been amazingly still, despite the cold. He had forced his brain into forgetting about the usual shivering. He didn't want anything affecting his next sale. He wanted absolute perfection in this, and demanded it from his bodies very limits. Then he heard a faint yell. That of a women, and looked over at Sayre. He just shrugged, and looked about the place for any outlying danger to them both.

Still he turned his head in every direction, Sayre doing the same, both of them looking for answers to something they had not planned on, when a rather happy looking man, walked around the corner with an odd accessory in his hands. It was a bag of sorts, but a more feminine looking product. This worried him, it could be concealing a weapon, and he had no intentions of killing the man instantly, or in cold blood. He needed his death to be observed. The future depended on it.

Still, he walked, smiling and swinging the bag in his hands. He moved his left hand to open it, and Sayre immediately clutched his weapon as the man walked by him, heading towards his master. He unzipped it, and pulled out, what they then realised, was a sizable amount of money.

"That scream, was of his doing?" Sayre had asked.

"Desperate man, with deadly habits . . ." His master had chuckled, even through mind. He lowed his cap a little more, clutching the substances in his had, more this time. He pulled them out, and held out his other hand in waiting for the money. He had little use of it, but remaining to the role was important this time.

He made a brief peek below his cap at the man, noticing he was still smiling giddily, for what seemed like no apparent reason. Madness was all that could explain it.

He made no conversation to the target, simply making the transaction, then turning away, ensuring the end of the situation. All they had to do now was wait a short while and the show would begin.

The man had walked away, maintaining his psychotic emotions as he walked away, now dropping the woman's bag on the floor, having no more use of it. He had got what he wanted, and would need nothing else for his future. Sayre got up, and walked towards his master who now began to walk towards the bench Sayre was at first seated.

"We follow him, first with out minds, then with our eyes. This is something I will enjoy watching."

Sayre nodded, and they both stood their, concentrating on nothing physical in particular, but maintaining an inner eye on the man's mind they were soon poisoning. Psychosis was easily inflicted in those who already suffered from it, only this time it would be the worst the man had ever felt. The master had power over mind, in more than just mental ways. As they felt his presence become distant, they began a brisk walk towards him, knowing full well that his residency was nearby.

They found themselves noticing his change in height from the floor sooner than they expected. He had almost run *home. They quickened their pace, not wanting to miss the essential time ahead, coming close to their observation spot.*

Then he saw him. The person he was trying so desperately to bring down. The now young boy who would be slightly older the next time they met. He was there, walking along the street, opposite to the place they now stood, waiting for their victim to make his move. They stood there, watching the window, waiting for a troubled yet relaxed face to appear, make his move on the world, seeing it as something that it was not. The wind on this day would help them. His mind would amplify the feeling; make him feel like it was something a little more . . . physical. *Like clockwork, they saw it. The look of a man, begging to do something stupid. Asking for the world to take hold of him, take him places that only existed in his mind.*

The window opened.

The man stepped out.

The people looked.

Smiling now, both the master, and the apprentice gazed above, noticing a few people walking about the streets stop and look up at the spectacle. The young boy, too, now staring in horror and what appeared to be sheer bewilderment.

First came the lean, and then came the drop. Last came the crack of bones. A faint thought went through the master's mind, as he read it.

"How sweet. The last thoughts of a boy who had lost what we needed him to lose." He sent to Sayre, and then turned, heading back towards the van. His work here was done, all went perfectly, and the final processes had been put in place. It was now all a matter of time, and time they had, in ample supply.

* * *

He couldn't bear to sit in the van once more. What great happiness he received in succeeding in his work, didn't give him enough reason to cope with numbing the rest of his body. He had been slowly freezing where he stood yesterday, and the van made little help in warming their bodies. They had stayed in their makeshift temporary rooms where his travelling building was. They had set up a main rift area in another place nearby to the closest airport, which was one of the more common one way portals. They had to sleep in a building that did little more than the clothes they had worn the previous day at stopping the wind. Through the night they had been haunted by the sounds of the harsh weather battering against every wall, often making objects outside take on movement of their own.

Now they faced the prospect of waiting in the van once more. Their final task at hand this very day and they had employed the hands of some otherwise useless people from this world. They needed to make everything look like a large operation. They had their last seed to plant, and they would never really see it grow, however they would witness it in its final days—something for them to be proud of in future.

They had slowly stepped outside, and made way towards the van, which felt colder than ever. Over night it had lost the small amount of warmth the engine had generated, and Sayre worried himself, as he found difficulty starting it on the first twist of the key. After much reluctance, it awakened like a beast from hibernation. The engine roared, and at the same time, choked on the very coldness of the air, that was trying its hardest to stop the engine from doing what it had been engineered to do.

'Blast that hot air on, for the love of keeping our hands at least.' He said to Sayre, both of them now wearing gloves from

their world, far superior to the clothing of this world. Theirs hands were being warmed, but the rest of their bodies were being punished by the vans incompetence.

They drove out of the fenced area, this time ignoring the lock. It was doubtful they would find themselves coming here again. They need never see this world again after this day. This time Sayre turned in the other direction, following the course of the signs that showed the icon of the plane of this world. The airport was a few miles away, but they didn't need to go that far. Brinkley would bring them from their places to where they were needed. Sayre and his master would make preparations at the main Interior Union building, constructed around one of this world's key portals.

Nobody had ever seemed to notice its pinkish glow over the years. It had its own ways of masking itself, until those that came close, were found worthy of entering the other world. It accepted only those, which could attain to keeping its balance. Sayre had made arrangements for Brinkley's car to be fitted out with gas release systems, to ensure the passengers unconsciousness, and he had arranged for some capable security in the complex, in case they had uninvited guests.

Hired hands were easy to find in this world, most of them were inexperienced and sloppy, but they came with their own weapons, and never questioned a thing. When asked to be in the room with the pink light, most of them had shrugged it off in a "It don't make a difference to me, as long as I see my cash in the end" attitude. Deep in their minds, Sayre knew they had questions. Then again, he also recognised the feeling of fear they had when they were stood in front of him. He emanated an aura of fear which pierced into the hearts of the fearless ones. Or so they thought.

Sayre had ensured the buildings security was to his master's exact words. His master's number of obsession had become the verbal key for all the doors, a detail Sayre never quite understood. In every situation, he did the same sensible thing, and never asked. There were reasons for such things, and he was not of a high enough state of mind to understand the underlying traps and tricks.

The journey was long, and like a bad penny, the numbness in their legs came back to pester them frequently, causing both of them to constantly shift, every few minutes or so. The lack of feeling had made the road feel somewhat smoother to their joints, now locked and frozen in whatever form they sat. There was a little more traffic in this region of road, they had presumed, because of the volume of people that wanted to make their way towards the airport. It was incredibly early in the morning, almost seven thirty, and the roads were buzzing.

They passed a considerably amount of cars, and the master sat and watched them pass by in various lanes on the road, huddled into their vehicles, hands held over the heaters, others on mobile devices, held closely to one ear as they driver attempted to manoeuvre the cars with one hand. This was quite probably one of the countless reasons the roads were so dangerous, everybody had a lack of concentration on everything.

Sayre had stuck to the lane that kept close to the grassy area of the road, as opposed to the middle, where every other vehicle seemed to be going faster. They were in no particular rush, they had ample time to prepare, but both of them were mentally begging to be let out of the enclosed vehicle, and exercise their poor flattened muscles.

Neither of them showed signs of tiredness today, both of them were feeling extremely awake. They had one last job to do, and get right. Then they could return to their superior world of bliss, and await the results of their experiment. It was an important day, and they were relying heavily on the people they acquired for this task. Brinkley needed to do his job correctly, if not, they would surely make him suffer. Sayre had no intentions of letting the men live afterwards anyway. They were nothing but slaves to him, and they had no right to cross over into the world he valued so highly.

They had been driving at some speed before Sayre slowed himself, and tapped on an object that was sticking out from the wheel. They were here, and there was a nicely erected sign outside of the area where their bright clean building was. Sayre turned in; the gates already open, welcoming them home. They drove towards the main doors, and quickly hopped out of the van, desperate to stretch their legs. Sayre even made a comical jiggle with his legs to force more blood through them. He felt he had experience no greater feeling in his life. They made their way to the door, and his master uttered the door phrase, and then walked in.

The main entrance itself was bare, as were the rest of the rooms in the building. It was simply there mostly for show. The only rooms that mattered were the prison rooms and the rift room. Still, they had been kept in exceptional condition, showing no apparent marks on the clean white walls. They breathed what they thought was truly heavenly air, filled with warmth from invisible heating devices. They felt instant warming, and found themselves in slight ecstasy as they made their way to the rift room. It was a few minutes walk, and they had to go through one of the false walls. They had created hallways leading from the prison cells that only went in one direction. The direction they needed to go.

Sayre's master came to what appeared to be a dead end in the corridor, and pushed his mind through to the centre of the wall, urging the mechanism to one side, allowing them to pass through. With a slight click, they were greeted by a microscopic crack in the wall, which soon widened until it was large enough for them both to get through. Sayre slipped pasted, after his master, and the door became part of the seamless wall again. Sayre turned to approve of the work for a brief moment, and turned again, to follow his master to where their main interest was. The lines on the floor were evident enough of their direction.

Little was said during the time they took to journey through the winding corridor that slowly angled down, slightly beneath the main floors surface. Enough was on their minds, and they never needed to share any information between each other. They both knew what had *to happen, and exactly how Sayre's master wanted it to be played out. What they were doing was playing with people's minds. Once it had begun, all they needed to do was push the mind further, essentially making decisions for it.*

They had passed the signs clearly stating the rift room, and had come to a similar door to the one on the front of the building. His master saying that same number he had before, only this time, with more volume in his voice. The door clicked open, and they were consumed with the pink haze.

At first, it appeared to brighten the entire room, allowing almost no vision at all of the surroundings. After half a minute, Sayre and his master found themselves able to see slightly more clearly. The men were here, just two of them, leaning against the tables with their arms occupied by large bulky automatic rifles.

'Glad to see you stayed, gentlemen.' Sayre said. 'In a short while, we'll be expecting visitors, and then you can make your way through.' He offered a brief fake smile, to which the men merely nodded at.

'But don't expect to be followed by our friend Brinkley. He has no further part in a business once he gets here. Sayre will take care of him while we leave.' The master said. They had never heard or seen him before, and half expected a more

brutish man to be before them. They offered a similar nod to him as before. No questions asked, no wish to know anymore about the plan they were involved in than they already knew. This place was something incredibly special. They thought it possible to be to do with the government, hiding things from the public. Sayre looked like a man who would make it in their best interests if they kept quiet, so they heeded to their minds warnings about his character. They just stayed there, leaning against the tables.

'So uh . . . what now?' One of them asked, in a rather childish voice.

'Now? We wait for our man Brinkley to arrive. Then the act begins.' Sayre answered, with a broad smile on his face.

He and his master moved over towards the other end of the room, allowing full view of the door Brinkley would walk through. That was the time it would all begin.

* * *

He hadn't slept the previous night, too caught up in his work for this day. He had been assigned to pick up a lad travelling to the airport, and one arriving from it. He set off almost immediately, waiting outside the boy's house in the freezing weather. It was not a good day to be driving long distances, but it was his job. It paid the bills, barely, but he froze his backside off during the winter, and sat there sweltering in the heat, dressed in his ridiculous khaki shorts. The seats of his taxi were the worst part. They were stupidly hard in cold weather, and uncomfortably sticking during the warmer months. All in all, his life was hell at work.

He found himself this job, offered by a mysterious man named Sayre. He had been going through a bad patch of work in the late weeks, and even thought the job was a shady one, involving the abduction and knocking out of two boys, he was desperate. And Sayre knew that.

They had fitted his taxi with canisters filled with knockout gas, and made his taxi window air tight, so he wouldn't meet an unfortunate end when he released the first load on the young man he was due to ferry first. He was well aware of the risks of getting it wrong, Sayre said he worked for a powerful, and very dangerous man, one not to be messed with. Brinkley was a proud Scott, rarely put in his place by anyone. He learned to hide his usual outlandish style in this instance, valuing his life, as well as what he was being paid to do this deed.

He leaned across the empty passenger seat, after hearing the opening of the door, and saw the first boy, actually, more like young man, he was due to take first. He jumped out, offered a polite greeting in his thick accent, and packed what few bags the kid had into his boot. He wouldn't need any of it later; he needed to remember to dump it before he got onto the next guy.

He jumped back into the taxi driver seat, and waited for his passenger to jump in the back. He had purposefully filled his front passenger seat with ample paperwork, most of it years old. He heard the back door shut, and the young kids's seatbelt click in place, and then started up the car for the short journey towards the airport. His hand lingered over the switch, then he decided to save the gas for when he was a little closer to the destination he was on his way to.

The journey was a mostly silent awkward one, he only exchanged a few words with the kid, as he drove closer and closer to the point he would need to knock him out. The cold was getting to him, but the boy seemed not to notice. He had his heat on full, and then he allowed himself a quick glance at the cars around him, before he noticed the sign on the boy's window side. Now was the time. He offered the boy an incentive to sleep, and after he had shown no signs of doing it willingly, he pressed the button, half expecting it to let out some sound of released pressure. He heard nothing.

At first, he thought it had failed, and he was in deep trouble. Then, as if like magic, the boy's eyes started to wander left and right, so very slowly. He was out, just like that. Brinkley turned in to where Sayre and his master had previously, and darted now at a quicker pace towards the bright clean building he saw before him.

'What a sight.' He said to himself, as he drove towards to the entrance.

He unfastened his belt, and made it fast to the rear of the taxi, pulling out the boy's luggage, and throwing it into the overgrown bushes close to the surrounding fence of the compound. He doubted anyone would make a point of checking there. Then he considered how to get the boy to the cell he was directed. He had been told by Sayre, that to get anywhere, anywhere at all inside, all he had to do was give the verbal password of "eleven".

"Fancy things those verbal password doors." He thought, and gently hauled the boy out the passenger seat. He didn't even stir in his unconsciousness; he was out pretty damn good.

Brinkley was a strong man, it was in his blood as a Scott, and he slung Jane gently over his shoulder, and walked towards the front door. At first he was a little apprehensive about the verbal password, and then finally resolved it in his head that it would in fact work, not fail.

'Eleven!' He shouted, thinking the door would need the extra help in voice to understand what he was saying. Without any sense of recognition, the door simply opened, and he made his way towards where he was instructed.

"Bloody clean freaks." He thought to himself, as he came towards the dead end in the corridor. This place was unnaturally white.

He was about to say the password to open the door in the wall, which he knew was there, but couldn't for the love of his life make out where it was, when it opened by itself. The crack first appearing, and then he hopped through, as if fearing the possibility of being crushed inside. It closed behind him, and a voice came into his head.

"That door, is not opened by verbal access . . . rather, i am the key to that one."

It had an inquisitive undertone, that he could barely recognise, and thought himself to be going mad. He took a deep breath, and urged himself forward to the first cell, the one he was told to put both boys in. He purged the idea of being mad from his mind, and dropped the boy to the floor, with a rather heavy bump, and made a quick return back to his taxi for the next and final pickup of the day. He jumped back through the door in the wall, and jogged back to his taxi, ensuring it was all cleaned out, and showed no signs of its previous customer.

He sped off, kicking up some dirt with his tyres, and made the shorter journey towards the airport. He could barely feel the cold now, his attention was elsewhere. The road was all he was feeling now, and then he could clean his hands of this mess once; the other boy was put where instructed. He hoped the last would go as simply as the first. He had given himself a little more positivity now, having gotten through the first half of his task without error.

He stayed in the fast lane of the motorway, all the way to the airport, not wanting to waste a second of precious time. He pulled into the airport passenger area, and waited outside of his car, watching the people leave the building through automatic doors. Not knowing what his next passenger would look like.

He was the only taxi here, he suspected the person would just walk up to him, and make the first connection. Lupe was his name—he had been told that much. Pretty weird name, Brinkley presumed he was some Mid-European kid. What on Earth did these strange people want with him? It was possible he knew some secret he shouldn't; maybe he was part of some almighty bigger plan. In any case, he wanted nothing more of it. He would do the job he'd been asked to, and nothing more. At least, not if he could help it.

He stood their in the cold, the wind now dying down a little more as the morning went by, beginning to feel his body warn him of the lack of heat. He had been stood there a few minutes, holding up a makeshift sign with "Lupe Delgado" written across it, when he was approached by a tall, slender boy, with dark curly hair. He had asked the boy if it was indeed him, and to his surprise, it was indeed. The boy must have been about eighteen or nineteen, and had an accent Brinkley couldn't identify. The less he knew the better. He instinctively grabbed the boy's baggage, stuffed it once again in the boot, and gestured for him to get into the same door the previous kid had gotten into.

He started up his taxi, for what he didn't realise was the last time, and pulled away from the airport collections area, and back onto the motorway, this time, sticking to the slower lanes. He felt like a relaxing journey this time, the building was closer, and his nerves were on high. He decided to treat his curiosity to finding out what the boy's language was. He had said Bulgarian, and for a split second, Brinkley had left his attention to the so called slower lanes of the road, and all of a sudden noticed a car pulling in front of him, at woefully slow speeds.

He lurched forward in reaction, and his knee jolted against the button near the wheel, releasing the silent gas to his passenger.

He hadn't shut the window between him and the kid, and reached immediately behind him to slide it shut. Fortunately for him, the gas had acted quickly on the boy, and seemed only to affect a certain area. His passenger was out in seconds, and Brinkley could feel the strain on his brain as he fought to stay awake. He fumbled through the glove compartment, for his ever trusty caffeine pills. He hoped they'd do the trick, if not, he was in big trouble.

He began to slow speed, keeping below the speed limit, but not so low that the people behind him would be agitated. His eyes were heavy, and his reactions were slow. He could feel the steering wheel beneath his hands, drift slowly to one side, before he punished himself to keep his eye straight. His foot lost its pressure, and his speed dropped by another few miles per hour. He hadn't noticed the car behind him. It wasn't a normal citizen, but he remained unaware of being watched.

He had begun to do exactly what they expected him to do. He slowly veered to one side of the road in his half sleepy state, and the rumble of dirt beneath his tyres awakened him from his brief slumber. Then he heard it. Sirens. They had been closely behind him, watching his pace drop considerably; they presumed he had been abusing the working hour rate, working over twelve hours at a time to make more money. Veering to the side of the road made it clear to them; this man was dangerous to the people around him.

He was grateful for the ability to stop driving, he thought he might do something dreadful and not even be aware of himself dropping into a ditch, or hitting a tree. They might arrest him, but at least he would be alive. *The patrol car stopped behind him, almost touching his back bumper, in case he made the move of bashing the car backwards and making a run for it. One man stayed in, the other opened his car, and strolled over, with a seemingly good bounce in his step. They had been patrolling for hours, with no action happening across these usually boring roads. Now they finally got the chance to do their job, and boy, were they going to lay into him.*

He tapped on the window, with a little smirk on his face. Brinkley felt like rubbing his eyes, but thought it might give him away. He wound down the window. Here came the sprawl so many officers of the law began with.

'Excuse me sir, do you know why I pulled you over?' He asked.

"Because you're a bored little prick, that's why.' Pedley thought.

'Yeah, that little stunt of mine earlier, I'm sorry about that, my paperwork fell all over the place . . .' He pointed to the mass of paper that was once well seated on his front seat, but since his little jerk earlier, it had gone sprawling.

The officer's face dropped. He had gone for the bait, and his little bit of action was soon over. He stood up straight, after being stooped towards Brinkley's window.

'Well . . . you should uh . . . be more careful next time. Dangerous driving on busy roads and all.'

'I will, my apologies officer.' This came out "Awwffissah". By the time Brinkley had finished his little fake apology, successfully hiding his immense exhaustion; the guy had already given up on persisting, and was already halfway back to his car. A lucky escape it was, all in all.

Brinkley couldn't afford any more problems like this, it would surely get Sayre's irritation rising. He wasn't sure he could cope with that kind of man on his back. There wouldn't be much left afterward, of that he was sure. He rubbed his eyes extremely vigorously, and decided to leave his window open. The fresh chilling air would help keep his brain awake. He waited for the patrol car to pull out first, and then followed, this time at a lower speed than before. He checked his speedometer and kept his speed safely at fifty five. He couldn't care less about the people behind him now; they'd just have to take the faster lanes.

He had checked on his passenger, who still lay their looking half dead to the world. His eyes gently shut; the jolt had only made him lean slightly to the left. No permanent damage done. He had only a couple of miles to go before he arrived, and couldn't wait for them to be over. He sped up to sixty so he was sure he'd arrive in two minutes, or thereabouts. He found himself constantly pushing his head into the way of the air that was rushing through his window. He couldn't feel how cuttingly chilling it was, half his senses were asleep. All he knew was, it was keeping his face with the living. He couldn't afford another shut of the eyes, this time he'd surely end up head first into a bollard.

Those were the longest two minutes of his life, seeming to drag on and on, purely because they were the most important two minutes. Little did he know they'd be among the last few minutes of his life. He'd be dead within the hour.

He spotted the sign long before he did last time, as he found himself searching, yearning *for the damned thing to come as quick as it could. He made a quick indication, and bumped his speed up so he could zip between the oncoming traffic to the dirt road that led to the building. This last trip was over for now. He could dump the kid with the other, and then make his way down. He'd been told to hurry up with meeting them straight after he made the last drop, they were expecting some people, and they wanted to leave as they arrived.*

He pulled up, and braked quickly, sparing no time to jump out his taxi and grabbed the boy out the back, forgetting all about locking the car and throwing the luggage. It didn't matter anyway, but he didn't realise that. He darted through the front door, this time not wasting any time ensuring his elocution of the word "Eleven" was perfect. The door seemed to have a great band of understanding, and understood his almost unfathomable Scottish words. Feeling the weight of the boy on his shoulders soon taught him to stop his fast jog, and he found himself slowing down particularly as he got the wall. This time it opened just before he got there. He slipped through, opened the cell, and dropped the kid on the floor.

The door locked by itself, and he jogged down the long corridors with the lines on the floor, this time being thankful for the lack of weight on his shoulders. At first he thought he'd take too long getting their. The people they expected might be there, they all might have gone by now. He rushed further down the corridor, coming to another door, passing a sign he paid no attention to, saying something about a room ahead. He spoke his words out of breath, and the door opened as he supported himself with his hands on his knees. He needed to catch his breath. But it was soon all taken away, as his vision was consumed with a great pink glow.

He stood back upright, seeming to forget the breath as he gazed at the light. It was almost mesmerising for him.

'Ah, Brinkley, you arrive with such pace, though my master says the people you put in the cell awoke almost as soon as you made your way here. A lucky man indeed.' Sayre spoke at first, with the other men simply gazing at him with bewilderment. There was another man, stood far in the distance, looking almost familiar to him. He had no idea why, he knew he had never seen or met the guy before. There was something in his face, at this distance he couldn't make it out quite so clearly.

'I will make my way out, I will meet you, Sayre, and the other men on the other side.' The familiar man said, nodding his head at the other men. 'Take care of Brinkley will you?'

He turned, and his body became consumed by the pink light, almost instantly becoming part of it, leaving no trace of where he once was.

'So . . . uh . . . let's get the taking care of done and dusted shall we?' Brinkley said, with an awkward laugh to accommodate his nervous disposition.

'Yes, well . . . I have already made these men aware of the proceedings, the boys are making their way here, and even now they are not far away.' Sayre replied, looking down at his hands as he rubbed them together. In anticipation.

'And what exactly are *the proceedings?' He asked, this time, feeling a little vulnerable. He didn't understand the situation, and desperately wanted to know that everything would be alright. The other men around him, just two of them, made their way towards the light, particularly slowly. Sayre had told them to do so, in their minds.*

'Well . . . ?' He asked again, somehow aware of just what was happening to him.

Sayre pulled out a strange looking gun from the pocket of his jacket, it looked like a pistol, but a lot more intricate than most Brinkley had seen.

'I'm afraid you are no longer part of the proceedings.' Sayre pulled the gun up to his eye level, and stood there, waiting. 'Any second now, we need them to see you. Helps us make their decisions you see.'

He brought his hands up, hoping that offering his surrender would give them the option of sparing his life. He had rushed here thinking it was all over and done with . . . but now he realised his entire life *would be over and done with, in just a few seconds.*

Behind him, he heard the click of a mechanised lock, and in front of him, he saw the men walk through, holding themselves rigidly, as if expecting to be torn asunder the second they stepped through. They disappeared, the door opened, the feeling came. He put his hands to his chest, and felt warmness on his hands, but coldness in his body. Somehow, the bullet didn't just penetrate him, it corrupted *his very feeling. First he lost his feelings, then thought passed from him, and last to go, was the sight of Sayre in his mind, the sight of loss—gazing upon a man who could control great things.*

Sayre put the gun away, aware fully that the boys had seen his deed behind the bright glow they would now see. In his mind, he sent a very clear message. It was a message that he and his master had considered the ultimate seed—one that would grow into their plans.

"Welcome to the Rift room, young one, glad to see you made it here with such impeccable timing. Follow us if you will, for you are one of the few that may, you and your puzzling friend here." He received a question through his mind which he had not expected. The boy had quickly found his thoughts. He replied simply, making the curiosity unbearable for them. "You need not know a thing, follow if you will, but understand that you can either attempt to stop our plans of killing this monster, which I assure you will fail, but if you do I guarantee your questions will be answered."

He turned and walked through, feeling the imminent energies passing through his body, and he felt the air, the warmth, and the perfection of his world once again. He opened his eyes on the other side, a craft waiting in front of him with his master at the wheel. The other men however, had been waiting outside of it. To him, they were scum; he and his master had no more need of them.

Sayre had not relied on his ability of the use of weapons to kill people. He was fully capable of more, though not as much as his master. With a flicker of his mind, he sent the men a clear message. It was a message that would spread into their brain infectiously; they would never be able to resist the order.

"Walk, young men. When you feel you are able to walk no longer, keep going, to the Frozen Wastes you will go."

Like robots, their arms flopped down, dropping their weapons. They turned and began walking without question or sound, walking aimlessly in the direction of the wastelands ahead. Now they final pieces were put in place, their work was done. Waiting time was ahead, and the Interior Union were always good at waiting.

Sayre hopped into the craft without word, and his master flew them up, and away, towards the Spire on Cradle 11, miles and miles away, then more miles above.

18

Dropping from the Skies

They had awoken, in a cell they almost recognised instantly, though to Roland and Brax, it was a new experience. They had lost all sense of consciousness at the very bottom of the spire, and now found themselves in a cell that looked almost identical to the one in Jane and Lupe's world. It had one key difference: the place was made of stone. They were not lucky enough to have been graciously transported by Tailen's master. They were there for a single reason only. They had done what this master person had needed them to. Now was their time to be brought to him, and judged to death.

Jane had looked up from the floor, and found Brax sat up, with his head in his hands. He nudged Lupe, who in the previous instance had been the first to awaken and help Jane up. This time, it was Jane's turn.

'Come on wide old man, it's time to get your sorry ass up.' He said, pulling him up by the arms. They both stood their, eying up Brax, realising now, it was not a headache that pained him.

They turned to Roland, who was sat next to Tailen, looking particularly down at this time. Then Jane understood why. He had felt a certain presence lacking in the air. Tailen sat there slouched against the wall, with his leg showing huge blood stains across his trousers. His skin was almost pure white, and his life signs were non-existent. Jane looked down at the floor in respect, and Lupe turned to look for himself, his eyes filling with sorrow as he looked down upon the man, whom he had brought this undignified death to. Lupe put his forearm over his eyes, and leaned against the wall in emotional pain. He began his release all his emotions in one, his eyes exploding with tears, and he stood there for a long time bawling his eyes out.

Eventually Brax found it upon himself to step up to the situation, and put his hands on both of Lupe's shoulders. To him, now was the time the boy would need the most support. Now he was a man, who had witnessed an ample supply of death, and had now even dealt it. Now was the time to take it upon himself to carry on, get past the events.

"Do not burden yourself with his death. He was glad to have been stopped before he did further hurt on this world. What's more important is, I forgive you for your mistake. It was one we all would have made in your position." Roland now spoke, aware that Jane's link between them all had not broken even now.

'It's too late for that now . . .' He sobbed. 'Give me the chance, and I'll tear the place down to my last breath.' He turned, his face red with tears, and his eyes showing a fury, a huge hatred, even now, for the people who were responsible for it all.

"I pray you use it when the chance comes. Sayre and his master will not be easily broken." Roland said, still sat next to his brother, as if guarding his corpse from grave robbers.

'How long?' Brax asked. Everyone understood the question.

"He claimed he was expecting us. My brother said he was to bring us to him. Not long, I believe." Even now, Roland answered questions, with such composure; it was almost as if his brother were all but forgotten. The truth being, he hadn't really felt his death deep inside. Later, though, it would cut deep into his mind.

They sat there in silence, each of them slumped against the wall, rejecting the idea of conversation. They had gotten so close now, and had been captured instantly. They had been so stupid to not believe the master and leader of the Interior Union would not expect them to make an attempt to bring his small empire to nothing. It was almost obvious. What still remained to be answered was who this master was, and what he intended to do to the "monster" Sayre spoke of all that time ago. All would be apparent in the coming time.

"After much preparation, you're here. Now, you come and see all that is." The voice said to all of them, as if it had attached itself onto their little mental network. It echoed even now in their minds. The multitude of locks on the single door clicked, and the door creaked slightly open, asking them to open it further—to make their way to their doom. Curiosity was what killed the cat, and yet on the cat went, still begging for its answers.

They sat there for a few seconds, each of them staring at one another, Roland staring intensely at his brother's visage. He was the first to make a move. He had nothing to live for now, he would gladly meet this master to his needs, and do what he could to fulfil his duty to this world. Brax got up and followed Roland to the door, pushing it wider open, revealing the stony corridor ahead. It looked like the inside of an ancient decorated tomb. It had only one direction. Onwards.

They made their way out, leaving Jane and Lupe to their decisions. The boy's had small things to do, to help each other through this time. Then Jane mentioned something that shocked Lupe almost instantly. A strange piece of information, Lupe had not expected, and it brought him away from his self hate, and all other emotions. All he could feel was bewilderment in his brain. What his friend said to him, gave him an odd sense of hope. But Jane didn't tell him everything he now knew.

'I know him somehow. He . . . he can't read my thoughts, as if they're locked out, forbidden . . .' Jane trailed off, clearly considering a great deal in his brain, even now. He stood up, and offered a firm hand towards Lupe. He had faint hope in their situation, and he needed Lupe to keep this master's mind busy.

"Don't think about what I'm going to do, just make sure you make every effort to kill the man. Rush him if you have to. Subdue his mind in any way you can." He asked of his friend through mind. Lupe simply nodded at the information that had been passed on to him. He would do what he could.

They strode out to meet Brax and Roland, and made their way down the corridor. They all noticed that the room they were expected to head towards was not at the end. Rather, at a closer distance, they noticed that there was a faint light coming off from the right. They had been denied the visual anticipation of what lay ahead. What they would see, would probably pierce deep to their cores. They continued down the cold passageway, making small note of the markings on the wall, similar to the ones they had seen on the ground floor of the spire. They had to be near the top, the passage was short, and the room ahead to the right could be no bigger. They finally reached the end of the stone walls, and turned, each of them fearing something more personal in their minds. Love lost, family lost, no sense of belonging.

They had turned as a group, and now, there stood Sayre, his hands behind his back, on the right of a man who stood there with a genuine smile on his face. A face they all recognised, not as an enemy, but as a friend. Jane almost knew it; he could not possibly forget his own voice. He himself stood their ahead of him, only a little more worn in the face. He was staring at himself, as an older man late in his twenties.

He felt it impossible to imagine. *He* had been the cause of this Cradle's damnation, the initial cause of Cradle 1's destruction, and in wider terms, and the turmoil that struck this world. He had stopped in his steps, and noticed that his friends had done so, long before he had.

'It's good to see myself so young and harpy.' The master Jane said.

'Impossible . . .' Lupe whispered, he had forgotten all that Jane had said to him. He was now struck by the sight that was ahead of him, the man before him, the very reason he had lost so much of his happiness in life. He had been a cheerful upbeat person until this Jane lookalike figure had dragged him here. The master just stood there, smiling.

'Quite the contrary, very possible in fact.' Sayre said. 'You no doubt know these worlds need balance. You can't have such power in one, without an equal power in the other.' He chuckled.

'Our intentions were simple. I supposed I should call you my brother. The worlds cannot survive without balance.

All we had to do was bring you here, and the tender balance that was, would crash.' The older Jane said.

'The monster . . . it was *our* world?' Lupe asked, almost terrified beyond his soul.

'Hahaha. Yes! We gave you the reason to come here, following a blind trail; you did most of the work for us. You have no way of getting back, and now you're world is slowly crumbling to its foundations.' Sayre said, feeling an immeasurable amount of prominence. There was nothing more satisfying to him, than pulling his trump card on the unsuspecting ones. They had no idea all along, he simply watched with amusement as they wandered around, causing their own world's destruction without realising.

'I thought it suitable to tell you, before I put an end to your lives. You, young Jane, will not be thrown off this place. You must stay alive, and feel your own world crash in your mind.' Jane's older self now said. He brought down his brow, and Roland cried in pain. His brain was being assaulted, slowly.

It was probably possible for him to decimate the hound's brain instantly, but he far more liked the idea of crushing their brains slowly, all at once. He moved half his concentration to Brax, who was brought to his knees in one quick thud to the floor.

"Lupe! *Tear him DOWN!*" Jane screamed to him in his head. At that very moment, Lupe stumbled, and Jane thought his mind had been penetrated as well. It was all going to be over too soon, and they were going to be far too helpless.

Then Lupe took his body to the extreme. Without warning, he darted across at the older Jane, his arms outstretched to greet the man's throat swiftly. Sayre, however, had been waiting for anything sour to happen; he immediately focused his attention on the boy's body, and tried to paralyse him in his steps. But it was *so* hard. He was moving quickly, and what Sayre tried to do in his head that normally ended most lives in an instant, took longer than expected.

Now was Jane's chance.

"You can't kill me, you cannot stop me. If balance is what this world demands, then balance is what it shall have."

He made his sprint towards himself, an odd feeling. He never took his gaze from the man in front of him, his mind straight as a die, his concentration purely on one thing. If the world needed balance, which could only be attained by both of their ends, then Jane would gladly take his and his twin brother's life. For the sake of the others in this world. for the sake of his friends.

'You can't!' The older Jane screamed, but had he cried out, the wind was blown out of his chest as his younger self crashed into his chest. He had been standing in front of one of the many windows that decorated the building. As old as the stone was, the glass was not designed for strength or security. It was only designed to fit the ancient style of the rest of the building. They had indeed been at the top of the spire, and with enough push, they would find themselves falling far past the edge of the Cradle, down into the ground miles below.

Jane pushed with what little might he had left, Sayre now too caught up in stopping Lupe, and thrashed him and his brother into the glass, blasting through it like half melted ice. The terror on his own face, but on one much older, one that thought it was wiser and far superior. It made Jane smile to himself. To think, that it was possible to fool yourself.

He uttered a few cruel words to his older self as they fell, for what would be an eternity in the air, and a much longer lasting ending below.

'I don't believe in God, but I pray for you.'